Curses Are
for Cads

Also by Tamara Berry

Séances Are for Suckers

Potions Are for Pushovers

3 1526 05468929 1

Curses Are
for Cads

TAMARA BERRY

KENSINGTON BOOKS
www.kensingtonbooks.com

This book is a work of fiction. Names, characters, places, events, and incidents either are the products of the author's imagination or are used fictitiously. Any resemblance to actual persons, living or dead, events, or locales is entirely coincidental.

KENSINGTON BOOKS are published by

Kensington Publishing Corp.
119 West 40th Street
New York, NY 10018

Copyright © 2020 by Tamara Berry

All rights reserved. No part of this book may be reproduced in any form or by any means without the prior written consent of the Publisher, excepting brief quotes used in reviews.

All Kensington titles, imprints, and distributed lines are available at special quantity discounts for bulk purchases for sales promotion, premiums, fund-raising, educational, or institutional use.

Special book excerpts or customized printings can also be created to fit specific needs. For details, write or phone the office of the Kensington Special Sales Manager: Attn. Special Sales Department. Kensington Publishing Corp, 119 West 40th Street, New York, NY 10018. Phone: 1-800-221-2647.

Kensington and the K logo Reg. U.S. Pat. & TM Off.

Library of Congress Card Catalogue Number: 2020939642

ISBN-13: 978-1-4967-2933-0
ISBN-10: 1-4967-2933-1
First Kensington Hardcover Edition: November 2020

ISBN-13: 978-1-4967-2929-3 (ebook)
ISBN-10: 1-4967-2929-3 (ebook)

10 9 8 7 6 5 4 3 2 1

Printed in the United States of America

Curses Are
for Cads

Chapter 1

"Look at the witch float!"

"Nothing can keep her down!"

"Mama, see—she's just like my rubber ducky in the bath. He always pops right back up, too!"

With a stifled sigh and one final thrash of my legs in the water, I come to a stop at the end of the swimming pool. The water is balmy and the air scented with chlorine, the sounds of children's voices somewhat muffled by the earplugs I'm always careful to pop in before I go for a swim. I've heard it said about town that I wear them to keep the water demons at bay, but the reality is that I have extraordinarily small ear canals. If I'm not careful, I'll develop an infection.

I pull them out now. When combined with my nose plugs and the pearlescent swim cap I'm careful to tuck my long, black hair into before I go anywhere near the water, I look ridiculous. I also look nothing like a witch, but that doesn't seem to affect my audience in the slightest.

"Madame Eleanor, that was smashing." The most exuberant—and bravest—of my onlookers, a gap-toothed, freckled boy named George MacDougal, holds up the stopwatch he's carrying on a string around his neck. He's wearing swim trunks in a similar shade of blue to my suit, though he has yet to stick so much as a toe in the water. He's too busy timing my laps and encouraging every other child in the vicinity to watch the "unsinkable witch" go. "That's three seconds off the last one, and you aren't even winded."

On the contrary, I'm much more winded than I'd like to admit. I'd always heard that nothing can surpass the full-bodied exercise of competitive swimming, but it's never been an activity that appealed.

And not, as my gawking audience seems to think, because of the medieval superstition that you can always spot a witch by her ability to float. I mostly don't like getting my head wet. Chlorine tangles in waist-length hair are no laughing matter.

"Thank you," I say as I hoist myself out of the pool and accept the towel he holds out to me. I dab it at my face. I also don't like what the water does to my painstakingly applied eyeliner, but sacrifices occasionally have to be made. "I appreciate the enthusiasm, George, but wouldn't you rather go play on the water slide with the other children?"

He blinks up at me. "There aren't any children on the water slide."

After a glance at the opposite end of the community center, I'm forced to retract my words. My heart—apparently the only part of me capable of such an action—sinks. When I arrived here, the shallow end of the pool had been teeming with young swimmers, all of them splashing and playing and enjoying a rainy Saturday afternoon at the local indoor pool. It had been my intention to slip into the water as quietly and unobtrusively as possible to get my laps in.

Clearly, I didn't do that as well as I'd hoped. The kids are now gathered around the lap pool, watching with mingled excitement and horror to see if I'll succumb to an impromptu trial by dunking.

"You can hardly blame them for their curiosity." A male voice sounds behind me. "You do seem to have the uncanny ability to stay afloat. Neither circumstances nor finances nor, it seems, water can keep you down for long."

That particular combination of amusement and timeliness can only belong to one man. I turn to glare at my accoster. Nicholas Hartford III is the entire reason I'm here in the first place—a thing he knows very well for himself.

"Drowning witches is an unfair test and always has been," I retort. "That's why it was devised in the first place. Women are biologically predisposed to rise to the top of the water because of our bone density. Chalk one more up for ye olde patriarchy trying to keep us down."

"A thing we'd be much more successful at if you weren't so persistently buoyant." Nicholas chuckles and leans in to kiss my cheek. I'm dripping wet and not wearing a scrap of my usual makeup, but that doesn't seem to deter him.

Nor, it seems, does it stop the crowd of onlookers. As Nicholas pulls away, he waves to a girl in pigtails who's creeping closer, despite her mother's determination to keep her back.

He cocks a brow at me. "Does this happen every time you come to the pool?"

"Yes." I fix the towel around my waist. "It also happens every time I go to the grocer's, whenever I stop by the library, and if I happen to be walking down the street. I gather a line of children behind me no matter what I'm doing. I think they hope I'm going to whip out a broomstick and take flight."

"I wouldn't mind seeing that for myself."

"Me either," George says with another of his wide grins. "But she won't do it, no matter how many times I ask. She says it's too hard to get air traffic clearance in this day and age."

Nicholas's lips twitch in a familiar attempt to suppress his smile. He manages it—barely—and places a hand in the center of my wet back to direct me toward the changing rooms. I've been dating this man long enough to know that the gentle pressure is deceptive. When it comes to having things his own way, Nicholas is king.

Technically, he's not royalty in the traditional sense. He doesn't even have any claims to nobility. However, he *is* one of the richest men in all of Sussex and lives in a bona fide castle to boot. In other words, a spade is a spade, and Nicholas Hartford III knows how to get what he wants.

Most of the time, anyway.

He stops me outside the door to the women's changing room. The children seem to have dispersed into the background, leaving us in relative seclusion, but that doesn't stop him from lowering his voice. "As pleased as I am to find that the swimming lessons are coming along in time for our vacation, I'm afraid I have good news."

"I don't think you understand how that phrase works," I say as goose bumps break out over my upper half.

Neither my sarcasm nor the state of my puckered skin has any effect on him. In addition to being supremely autocratic, Nicholas is also impervious to things like freezing cold air after a dip in the pool. He clears his throat. "What if I were to tell you that I won't be making you go scuba diving with me in Malta, after all?"

"Then I'd tell you not to be such a liar. That's not good news, Nicholas. That's *fantastic* news."

I cast my eyes up in thanks before he can respond. The ceiling is made of corrugated tin and appears to have rust growing in several spots, but that doesn't deter me. A month of swimming laps has in no way, shape, or form prepared me for a two-week Mediterranean vacation with a millionaire. Not for him a relaxing sojourn to the beach to drink fruity cocktails and soak in the sun. Oh, no. Nicholas scuba dives and jet skis and jumps from cliff tops with nothing but a triangular kite at his back.

It's unnatural, if you want my opinion, which you should. When the village witch—and a woman who can commune with her dead sister, no less—draws a line, it's usually for a good reason.

"Bless you, Winnie," I say as if to prove it. "You are the best of sisters, and I'll put an altar up to you tonight. No, I'll put up *two* altars, and you can flit between them as the mood strikes."

When I glance back down at Nicholas, he hasn't lost any of his amusement. "You could have just said you don't want to go."

"Oh, I want to go. I never pass up an opportunity to enjoy myself somewhere that it doesn't rain six days out of the week. What I don't want to do, however, is risk life and limb and my entire oxygen supply to go stare a few fish in the face. Are you sure you wouldn't rather lounge poolside for eight hours every day? We can always watch the fish simmering in butter sauce later."

He lets this comment pass, but an earnest expression arrests the handsome features of his face. He's everything a non-royal, non-noble British millionaire should be, which means it's impossible to read him 90 percent of the time. His face is well-lined, but not with either gaiety or sorrow, and his gray eyes are incalculable. In fact, unless he smiles, most people assume he's some sort of superhuman.

But I know better. Not only am I skilled at reading people—a must when the entire village looks to you to solve their problems via witchcraft—but I'm skilled at reading *him*. I reach out and touch his forearm.

"Hey," I say gently. "It's okay. I understand. If we have to postpone the trip, we have to postpone the trip. I won't die from lack of sunlight for at least another two months. And even then, I know some great fungal folk recipes that will take care of it in a flash."

At this, a small smile twists his lips. "Why does that sound like something you just now made up?"

"Because you're a cynic," comes my easy reply. "But I'll

have you know that mushrooms are very high in vitamin D. All my spells come with a side of science."

I'm speaking no more than the truth. Some people might believe that the work I do tips toward the shady side of the morality scale, but I have a large—and happy—clientele. Love spells, sleeping spells, spells to pass a test or get a promotion at work . . . If it can be fixed with an herbal remedy and/or a slight boost of confidence, I'm your witch.

As if just noticing that I'm dripping onto the concrete floor and rapidly losing all feeling in my extremities, Nicholas makes a tsking sound and rubs his hands up and down my arms. "You're freezing," he says. "And I'm late for a business call."

I'm about to reply that I've been freezing for pretty much the entire year that I've been living in England, but he stops me by reaching into the inside pocket of his suit jacket and pulling out an envelope.

"Here." He hands it to me. "Read this. It's not Malta, but I think you'll like what it has to offer."

I dangle it between two damp fingertips. "What is it?"

"Read it," he says again. "It's from an old school friend of mine. And meet me at the castle tomorrow by seven. If we leave before breakfast, we can be there in plenty of time for lunch."

"Be where?" I ask, but I already know there won't be an answer. Nicholas's delight in being mysterious is secondary only to my own.

His response is to lean in for another kiss. This one bypasses my cheek and lands on my lips. The outbursts of "blech" and "ew" in the background indicate that some of the children must have still harbored hopes of my bursting into flames or transforming into the shape of one of my cats.

Their disappointment is my gain. Nicholas is a good kisser.

"You can thank me later," he says as he pulls away. He shows no signs of lingering, this time offering *me* that friendly wave. "See you tomorrow, Eleanor. And pack warm. If you're suffering from lack of mushrooms now, I shudder to think of what will happen once we get there."

It's on the tip of my tongue to demand what the *there* in question is, but I won't give him the satisfaction. He might think he has the power to tell me what to do, brandishing mysterious letters and demanding that I rearrange my travel plans at the last minute, but unless there's something downright amazing in this envelope, I'm staying exactly where I am.

"Ha! That's ten quid you owe me, Grandmother." Rachel pulls open the front door to Castle Hartford and immediately turns on her heel. "She totally caved. She's got three bags, and there's not a bikini in sight."

"Good morning to you, too," I call after the pretty blond girl, but to no avail. Nicholas's niece is one of my favorite people in all of England, but she's as much a Hartford as the rest of her family. I'm forced to struggle through the door with my stack of luggage on my own.

To be fair, I don't mind too much. I might have to carry my own bags for now, but I'll be steeped in luxury soon enough. Wherever Nicholas Hartford goes, he goes in style.

And by *style*, I mean he flies his own airplane.

"I don't believe it." Vivian Hartford pokes her head into the foyer. In the manner of grand castles everywhere, the entry to their home is a huge, cavernous space complete with black-and-white marble tiles spread expansively across the floor. There's also a grand staircase, a dust-covered chandelier, and a suit of armor bearing an axe that's likely to fall at the least provocation. I adore it.

Vivian, the matriarch of the family and a woman who delights in being an oddity, isn't so impressed by her surroundings. Nor, I need hardly add, by the sight of me.

"Eleanor, how could you?" She steps closer and takes in my scarf-covered person with a frown. I have three scarves in total, each one layered over the other to keep out the chilly blasts. I'm going to need them if I'm making it through this trip in one warm piece. "You're supposed to be better than this."

I've finally managed to get all my suitcases through the heavy wooden door and allow it to fall shut behind me.

"You think I'm better than an all-expenses-paid trip to the Outer Hebrides to commune with a Scottish patriarch from the great beyond?" I tsk gently. "And here I thought you knew me."

Nicholas certainly does. I was fully dressed by the time I opened the letter yesterday, but that hadn't stopped chills from moving up and down my spine as I read it. Phrases like *dead father*, *missing heirlooms*, *don't know who else to turn to*, and *your friend the medium* had been all that were necessary to have me consigning Malta and its exotic splendors to perdition.

If there's one thing I enjoy more than dead fathers, it's dead fathers who require the immediate aid of a medium. And Nicholas, drat him, knew it.

"It's been ages since I got to do any real ghost hunting," I say eagerly. "Apparently, this Glenn Stewart guy died last month without telling anyone where he stashed a bunch of valuable family heirlooms. His kids seem to think he squirreled them away somewhere on their private island, but they're at a loss to locate where. What could be more natural than hiring me to contact him via the spiritual world?"

Vivian snorts. "Buying a metal detector and going about things in the usual way?"

Rachel and I take this response as it's intended, which is to say we ignore it. Vivian Hartford has never been known for her tact. The younger woman sticks out her palm and gives her fingers a waggle. "Pay up, Grandmother. I told you she wouldn't be able to resist."

Vivian grumblingly acquiesces, but it's obvious she holds me personally responsible for this drain on her purse. Rachel is gleeful as she tucks the money into the pocket of the heavy parka she's wearing to keep out the chill of the castle they call home.

It doesn't occur to either of them that they have enough money to pay several million such debts—or to install a good heating system—and it doesn't occur to me to question it. A large part of this family's charm is how oblivious they are to how the real world works.

"Where's the man of the manor?" I ask, making a show of peeking around the foyer in search of my absent beau. "I was up half the night repacking my bags for the wilds of coastal Scotland instead of Malta. The least he could do is be here to appreciate that I made it on time."

A stricken look fills Rachel's wide, violet eyes. Although she'd be considered a beauty even without such strangely compelling irises, that purple tint gives her an almost supernatural attraction. "Uh oh. Didn't you get his message?"

A sense of doom fills me. Another medium-turned-witch might call it a premonition, but I know better.

"Don't tell me. He was called away on business?"

Rachel nods. "Early this morning. He had to fly out first thing. I'm supposed to tell you that he'll join you up there as soon as he's free." She reaches into the pocket of her parka once again and extracts an envelope. This one I recognize almost immediately as a ticket.

A *train* ticket.

My sense of geography isn't nearly as strong as my sixth sense, but I know enough about the United Kingdom to recognize that train travel that far north will take me at least twelve hours. I accept the proffered ticket and stare at it.

"There weren't any flights?" I ask doubtfully.

"I didn't ask." Rachel shrugs. "Besides, Uncle Nicholas thought you'd prefer to go this way. So you'd have time to prepare your incantations."

"He said that, did he?" I ask in a purely rhetorical spirit.

That sounds *exactly* like something Nicholas would say, if only because he believes in my incantations as much as he does Santa Claus. "Of course he did. He wants me to suffer."

Rachel watches me under knit brows. "You don't mind, do you, Ellie? Perhaps I could skip my art class next week and come with you—"

I hold up my hand to stop her before she can finish. "If you came with me, who would stay at the cottage and watch over Beast and Freddie?" I ask, and not only as a way to keep Rachel from rearranging her plans on my behalf. I've been worried about leaving my two cats behind ever since Nicholas first broached the idea of going on vacation together. Beast, an all-black cat who occasionally masquerades as my witch's familiar, has been with me since the start of my sojourn in England. I have no doubt that she'll view my absence as nothing more than an opportunity to glory about, catching mice and letting in evil spirits, but Freddie is still just a kitten. And considering the way both Beast and I coddle her, she's not a very self-sufficient kitten, either.

"It's best this way," I say with a decisive nod. I left my fur babies curled up before a banked fire, but it won't be long before they'll need Rachel to get the flames roaring again. I'm not the only one who finds this fall weather chilly. "Besides, your uncle is right. I *do* need time to prepare, and it'll be lovely to see something of the country. The ride up to Scotland is supposed to be beautiful."

At this, both Vivian and Rachel cast a doubtful look out the nearest window. The gray drizzle of a ceaseless rain isn't up there with, say, the azure skies over a Mediterranean archipelago, but what can you do? There's a ghost somewhere in the Outer Hebrides that needs my attention.

"Well, is one of you going to drive me to the train station, or do I need to call a taxi?" I ask. "Spirits don't lay themselves to rest, you know."

"I'll take you," Rachel offers, and once again reaches into her capacious pocket to extract the keys to the family's Land Rover. She twirls them on one finger. "But we're stopping for breakfast on the way."

"Are we?" I ask without surprise. Keeping this girl fed is practically my second job—and one that doesn't pay very well.

She knows this, which is why she flashes me the ten-pound note. "And for once, it's my treat. To repay you for your predictability."

"I am *not* predictable, thank you very much," I retort as I gather up my bags and follow her out the door. In the name of fairness, I pause to add, "But the day I say no to hunting a ghost is the day I am one myself. And even then, I'm not making any promises."

Chapter 2

Incantations—at least, the kind of incantations *I'm* used to performing—don't require much preparation, so I spend the first half of my trip to Scotland pouring over the letter Nicholas gave me.

He's never been the kind of man to overindulge in details, so the fact that I have nothing to go on but two handwritten pieces of paper isn't as strange as it sounds. In all honesty, these papers tell me a lot more about what I can expect at my destination than any number of long conversations could.

For example, the fact that Nicholas's friend Sid sat down and penned a letter to ask him for help is a marvel in and of itself. People don't write letters in our day and age—and if they do, they're not done in this florid style of handwriting. There's even a seal on the outer envelope in bulbous red wax. This tells me that Sid is either a lover of history and tradition, or he's a pretentious windbag. It could go either way.

There's also the little matter of just how *little matter* is divulged. Instead of giving me particulars about the death of Glenn Stewart or the ways in which I might reach out to his ghost, the letter focuses mostly on reminiscent stories about the boarding school Sid and Nicholas once shared. From everything I can glean from the rest, it seems that Glenn hid a small fortune's worth of family heirlooms before he passed. No amount of searching has uncovered them, which is why they've resorted to a woman like me. When logic and common sense fail, only communion with the dead will work.

Or so they believe. The only dead person I've ever been able to talk to is Winnie, and she's much more like a sarcastic commentator on my life choices than a helpful spiritual guide.

Gee, thanks. And here I was going to tell you exactly where to find the money.

I can't help a grin from spreading across my face. I'm never entirely sure when or where my sister will reach out to me, but her visits are always welcome.

"That shows what kind of help you'd be," I say, heedless of the impression that talking aloud to myself on a train might give the other passengers. There's a gentleman in a kilt the next aisle over who's busy clipping his fingernails. I'm obviously not in the classy car. "It isn't money that's missing. It's family heirlooms."

Um, hello? Money can be an heirloom.

I tamp down a snort. "Only if you're some crass American. These are fancy people, Winnie. They own an island."

What about gold coins? Those are both currency and collectible.

She has me there. I'm about to dig deep into my upholstered seat and settle in for a long chat when a loud, deeply fluting voice interrupts from the doorway between the train cars.

"This is the one," it announces. When I glance up, it's to find a tall, gaunt woman standing on the threshold. "There's no need to keep following me about, young man. I'll sit here or nowhere."

"But, ma'am . . ." The young man she's speaking to is wearing the blue uniform of an employee, his face flustered as he struggles under the weight of the carpetbag in his arms. "You have to sit where your ticket says."

"There." She lifts a finger and points at me. "I'll sit there, or I'm flinging myself out of this train at full speed. Try explaining *that* to your superiors."

I blink, thinking at first that she wants my exact seat. The train car is only half-filled, which means there are plenty of open places—some of which are well out of the way of the flying fingernails of my nearest neighbor. I'm about to point this out when the woman starts making her way down the aisle toward me.

As she draws nearer, I blink again. Now that I'm seeing her in her full glory, I'm able to take in the full spectacle of her appearance. This is marked primarily by a pair of eyebrows so thin and arched they look as though they were drawn on with a pencil, a row of glittering rings on each of her ten fingers, and a sweeping purple robe with a fringe that drags along the floor to hook on each passing seat. She seems blithely unaware of this, causing the porter with her bag to fumble to release the strings every few steps.

"No, no. I'll take that," she says as the man makes a motion to stow her bag overhead. She drops into the open seat next to me and lifts her arm to take it from him. Each movement she makes is accompanied by a waft of patchouli-scented air. It's not an unpleasant smell, but it is a strong one. "Thank you, young man. I'll be quite comfortable now."

He pauses in the manner of an underemployed worker expecting a tip for services rendered, but the woman makes no move to pay him. He looks so crestfallen that I reach into my own wallet and extract a bill. Since Rachel paid for our breakfast with her honeyfall, I'm feeling generous. I also get the impression that he thinks the two of us are traveling together. If I want my tea later, I'm going to need to smooth the waters.

"Thank you," I say. "You've been a big help."

His shy nod is enough to convince me that I made the right choice. Since there's little likelihood of Winnie returning to chat now that I have a *real* person to talk to, I turn my attention to the woman by my side.

She's no less alarming now that she's up close. Her eyebrows are, in fact, drawn on with a pencil. So too is a line of lipstick well outside the physical boundaries of her mouth and, unless I'm very much mistaken, a mole placed at a jaunty angle on her cheekbone. Something about her feels vaguely familiar and unsettling, and it only takes me a moment to figure out why.

She looks exactly like a puppet that Winnie and our brother, Liam, had as children—a gift from a neighbor who'd probably wanted it exorcised out of her own house. We were *terrified* of that puppet. Its limbs were so loose and poorly jointed that it had a tendency to shift and settle in the night. No matter how we stored it, we'd go to bed only to wake up and find it in a new position every morning.

I barely manage to suppress a shudder at the memory before the woman speaks, once again in that low, musical voice. "I thought I'd find you here," she says, and zips open her floral-patterned bag. "Terrible weather for our trip, isn't it?"

"Um." I'm not sure how to take her familiarity, but I decide that bland acceptance is best. "I rather like the rain. As long as I'm indoors and warm, I find it soothing."

She hands me two plastic tumblers and continues rummaging inside her bag. "There will be nothing soothing about it when we reach the Western Isles. The rain has a tendency to go sideways once it hits the ocean."

I'm careful not to show any of the surprise I feel. The train we're on is bound for Oban in western Scotland, at which point I'm supposed to transfer to a ferry that will take me to the island of Barra in the Outer Hebrides. From there, Nicholas's instructions have informed me that a fishing vessel will carry me the rest of the way to Airgead Island, where his friend Sid's home is located. In other words, both the Western Isles and rainy ocean views are in my immediate future.

But unless this woman somehow managed to pick the letter from my pocket in the two minutes she's been sitting here, there's no way she can know that.

"Don't worry." She finally finds what she's looking for and pulls out a tin water bottle. "It'll be calm for our crossing. I made sure of that. Hold those still, would you?"

I've seen too many weird and wonderful things in this world—and met too many weird and wonderful people—to feel alarm as the woman proceeds to open the bottle and pour its contents out into the tumblers. That alarm comes into play once I realize that what she's pouring isn't water but a gin and tonic, the piney scent of it at odds with her patchouli.

She lifts one of the tumblers from my hand and touches it with the remaining one. "Cheers," she says, and takes a long sip. Glancing over at me, she adds, "You might as well have some, dear. The train is going to be delayed for several hours outside Shap."

"Is it?" I sip delicately. "That's too bad. It's already such a long trip as it is."

"Not nearly as long for us as for the poor man who's going to have a heart attack. His journey, as you and I both know, will have only just begun. He'll have a hard time finding his way home again after a passing like that."

"A passing like that?" I echo, starting to feel a little queasy. I'm not sure if it's the movement of the train or the fact that this drink is much stronger than I was anticipating, but a tight, queer feeling settles in the pit of my stomach.

"I don't *think* he's in this car." She casts her eyes around the train, taking a moment to appraise each male she lands on. "It might be that gentleman in the tweed cap near the front, but I expect he's only dyspeptic. Most of the vibrations are coming from the next car up. What say you?"

For once in my life, not a lot. In the ordinary way of things, knowing what to say—and how to say it—is a large part of what I do. If one's name is Nicholas Hartford III, one might argue that it's *all* I do. However, this woman isn't asking for my advice or even for my comfort. She's asking me to pick out someone on the train who's going to die just outside of Shap.

That's a trap I know better than to fall into. It's never a good idea to put a certainty like that on the line.

I place a hand to my head and take a deep breath. This signature move of mine is useless, since the only thing I can see when I close my eyes is the inside of my eyelids, but I feel as though I should put on a good show.

Don't do it, Ellie.

I jolt, startled to hear my sister again so soon—and at a time when I'm supposed to be concentrating on the great hereafter. One of the hallmarks of my ability to communicate with Winnie is that it's always on her terms. She comes when she wants, stays as long as she feels like staying, and nothing I say or do or concoct in my huge, showy cauldron is able to change that.

Get out of your seat and get off this train. Do not pass Go. Do not collect two hundred dollars.

I'm about to laugh at Winnie's obvious attempts to mess with me when a sudden image flashes across my vision. It lasts for only a second, almost like a slideshow picture turning on and off, but I see it as clearly as if it's taking place in front of me.

A man in a train car similar to this one but with red seats clutches his chest. His paper cup of tea falls to the floor, the thick, chalky liquid splashing all over his brown Oxford wing tips.

My eyes pop open again, and I turn to stare at the woman next to me. She's watching me curiously. "Well?" she prods.

"The red car," I manage, even though the last thing I want to do is say the words aloud. It's almost as though I'm no longer in charge of my own tongue. "Oxford wing tips."

She checks for a moment, her gaze intent. "Yes. Wing tips. I think you're right." With another long, careful sip of her gin, she adds, "It's a shame, really, but what can you do? Death comes for all of us in the end."

A chill moves through me—through the entire train car, in fact, sweeping down the aisle like a gust of arctic air. It's the exact kind of thing I've fabricated in the past through the use of fans, portable air conditioners, and natural draughts, but no one else seems to notice it.

No one except my companion, that is. She shivers and pulls her fringed purple robe tighter around her.

"What did you say your name was?" I ask.

She glances at me with wide-eyed astonishment, her already arched brows practically reaching her hairline. "Oh, dear. Don't you know?"

I shake my head. There are countless ways to glean information about someone's identity—I might ask unrelated questions, make casual references, or, if all else fails, take a quick peek in her bag while she slips off to the restroom—but I'm in no mood for games.

The tea was still warm. I can practically feel it seeping into the toes of my tights.

"Should I?" I ask.

She shifts to face me, her gin sloshing onto her lap in the process. Since I'm still holding my own tumbler, there's little I can do to help her as she dabs and wipes at the spill, muttering to herself all the while. By the time she's done, the chill has left the train car, and I'm starting to feel as though the vision was a figment of my imagination.

But then she speaks. "Why, I'm Bridget Wimpole-White."

The name is as familiar as her face. It nags at me, tugging at some long-distant memory, but I can't seem to pull it all the way out. To buy myself time, I extend my free hand. "It's lovely to meet you, Bridget. I'm—"

"—Madame Eleanor Wilde," she finishes for me. "I know that. But please, call me Birdie. All my friends do."

The memory snaps into place. "Birdie White?" I ask. "Not—"

She nods, pleased to find that her fame precedes her. "The one and only. I can't tell you how excited I was to hear that you'll be joining our little party up at Airgead Island. I've been dying to meet you." She rolls her eyes toward the front of the train and adds, "That's a touch gauche, considering our poor friend in the Oxfords, but you know what I mean."

"But I don't . . . I can't . . ." I take a deep breath and a fortifying gulp of my gin before speaking again. *Don't* and *can't* are words that belong nowhere near a medium's vocabulary—a thing both I and Birdie White know full well. More composed this time, I say, "I was under the impression that I'd be the only medium helping out the Stewart family. There was no mention of anyone else joining the party."

"Oh, as to that, I doubt the family knows I'm coming. Terribly rude of me, I know, but I was invited by Glenn himself."

I have to hold the drink firmly in my hand to avoid downing it in one incredulous gulp. The last thing I want is to be drunk on a train with Birdie White. Her name might not mean much to a layperson, and her fame is restricted to a rather select circle, but I've been studying her methods for years.

When it comes to faking communion with the dead, no one does it better—or more convincingly—than she does. Her ability to cold read a stranger is the stuff of legend. In fact, I've probably inadvertently given her enough information to tell my entire life story from start to finish.

"Mr. Stewart invited you directly?" I ask in what I hope is a politely noncommittal tone. Birdie might have taken me by surprise, showing up as she did, but she's not the only one who knows how to read a person. Not only do her fringed shawl and terrifying eyebrows make sense to me now—I own quite a bit of fringe myself, and have been known to darken my already black eyebrows for effect—but her noisy arrival to this train car is a tale unto itself.

It would have been very easy for her to sneak in when no one was looking, to carry her own bag and come find a seat next to me with the porter being none the wiser. But she wanted to be seen, meant to be heard. Even the contraband gin is most likely for show—and I am her intended audience.

"I had no idea he was already reaching out," I say as though it's perfectly ordinary for ghosts to invite people to their former homes. "It usually takes spirits a few months to realize they're dead."

"Oh, of course, of course," Birdie agrees, perfectly bland. "It took me by surprise, too. I have an incredibly full schedule right now, but when the spirits call, you know . . ."

"Such impatient creatures, aren't they?" I agree. "When they have all of eternity at their fingertips?"

Birdie chuckles, but in a condescending way rather than an amused one. "I doubt a man like Glenn Stewart ever waited on anyone's convenience—living or dead. He had more power than was good for him."

I glance out the window, watching the endless swatches of green and gray as they pass us by. There are so many things I want to ask this woman—including how she knows about me and discovered that I'd be going to Airgead Island on this train—but I don't dare. Admitting ignorance is tantamount to admitting fraud.

"He also had more money than was good for him, which is the root of all this trouble in the first place," Birdie adds with a cluck of her tongue. "Hiding perfectly good heirlooms like that and then refusing to divulge their whereabouts. Who ever heard of such a thing? If you'd like a piece of advice from a woman who's been around the world a little, dear, you'll have nothing to do with millionaires or their family dramas."

I'm unable to mistake her meaning. Although Nicholas is an intensely private man, it's natural for anyone as wealthy as him to be in the public eye—especially if he's been seen escorting a suspected witch.

"I think it's a little late for that, don't you?" I counter, not mincing matters.

Her lips curve in a tight smile. "It's never too late, dear. Women of our profession are better off living and working alone, relying on no one but themselves. You'll see what I mean soon enough."

I don't much care for the implication behind her words, but there's still a long way to go to our destination, and I don't see her moving seats again anytime soon. I might as well get some use out of her.

"Is that your opinion or a premonition?" I ask.

"A little of both. I'm surprised you haven't seen it for yourself yet. But then, Nicholas Hartford the Third can be rather persuasive, I imagine."

Oh, he's persuasive, all right. So persuasive that I'm sitting on a train next to one of the most famous mediums in the world instead of next to him in his Cessna. I have no idea how much of a hand he had in this particular situation, but I wouldn't be Madame Eleanor Wilde if I didn't suspect at least a little foul play. This is the exact sort of situation that would tickle his twisted funny bone.

"He has a high-handed way about him, that's for sure," I concede.

"Ah." She nods. "You *have* seen what I mean."

I'm startled into a laugh. "He was supposed to fly me up to the Stewart estate today," I admit. "But when he was called away on business at the last minute, he decided I'd prefer the train."

"I know." She smiles again, this time with real warmth. "I did that, too. I hope you don't mind, but I do so hate traveling alone. This way, we can have a comfortable coze before we arrive."

I swivel to stare at her. It's not out of the realm of possibility for this woman to have pulled some strings or faked a phone call that would sweep Nicholas temporarily out of the picture. It's the exact sort of thing I might do if I wanted to impress a client. Additionally, there are a limited number of trains that will carry us to our destination. It would have been very easy for her to narrow the window to a few possibilities and then cadge a passenger list to find me.

In other words, nothing she's telling me should be alarming, especially considering who I'm talking to. Birdie White has acted as a spiritual adviser to royalty—*real* royalty—and has even been called to assist Scotland Yard on missing persons cases. Although I've been of some help to our local police inspector, Peter Piper, it's always been with profound reluctance on his part.

Just as I'm about to compliment her on her technique, the screech of the brakes rips through the air. It's accompanied by a jolt as the train begins to slow. I glance at Birdie, my eyes wide, to find her nodding and heaving a sigh.

"Right outside Shap," she says, and points out the window. "What did I tell you?"

I follow the line of her finger to a tiny collection of houses above a rise in the distance. It's barely enough to constitute a village, let alone a town, and there are no signs to denote where we are. However, there's no denying the murmur of voices as a quick-footed employee rushes down the aisle toward the car in front of us.

"A doctor," I hear someone say as he brushes past us. "We need a doctor."

The kilted man who had been cutting his fingernails springs to his feet at once. I'm not much impressed by someone who grooms himself on public transportation—or who thinks a comb-over like his is doing anything to hide his balding head—but he's the only one who makes a move to come to the rescue.

"I'm a doctor," he says with a highly accented Scottish burr. "How can I be of service?"

I watch the pair depart with uneasiness, but Birdie only lifts her glass to me in a mock toast. "Silly creatures. A doctor isn't going to be of the least use at this point." She heaves a sigh. "But they will insist. They always insist."

I open my mouth to demand an explanation but am stopped by a cold gust moving through the train again. It could be explained away by the doctor and various employees rushing to the scene, throwing open doors and bustling about, but there *is* a possibility of a dead man in the next train car. I'm not making any promises.

"Ah, well," Birdie says as she pushes back into her seat once again. The cold, if she feels it, has much less of an impact on her this time. "At least we have all the time we want for our chat now."

"Our chat?" I echo.

"Oh, yes. We have so much to talk about, you and I."

I hold my breath, wondering which of my questions to ask first. The most pressing seems to be how she knew about the train getting stopped like this—if there is, indeed, a death taking place, or if it's a luckily timed bout of appendicitis that's done the trick—but Birdie clearly has other plans.

"Tell me, dear," she says, nothing but friendly disinterest in her expression, "what are your thoughts on the use of grounding stones during a séance?"

Chapter 3

By the time we arrive at Airgead Island, I'm almost convinced that I've made the journey in the company of a real medium.

Despite the fact that the train deposits us at our destination well past the appointed hour, we're able to exchange our tickets for the Barra ferry without any trouble. If that alone isn't enough to convince me that Birdie is smiled upon by the travel gods, then the fact that the rain, which had been pouring ceaselessly all day, clears the moment we board does.

"Ah, you see?" Birdie says as she points out the moon bursting through a sudden break in the clouds. "It'll be a fair crossing, just as I said. Enjoy it while it lasts, Madame Eleanor. The way back won't be nearly as calm."

Between the ominous glow of the moon and those words, which are uttered simply and without ceremony, it's a wonder I'm able to make it up the gangway. In fact, the only way I succeed is by promising myself that if she says one word about me plunging into a watery grave, I'm heading straight for the nearest airport and buying a one-way ticket to Malta.

She doesn't. She merely finds herself a comfortable spot near

CURSES ARE FOR CADS

the stern of the ferry, asks me to wake her upon arrival, and closes her eyes for a restful few hours. Not even the sight of the small, rickety fishing boat waiting to take us to the castle has the ability to move her.

It moves me, though. Up and down. Back and forth. Crashing through waves with an utter disregard for the realities of nautical physics.

"Oh, thank the Good Goddess," I mutter as we finally approach the dark, huddled form of Airgead Island. My hands are clutched together in my lap, my feet pushing against the wood planks in an effort to keep from being thrown overboard. Never before have I been so grateful to see solid ground. "We made it here alive."

"Of course we made it here alive," Birdie admonishes me with a cluck. "I told you we would. And not a scratch on us."

She obviously hasn't seen the half-moon impressions of my fingernails in my palm. They started to bleed half an hour ago.

"You two can leave them bags at the end of the dock," says the old man piloting the fishing vessel. He told us to call him McGee, and a more fitting name I couldn't have devised on my own. There's something profoundly appropriate about his knit hat and heavy cable sweater, which is as gray as his beard. He looks as though he's been traversing these seas since the eighteenth century—which, considering he's impervious to the cold and seasickness alike, seems a valid theory.

He cuts the engine. Unceremoniously tossing my three suitcases and Birdie's sole carpetbag onto the dock, he says, "One of the boys will come get these and take 'em up to the castle. No need for you to trouble yourselves."

Since the idea of lugging my bags another inch is one I don't much relish, I go along with this plan. Especially since it takes some serious hoisting and grunting to get Birdie safely disembarked. To her credit, she takes this in good part, merely pausing to straighten her shawl before thanking the man with a dignified air.

"Wait—aren't you coming in with us?" I ask as McGee makes a motion to start the engine once again. "I thought you said this boat is the only way on or off the island."

"Aye, so 'tis," he agrees. "I'll be back in a week's time with the supplies."

I glance at Birdie, hoping she shares my horror at being stranded for an entire week, but she accepts this decree with the same calm she evinced at foretelling a man's death.

"Don't look so alarmed, Madame Eleanor," she says with her low laugh. "It's a lovely old place—medieval, actually. There aren't many castles of this antiquity in private use anymore."

I have no way to ascertain for myself the truth of her words. It's well past midnight by this point, and the moon isn't nearly full enough to give me a good view of my surroundings. All I know is there's something about all those jagged outcroppings and the sole dark tower rising from them that's seriously unsettling.

I'd expected, when I'd heard that Airgead Island is a centuries-old stronghold just large enough to house a single castle, that it would be a forbidding place, but not like this. The dock where we've landed juts out from a rocky coast that seems treacherous to look at, let alone traverse. Those rocks lead to bigger rocks, which keep escalating in size and slope the higher I look. There's not a single tree, not a blade of grass, no weed pushing its way determinedly up through a crack. Just barren rock and the incessant splash of water against the pebbled shore.

There's something oppressive about it, something dark. And I don't just mean the fact that I'm seeing it in the middle of the night.

"What is it?" Birdie asks as I continue standing on the end of the dock, staring up into the barren shadows. There's an excited undertone to her voice. "What do you see?"

I shake my head, unwilling to give my thoughts a voice. Exhaustion will make a person do and feel strange things. Much more than ghosts and premonitions, at any rate.

"I don't see anything," I say. "I was only thinking that there's no reason why they couldn't keep their own boat for emergencies. What good does it do to strand people out here? We live in the age of global satellites."

If Birdie has a response, it's swallowed by the roar of the boat engine as the old fisherman places his hand on the tiller and plunges back into the sea. It's on the tip of my tongue to call to him, to beg him to take me away from this place so I can put up in a reasonable bed and breakfast on the main island, but it's too late. By the time I find my voice, he's already become a dark dot in an increasingly dark distance.

"Well, then." Birdie crooks her elbow at me. "I don't know about you, but I'm ready for a nightcap."

I'm not averse to a nightcap of my own, but the thought of navigating my way up those rocks with only the moon to guide me has me questioning every life choice that brought me to this place.

Birdie must sense my doubt, because she laughs and adds, "McGee told me the way to go. There's a hidden stairway at the end of the dock."

Remembering similar encounters in dark corridors, it's all I can do to suppress a shudder. "Of course there is. Tunnels, too, I presume? Places like this *always* have tunnels."

"On the contrary, places like this can't have tunnels," she responds. "How could they? Any underground passageway would flood every time the tide comes in."

This reasonable remark goes a long way in reconciling me to being dragged up the stairway. It's not, as I assumed, a barren, slippery ascent up even more rocks. The structure is made of wood and sturdily built, lined with flower boxes and with lights recessed into the sides.

"Oh," I say, feeling somewhat foolish. Although there's no mistaking the cold and damp of all the rocks around us, this looks more like a stroll through a well-tended garden than the climb through a tomb I was anticipating. "This is pretty."

Birdie just laughs. "Were you expecting skulls lining the walls and flaming torches leading the way? I don't know what you were told, but the Stewart family isn't hurting for money, even with half the family heirlooms hidden away somewhere. You won't find anything but comfort and elegance inside those walls."

"Elegance?" I echo dubiously. I've spent far too many hours at Castle Hartford to accept the British idea of *elegance* at face value.

"Oh, yes. Visitors here have a tendency to linger." She gives my arm a squeeze before releasing another one of her low laughs. "With any luck, so do the dear departed. Between the two of us, we should have old Glenn up from his grave in no time."

"Birdie—" I begin, but I'm not sure where I plan to go from there. Perhaps it's the length of the journey getting to me, or maybe it's that I'm thrown off balance by embarking on this expedition with a fellow medium, but I'm hesitant to put any of what I'm feeling into words.

To be perfectly frank, I don't know what my feelings *are*. Some of it is the natural excitement of a new case, true, but it's more than that. Something happened to me on that train. Something unknown. Something *new*.

"That incident on the train," I say somewhat feebly. "We couldn't have stopped it, could we? Warned someone of what was coming?"

The look Birdie bestows on me is kind. "They wouldn't have believed us if we had, dear."

They're wise words but not very comforting ones. People don't believe me all the time. It's what makes me so good at my job. When doubts creep in and the world stops making sense, I step in to explain the unexplainable.

"Yes, but maybe if we'd—"

She doesn't let me finish. With a strong tug, she continues leading me up the stairs. "Until the day one of us figures out how to reverse time, it does no good to dwell on the past," she says with a remarkable show of common sense. She immediately ruins it by dropping her voice to an ominous note and adding, "The future, however, is another matter entirely."

"I'll stay in Glenn's room." Birdie makes the announcement in the middle of a sitting room that looks as though it's been dipped in gold and tempered into shining malleability. She casts a look around her surroundings as though she's been born to them. Not even the monstrosity of a chandelier overhead, which looks to weigh a thousand pounds, has the ability to awe her. "I'll need the psychic vibrations to help me make a strong connection. You don't mind, do you, dear Ella?"

I blink at her, somewhat taken aback to hear myself addressed in such an informal fashion—and by a name I've never used in my life. "Uh, no. Feel free to stake your claim."

Birdie nods before returning her attention to the slight, delicately built woman who led us to this room. Although the setting is every bit as elegant and comfortable as Birdie promised, the woman doesn't seem the least bit ostentatious. You'd think that regularly sitting in a room that looks like the inside of a gold toilet bowl would require a wardrobe of silks, satins, and brocades, but she's dressed in flowing linen slacks and has her deep auburn hair pulled back in a loose knot at her neck.

"I'm so sorry," she says now, her somewhat anxious gaze moving back and forth between me and Birdie before finally setting on the latter. "I don't mean to be rude, but I was under the impression that you were coming alone."

"Alone?" Birdie gives one of her deep, musical laughs. "Why, none of us are ever alone. The spirits are always with us."

"Oh, of course," the woman murmurs, worrying her hands in front of her. "How silly of me. But you must forgive me . . . I was also given to understand that . . . How do I put this delicately?"

My sympathies are instantly roused. I may have been able to accept the advent of Birdie White into my life with complaisance, but that's only because I'm familiar with her work and background. To a woman who looks as though a strong wind might blow her over, Birdie must be quite a shock.

"There's no need for delicacy in cases like this," I say with a warm smile. "It's best to come out and say it. You can't hide much from a medium."

The woman turns to me with a look of such profound relief that I'm tempted to laugh. You *can't* hide much from a medium—at least not a medium like me—but that doesn't stop people from trying their best.

"That's true, isn't it?" she asks. Without waiting for me to answer, she extends both of her hands toward Birdie. "I'm delighted to finally meet you, Madame Wilde, and can only apologize for being caught off guard. Any friend of Nicholas's is a friend of mine. And your assistant, too, of course."

Since this last part is addressed to me, clarity strikes like a starting bell. I've dressed for the occasion in my usual ghost-hunting garb, which means layer upon layer of dark vintage glory. My favorite T-strap heels, a calf-length velvet shift dress tied around the waist with a paisley scarf, and the intricate coils of my braids tell their own story—namely, that I'm a woman with ethereal timelessness and a flair for the dramatic. When compared with Birdie White, however, I look like a schoolgirl playing dress-up.

A much shorter, much less grandiose schoolgirl playing dress-up. In other words, an *assistant*.

"I'm afraid there's been some confusion—" I begin, but the woman cuts me short and addresses Birdie again.

"Nicholas has always kept unusual company," she adds. "I should have known better than to be surprised by anything he says or does. I'm Sid, of course, but you must already know that."

"Indeed, my child," Birdie agrees. "How could I not? You're the spitting image of your father."

Now it's *my* turn to be confused, but it's a short-lived sentiment. Nicholas's old school friend Sid is not, as I originally suspected, a pretentious windbag with a love of tradition.

She's a woman.

She's a beautiful woman.

She's a beautiful woman who thinks that Birdie White—a walking puppet with eyebrows like the Gateway Arch—is dating Nicholas Hartford III.

It's all I can do to tamp down a giggle in time. I manage it, though, and not just because giggling is beneath a woman of mystery. Now that I have a better understanding of the situation, it's time I regain a semblance of control. Birdie White might be skilled at the art of being a medium, but *I* was the one who received an invitation from someone with a pulse.

"I'm afraid there's been some confusion," I say again, more firmly this time. I hold out my hand. "*I'm* Madame Eleanor Wilde. This is Bridget Wimpole-White. We met coming up on the train. When we discovered we were bound for the same place, we decided to travel together."

"We're all bound for the same place," Birdie says. "Death takes everyone in the end."

The effect of this gloomy pronouncement is to cause Sid's

eyes to open wide. They're a warm, rich hazel that reflects the light of all this gilded illumination perfectly. "Oh, I see," she says somewhat vaguely.

"No, you don't," Birdie says frankly. "But you will."

On those depressing words, she seems content to step back and allow Sid to turn her attention toward me. The other woman does this with interest, taking in the details of my dress and demeanor with something like relief.

"Everything makes so much more sense now," she says, her sigh tinged with laughter. "I can't think what made me so stupid."

"We came barreling in incredibly late, and you've recently experienced a major loss," I say. "Please, don't think anything of it."

Her relief grows, accompanied by a smile that causes twin dimples to appear in her cheeks. "You *are* a comfort to have around, aren't you? Nicholas said you would be."

My eyelid twitches, but I'm careful not to give anything away. *Comforting* is the last word Nicholas would willingly use to describe me. Conniving, sure. Cheeky, absolutely. But he's the first to point out that nothing in his life has been ordinary since the day I entered it.

However, this woman seems to both want and expect comfort from me, so that's what I plan to give her. She'll be much more likely to open up to me about the secrets of her family that way.

"I'll do my best to make this as easy on you as possible," I promise, and cast a glance back the way we came. "Speaking of, the man who brought us to the island had us leave our bags at the dock, but I'm wondering now if that's too much of an imposition. Would it be better if we . . . ?"

"Oh, I sent my brother down to fetch them as soon as we heard you arrive. He should be here any moment." She glances at a grandfather clock to my right and furrows her brow. "Were you two the only ones on the late ferry?"

I look to Birdie in an attempt to include her in the conversation, but she's taken a keen interest in a gold-framed painting of a hunting dog and doesn't appear to be listening. "There was a family on board with us as well as a young woman who looked like a college student on holiday," I say. "Why? Were you expecting someone else?"

We're joined just then by a man in a peacock-blue satin robe and matching slippers, both of which are lined with velvet of a deep, rich fuchsia. He appears in the doorway as if materializing from out of nowhere, looking like a silent film star who was only recently colorized and digitally enhanced. An image like that isn't easy to pull off, even allowing for a setting as decadent as this one, but this man manages it with panache. Even his pencil-thin mustache seems to have been contrived to set female hearts aflutter.

My heart is already taken, so I'm able to withstand such charm. Besides, he appears to be about my age and bears a full head of Sid's same rich, auburn hair, so I can only assume this is the brother . . . A brother who doesn't appear to be carrying bags of any kind.

Sid notices at the same time. "Oh, Ashley—what are you thinking? Don't tell me you went all the way down and didn't bring the bags up?"

"There weren't any bags," he says, blinking somewhat dazedly around him. Since I can only presume he's been inside this room before, it must be Birdie who's eliciting that response. Well, either Birdie or me, and I like to think that I'm a *little* bit less startling than her. Upon first acquaintances, at least.

"You wretch. You didn't even go look, did you?"

"I did," he protests. "There wasn't anything on the dock."

"Well, you'll have to go back and check again," Sid insists. "They can hardly have sprouted legs and walked away."

The scolding note in Sid's voice goes unheeded by her brother. He's still wearing that slightly bewildered look. "Don't be fussy. The bags aren't important." I'm about to politely disagree with this when he adds, "Sid, I got word that Harvey wasn't on the ferry. A man called from the station."

"Yes, I was just asking Madame Eleanor whether or not he came that way. If the trains are running as far behind as it seems, perhaps he's been delayed. I'm sure he'll come up tomorrow." She turns to me with a nod. "Harvey Renault is our father's solicitor. He's been very helpful in getting everything sorted since Father's passing, and he knows more than anyone about the estate. We thought you'd like to include him in the, ah, proceedings."

"How kind of you," I murmur noncommittally. A solicitor *might* prove an invaluable source of information in a case like this, but those in the legal profession have a tendency to view my kind with suspicion. Harvey's presence could end up swaying the family in either direction. "I look forward to meeting him."

"McGee won't like taking a second trip so soon after the last one, but he won't turn Harvey away." Sid releases a sigh. "At least, I don't *think* he'll turn him away. I don't remember him being so unpleasant. He was always a bit naggy when we were children, but—"

"Harvey's not coming tomorrow," the young man says, cutting his sister's commentary short.

"He's not?" Sid blinks at him, her lashes so long and curled they almost catch together. "Then when will he be here?"

"Never. It's happening again—cursed 'with book and bell and candle.'" There's barely time for this bizarrely poetic phrase to penetrate before he adds, "Sid, he's *dead*."

At those heavy words, every muscle in my body seizes up at once. I find I can't move—not to blink, and certainly not to breathe.

I warned you, Ellie, my sister says suddenly. *I told you not to do it.*

"He died on the train up," Ashley adds. I strain to hear the next part, even though I already know, deep in my gut, what's coming. "They're saying he suffered a heart attack."

Chapter 4

"Nicholas Hartford the Third, if you know what's good for you, you'll cancel all your plans and get here immediately." Even though I'm only talking to a messaging service, I'm careful to hold nothing back—not my fear nor my anger, and certainly not my annoyance. "You sent me on that train with a murderer. A *murderer*. Well, either that or a real psychic. I'm not sure which is worse."

The sound of footsteps in the hallway has me lowering my voice to a near-hiss. "If I'm found tomorrow morning dead in my bed, you have no one to blame but yourself. And I'll haunt you—don't think I won't. I'll haunt you so bad that you'll *wish* I was still alive to lay myself to rest."

On this nonsensical threat, I click my phone off and toss it onto the bed. I'd also called and left a message with my brother, Liam, telling him I loved him and that he's duty-bound by blood to adopt my two cats should I meet with an untimely end, but my connection was cut off about halfway through, so I don't know how much of it he'll understand.

To be perfectly honest, I don't know how much of it *I*

understand. All I know is that our dead man now has a name. A name and a personality and a knot that ties him inexorably to this case.

Harvey Renault. Oxford wing tips. Heart attack.

"Madame Eleanor! Oh, Madame Eleanor!" Birdie knocks on the door to my room, her voice carrying nothing but cheer and goodwill. If the night's events have upset her, she's doing a much better job than me at hiding it. "Have you gone to bed, dear? I brought us that nightcap."

I toy with the idea of climbing out onto the terrace and scrambling down the rocky exterior to escape my fate at Birdie's hands. There's something altogether appealing about a young woman descending several stories into the bosom of the dark, swirling sea, but I decide against it. My chances of surviving an encounter with Birdie are probably better. I didn't get in *quite* enough swim practice for ocean currents in the dead of night.

Tiptoeing to the door, I pull it open just enough to reassure myself that my visitor isn't carrying any weapons on her person. There's always a chance that the wine bottle in her hand is poisoned, and I wouldn't put it past her to have a knife concealed somewhere underneath the voluminous folds of her purple shawl, but she seems safe enough.

"Splendid." Birdie shoves her foot into the open space of the door and nudges it the rest of the way open. "I didn't think you'd be asleep yet. There's always so much to do when one arrives at a new house, isn't there?"

As a matter of fact, yes, there is. One of the first things I do whenever entering someone's home is to spend literal hours poking into every nook and cranny I can find. When there's a "ghost" present and in need of exorcism, I look for loose boards and draughty windows, check into heating appliances, and search for vermin in the walls. It's amazing how quickly the things that go bump in the night will stop bumping once you nail down a few boards. When there isn't a ghost but the family expects me to somehow manifest one anyway, as is the case here, my activities are more about squirreling out old family photos and checking the medicine cabinet in search of clues.

So far, I haven't had much time to do anything but berate Nicholas for sending me to my death. But the night is young, so there's no telling where things will lead.

"How's Glenn's room working out for you?" I ask as Birdie floats past me. Her patchouli scent is much less pungent as time goes on, but it still cloys my senses. "Any signs of our ghostly host?"

"Oh, nothing worth mentioning," she replies in a tone that matches my own. "Just the usual settling-in antics."

I give a sympathetic tsk and gesture for Birdie to take a seat in one of the plush red-velvet chairs by the dwindling fire. My room might not be the former domicile of the dead man I'm supposed to be conjuring, but it is beautiful. Unlike Castle Hartford, where everything is either worm-eaten or recently purchased from a discount store, this castle has been meticulously kept up and maintained throughout the centuries. My room manages to strike a perfect balance between gorgeous and gothic—full of oversized furnishings and heavy fabrics and all the more delightful because of it. There's even a metal-cast coat of arms on the wall.

"Cold draughts and flashes of light?" I ask. "You won't get any sleep that way, I'm afraid."

Birdie heaves a long-suffering sigh as she lowers herself to the nearest seat. "Likely not," she agrees. "But then, I didn't expect this to be a relaxing sojourn. As I always tell my clients, I can't rest until the spirits do."

"Very wise."

"And now we have poor Harvey on our hands, too." She looks at me with a smile that holds nothing but bland interest. Extracting two glasses from underneath the folds of her shawl, she pours out the wine and pushes one at me. "What do you make of it, dear? I had no idea that our dead man was going to be tied up in this business. Did you?"

To an outsider, Birdie and I probably sound like friends settling in for a comfortable chat about murder before bed. To me, we're strangers approaching dangerous ground. I have no way of knowing how much Birdie is involved in Harvey's death—if at all—but I don't care for the odds.

Theoretically speaking, *my* vision could be called nothing more than a fluke. I never confirmed that the body carried out of the train was wearing Oxford wing tips, or that he was drinking tea when he died. In fact, the only thing I got verifiably correct were the red seats in that particular car, and I could have easily absorbed that information without knowing it when I walked past the train on the platform.

Birdie, on the other hand, knew when and where he was going to die, right down to the village where the train would come to a stop.

People don't know that sort of thing. People *can't* know that sort of thing.

"No, I didn't," I say carefully. "All I got were the shoes."

"Yes, you did get those, didn't you?" she murmurs. She lifts the wine to her lips, her eyes never leaving mine over the top of the glass. "Have you felt his presence yet?"

"Whose, Harvey's?" I accept the other glass but don't drink. I get the feeling I'm going to need all my wits if I'm going to make it out of this interview intact. This is no mere social call. "No, I haven't felt anything from either man, but I also haven't made any attempts to reach out, so that's not surprising."

It's obvious she was hoping for more. A flash of something like disappointment crosses her expression, but she quickly tamps it down and tries again. "A solicitor and close family friend dying like that . . . rather suspicious, wouldn't you say? When there are valuable heirlooms missing?"

I'm tempted to point out that it's equally suspicious for her to descend on the Stewart family at just such a time—and on a train carrying the solicitor whose death she predicted—but I don't. Until I know what this woman's game is, I'm not giving anything away.

"He can't have known where they're located, or he would have told Sid and Ashley weeks ago," I point out. "It may have been nothing more than unfortunate timing. People die of heart attacks all the time."

"True." She purses her lips and nods at my glass. "But you're not drinking, Madame Eleanor. This is a lovely port. The wine cellar here is one of the best in the country. Glenn Stewart was known as something of a connoisseur. I was going to grab a merlot, but he recommended this one especially."

Which makes me *especially* loath to drink it. I don't trust dead men's motives any more than I do Birdie's. I lift the glass to my lips and feign a sip. "Very nice," I murmur.

She beams as though she had hand-pressed the grapes herself.

In an effort to keep the conversation on topic, I add, "It could prove useful that you and Glenn are so close. If he's helping you select wine already, then you should be able to find the money in no time. You'll have me out of work before the week's over."

"Money?" she echoes with a laugh. "It's not money that's missing, dear. You've been misinformed. It's family heirlooms we've been called to find."

I think back on my conversation with Winnie. "Money can be an heirloom."

Birdie only stares at me.

"Gold coins, for example. One might consider them both currency and collectible." I smile blandly to show I'm joking. "I'm sure all will be revealed to us tomorrow. What do you think of the family so far?"

This is meant as little more than a conversational gambit. I've made my own conjectures about the Stewart siblings, and my first impressions are rarely wrong. They have money—too much of it, if you ask me—and little worldly sense. It's a dangerous combination, especially once you start introducing them to the Birdie Whites and Eleanor Wildes of the world. How easy it would be for a medium to take advantage of their fear and grief for her own gain.

How easy it would be for *anyone* to do it.

Strangely enough, Birdie seems to agree with me. "Sid Stewart is a beautiful widgeon, and the brother isn't much better. But their family is an old and respected one—not just in Scotland, but everywhere. Glenn had a good head on his shoulders."

I don't know how good his head was if he managed to misplace a batch of important family heirlooms, but I keep that to myself.

"I like them," I say with perfect truthfulness.

"Do you?" she asks, blinking. "Already?"

I could easily tell her that my like of the Stewarts is matched by a *dis*like of her, but I don't. There's still that chance of a knife tucked underneath her shawl. I might be exhausted, but I'm not stupid.

"Oh, yes," I say instead. "I'm not as adept as you at controlling the weather, but I'm not without my uses. I always seem to have a sense of when someone is hiding something."

Birdie eyes me speculatively but doesn't show alarm. "I couldn't agree more. Innocent little lambs, those two. Perfectly unobjectionable."

I don't know that I'd go *that* far, since beautiful widgeons and resurrected silent film stars can be pushed to extremes like anyone else, but I'm willing to play along. "Indeed," I agree. "They're nothing but victims of circumstance. You and I, on the other hand—"

The large grandfather clock on the far wall of my room

chimes just then, ringing in the two o'clock hour with somber glee. It's as good a reminder as any that if I want to get my usual poking done before the family rises for the day, I'm going to need to get started soon. As enlightening as it is to sit trading commonplaces with a woman I trust as much as a baited bear, I need to find a way to get rid of her.

Fortunately, the clock's chime seems also to recall Birdie to a sense of her surroundings—and, I assume, her duty. Like me, she's going to have to do some serious legwork if she plans to convince these people that she's the real deal. Under normal circumstances, I might try to band together with her, combining our forces for the sake of a happy ending for this family. Under *these* circumstances, I'm not going to risk it.

Especially since she's looking at me with a strange, almost calculating gleam in her eye. If she doesn't have murder on the mind, then she has something else I won't like—that much I know for sure.

"I'll just take this with me, shall I?" she says as she grabs the bottle of wine by the neck. "For safekeeping, you understand."

"Absolutely." I get to my feet and walk her to the door. If that thing is poisoned, I don't want the evidence anywhere near my room. I exercise no hesitation in ushering her into the hallway and shutting the door in her face. "I hope you sleep well, Birdie. I fear that you and I may have our work cut out for us tomorrow."

"Oh, yes," she agrees, still with that speculative look in her eye. "I have the oddest feeling that our journey has only just begun."

Chapter 5

Much to my dismay, I'm the last person down to breakfast.

In the manner of all historic estates across the United Kingdom, our meal is served in a series of chafing dishes set on top of a sideboard that looks to be as old as the castle itself. The contents of those dishes, however, are mouthwateringly fresh. Eggs, ham, some kind of smoked red fish swimming in oil . . . Not since I treated my brother, Liam, to one of those all-you-can-eat pancake buffets have I seen so much breakfast food in one sitting.

"Dear Ella, how naughty you are," says a voice from the table. I don't have to look to know it's coming from Birdie White, if only because of that *dear Ella*. I don't like it any more this morning than I did last night. "Having a lie-in while the rest of us spend the morning in toil. For shame."

I feel a sheepish blush mount to my cheeks. It *is* rather late for a working guest to be making an appearance on her first day, but that was Birdie's doing. After leaving my room last night, what did she do but park herself at a reading nook at the end of the hallway to finish off her nightcap? Never has a woman consumed a bottle of wine so slowly or with such determination. I had to keep stealing peeks through the keyhole before I finally gave up and went to bed.

"*Has* your morning been spent in toil?" I ask as I spoon a little of everything onto my plate. I'm not accustomed to being fed like this—or at all, really—so I intend to make the most of it. "How strange. I've always found spirits to be the least communicative in the morning. There's something about a fresh new day that sends them into hiding."

Granted, the day isn't the least bit fresh or new, with rain spattering on the windows and storm clouds rolling thickly over the horizon, but the sentiment remains true. Somewhere in this world—say, Malta—I'm sure the sun is shining.

"Sid was kind enough to sit down for an aura reading with me," Birdie says.

My plate now full, I take a moment to examine the three people sitting at the long oak table. Birdie has improved on yesterday's purple fringe by twisting it around her head instead of her body, complete with a long white feather stuck in the top. I have no idea where she managed to get her hands on a feather, but she looks like a Regency matron from a period drama and—I'm forced to admit—exactly the way a medium should. My own recycled black velvet dress from yesterday seems paltry by comparison, but I don't have any other choice. Much to my dismay and not at all to my surprise, our bags didn't materialize overnight.

Sid also looks like a wakeful, elegant facsimile of her former self, but at least her smile is genuine. She's pouring tea from a huge silver pot, the steam wisping up in enticing coils.

"I don't know how helpful the reading was in finding the missing heirlooms, but I enjoyed it," she says, dimpling. "Apparently, Ms. White sees a man in my future. A tall, handsome one."

"Please, call me Birdie," comes the instant reply. Birdie spears a fish from the plate in front of her and waves it across the table. "And don't forget that I told you he's rich, too. A man of substance in more ways than one—provided you make the push to capture him."

Sid laughs. "How could I possibly forget? The moment such a paragon crosses my path, I promise to do my utmost to catch him in my toils. I don't suppose you know of any, do you, Madame Eleanor?"

The only tall, rich, handsome man I know is the one I'm dating, and he's proving hard even for me to pin down. There wasn't so much as a text from him on my phone this morning. Apparently, my imminent death at Birdie White's hands isn't a cause for his concern.

"Alas, no," I admit. "The village where I live is mostly retirees and schoolboys. Unless you have an interest in a police inspector embittered by a painful divorce, I'm fresh out of eligible gentlemen."

"A police inspector?" Birdie says, her expression one of sharp interest. It looks a lot like all her other expressions, which is to say exactly as though she's been taken by surprise. She's somehow managed to re-create the arch of her eyebrows this morning, but I note that her mole has slipped a good half inch to the right. "You're friends with a police inspector?"

I nod. "*And* the local vicar. I haven't yet cracked the mayor, but I'm making inroads that direction. Sorry, Sid, but he's happily married."

From the other side of the table, Ashley stifles a yawn. He's in the same dressing gown from last night, his hair a little askew, so I can only assume that he's no early riser, either.

"I know for a fact that Sid has turned down marriage proposals from no fewer than three tall, wealthy men," he says, and holds out his cup for his sister to refill. "Fitting, isn't it? 'All tragedies are finished by a death, all comedies are ended by a marriage.' Given last night's news, I think we can safely preclude the possibility of matrimony in our future."

Sid pours out the tea with a frown. "Byron, I think?"

"Naturally. Who else would do for a morning like this one?"

As was the case last night, Birdie pays little heed to the conversation taking place around her, but I find myself taking a keen interest. The shock of Harvey's death seems to have abated, leaving a pair of siblings able to eat breakfast and quote torturous poetry as if nothing untoward has ever happened. This doesn't necessarily make them *bad* people, but it does mean that however much they might have been upset by their father's solicitor's passing, his death didn't touch anything deep within them.

This idea is borne out when Ashley turns to me with another yawn. "Pass the milk, won't you, Madame Eleanor?"

I search in vain. The table is laden with butter and salt and tiny egg cups with even tinier egg spoons, but nothing resembling a pitcher is within my line of sight.

"He means the powdered milk packets to your right." Sid gestures at a porcelain holder filled with small blue envelopes. "It's ghastly, I know, but it's a tradition whenever we visit the castle. Father couldn't always get fresh foodstuffs delivered in bad weather, but powered milk is eternal."

I hand over the items in question and watch with mild interest as Ashley tears open two packets and sprinkles the contents into his cup. It takes some careful stirring before the clumps dissolve in the liquid, but the end result is a thick, pale brew that I immediately recognize.

"It looks chalky," I say.

"It tastes chalky, too," Ashley admits as he lifts it to his lips. "But in a good way. You should try some."

I shake my head and try not to stare too hard at the contents of Ashley's cup. His tea is the exact same color and viscosity as the liquid from my vision. All he needs to do is spill it on his shoes, and he'd be emulating Harvey's death down to the last detail.

"Is that the same kind of milk they serve on the train?" I ask, unable to stop myself.

"Probably." Ashley shrugs. "It's fairly popular hereabouts."

"Would Harvey have used it?"

Ashley and Sid share a meaningful glance. "Yes, most likely," Sid says with a slow, careful blink at me. "He grew up on Barra. Why do you ask?"

I can hardly tell them that I'm trying to ascertain whether yesterday's vision was the product of an overactive imagination or not, so I strive for neutrality. "I'm just getting a feel for his character—both his and your father's," I say. "It can be easier to make a connection when there are personal details to draw on. For example, would you say that your father—?"

Birdie interrupts me with a sweep of her arm across the table, still brandishing her fish-speared fork.

"I knew your father's solicitor was going to die," she announces in the gloomy tone I'm coming to recognize as her soothsaying voice. "I predicted it the moment I stepped onto that train, saw it as clearly as if it happened in front of my eyes. Didn't I, dear Ella?"

Instead of turning their heads toward the woman claiming the power of clairvoyance, Sid and Ashley glance at me. It goes against every grain I have to give Birdie any spiritual authority, but she's not wrong. She *did* predict his death.

I mean, she may have also caused it in the first place, but I'm not about to throw around those kinds of accusations willy-nilly. I'm a professional. I'll make sure I have proof first.

"She did," I admit. "Quite accurately, in fact."

Birdie lifts her head in lofty recognition of my praise. "It's a terrible burden to hear Death knocking before he arrives, but it's a burden I've carried my entire life. I wouldn't know any other way."

"Well, really," Sid breathes, her eyes wide.

"How unfortunate," Ashley adds, his lips and mustache pursing as one. "Couldn't you have done anything to help him?"

I almost wish I had my phone out so I could send Liam the look that Birdie levels on the young man. It's so dark and so much like that terrifying puppet of our youth that there's no way my brother would believe me without picture evidence.

"One does not interfere with Death," Birdie says coldly. "One merely—if one is lucky—bears mute witness."

Even *I* feel a bit of a tremor after a pronouncement like that one, so I can't blame Ashley and Sid for not following through. Unfortunately, it means I have to do the heavy lifting.

"I'm so sorry for your loss," I say with genuine sympathy. Since shoveling scrambled eggs into my mouth during a conversation like this one seems a touch gauche, I set my fork down. "His death must have been a shock, coming as it did so soon on the heels of your father's passing. Have you heard anything more from the authorities about what happened? Spoken with his family at all?"

"He doesn't have any family," Ashley says.

"*We* were his family," Sid corrects him. "Or as close as he had to one, anyway."

"Poor Harvey," Ashley murmurs. "He could have done so much better. 'All happy families resemble each other; each unhappy family is unhappy in its own way.'"

I'm ready for the quotation this time around. Ashley Stewart isn't the only person around here who's read a few books. Heavy Russian literature is the cornerstone of every angsty teen's bookshelf. "Tolstoy," I say. "*Anna Karenina.*"

Ashley looks at me with burgeoning respect, but Sid merely continues unchecked. "Harvey was more like a brother to Father than a solicitor. They practically grew up together. It's why I invited him to join us for this. He wasn't too keen on the idea, but if anyone would have been able to reach out to Father, it was Harvey."

Birdie gives a low chuckle. "Who's to say he won't be just as valuable to us now?" She raises a hand to her temple in *my* signature move. "There are so many vibrations in this place, so much energy . . ."

Once again, Sid and Ashley look to me for confirmation. This time, I decide not to support Birdie's theatrics with my own. Is that what I look like when I do it? *Talk about pretension.* I feel nauseous watching such a display.

"I haven't felt much yet, but that's not surprising considering the long journey up here." I give up on the idea of eating and push my plate away. No good can come of sitting here and letting Birdie take center stage. "If it's not too painful, would one of you mind telling me a little about what you're hoping I can do for you? Nicholas gave me to understand that there's a missing cache of family heirlooms, but he wasn't very forthcoming about the details."

Sid smiles her understanding. "He never is. Not if he can help it, anyway."

This moment of amity is exactly what I was angling for. I might not be able to match Birdie White in terms of showmanship, but Sid likes me. She trusts me. That kind of honest connection is worth much more than a dozen plumes shoved into a makeshift turban.

"In this instance, his reticence is my fault," Sid says. Like me, she gives up on breakfast and clasps her hands together on the table. "It isn't our family's custom to discuss the heirlooms in the open. Or to discuss them at all, really. Even inviting you here for the purpose of finding them, putting their existence into words—"

"Don't do it, Sid." Ashley raps his knuckles on the table in a show of superstition. "Think of Father. Think of *Harvey*."

For the first time since I embarked on this long, exhausting, and death-filled journey, I feel a surge of gratitude toward Nicholas. There's more at work here than a box of valuables tucked away in a long-forgotten cupboard—more, even, than a crackpot of a medium presiding over the breakfast table with promises of doom. I *knew* he wouldn't have sent me here unless it was worth my while.

"We have to find them, Ashley," Sid says. She places her hand over his fist to prevent him from knocking on wood again. "It's dangerous, obviously, but what other choice do we have? I can't live like this any longer. I *won't*."

"Yes, but—"

"And don't forget what Nicholas said," she adds in a low voice. "Madame Eleanor can keep us safe. She'll know how to protect us."

I'm about to protest any and all such promises Nicholas might have made on my behalf, but Sid isn't done yet.

"She's our only real hope." As if in confirmation of this, Sid turns a pair of misty, hopeful eyes my way. "If Madame Eleanor can't break this thing, then no one can. We have to trust her."

I open my mouth and close it again, unable to find the right words to bring Sid the comfort and confidence she seeks. Modesty isn't a trait I normally wrestle with in moments like these, so it's a new kind of struggle for me. I've always been more of a shrieking eel than a shrinking violet, slippery and vociferous about my psychic abilities, but something about this particular case has me feeling uneasy.

For the first time in my life, I don't *want* to stand up on a table and mystify the room with my capabilities. Perhaps it's seeing what Birdie looks like when she's trying so hard to be profound, but it feels like something more, something deeper.

Something real? Winnie suggests.

Sid speaks again before I have an opportunity to examine

Winnie's timely intervention. "If we don't so something soon, we're all in danger. It won't stop until we're dead. It never does."

This sounds like a piece of dramatic and utter nonsense to me, but Birdie stands abruptly. She pushes off the table as she does, which has the effect of sending dishes and forks clattering. My eggs slide off my plate and onto the delicate lace tablecloth with a *splat*.

"Gloriana's Curse," Birdie says. "My God. This isn't just some random treasure hunt you want our help with. You've brought us here to lay Gloriana's Curse to rest."

Before anyone has a chance to respond to this enlightening piece of news, a crack of lightning flashes in the distance. The room plunges almost immediately into darkness—or as much darkness as can exist at ten o'clock in the morning. It's hardly a cause for panic, since the windows are large enough to let in the feeble gray light of day and my cell phone has a fully functioning flashlight mode, but from the way the rest of the people in the room react, you'd think we were trapped in an underground bunker with a serial killer.

Ashley's chair topples over as he jumps back from the table. Sid runs to the sideboard and frantically pulls open several drawers in search of candles. Birdie stands ominously in the same place as before, soaking in all the drama as a woman born to it.

I start moving, too, but only to help a short, rounded woman bustling through the attached swinging door. She bears an ornate candelabra in one hand and a second pot of tea in the other. She's dressed neatly but simply in a faded blue calico dress that looks, like McGee's sweater, as though it's been in use for hundreds of years.

"It's that blasted generator, Miss Stewart, and so I told McGee last week when he was here." Her voice carries a light, pleasing burr native to these parts. She hands me the candelabra and flashes me a grateful smile. "It drips if you tilt it, so be careful of your fingers. 'One more storm, and it'll fizzle right out,' I says to him. 'And here the lot of us will be without hot water or the telly to while away the hours.' Well, I was right, and now how am I to wash the dishes?"

There's something about the woman's no-nonsense prattle that puts Sid and Ashley at ease. Ashley's hand shakes as he rights his chair again, and Sid closes the drawers with more force than is strictly necessary, but they no longer look as though they're facing their own mortality.

"Oh, Elspeth. Don't say it's out for good?" Sid draws forward and accepts the fresh pot of tea. "Surely we can fix it?"

Elspeth shakes her head resolutely. Her hair, a soft, mousy brown threaded liberally with gray, is pulled back in a bun that doesn't seem to shift no matter how much she moves. "No one can fix that old heap. With aught luck, McGee'll have ordered a new one, and we'll be all right in a week or two." She turns to me with a smile that looks particularly soft in the glow of the candles. "I haven't found your luggage yet, either, but not for want of trying. You're sure McGee didn't load the bags back on the boat before he left?"

Yes, I'm sure. I recall looking back with regret—and, apparently, prescience—as Birdie and I walked up those hidden stairs, the boat already heading out on its seaward journey.

But "It's possible," is what I say. It seems rude to harp on clothing and toiletries when the poor woman is going to have to wash all these dishes in cold water.

"Aye, then. I'll round up all the candles I can find and make sure we've fires laid in the grates." Elspeth looks around the room with satisfaction, apparently finding nothing amiss with the upturned plates and Birdie looking like a drawn puppet at the head of the table. "You just leave this here when you're done with breakfast. I'll take care of it, and don't you worry."

On that comfortable pronouncement, she bustles back out the way she came, leaving the four of us standing in a state of suspended animation. Once again, it's up to me to dispel it.

"Should I put this down?" I ask as I hold the candelabra level. Several drips of wax have already started running down the tallest taper, so I'm careful not to jostle it. "Or did we want to discuss the, uh, curse in another room?"

At fresh mention of the curse, Ashley and Sid share another of those wary, shifty-eyed glances. It's based mostly in fear, I know, but there's a mulish look about Ashley's mouth that forces me into an executive decision.

No way am I allowing us to lose this momentum. *Real* or not, we're making progress here.

"We'll take this up to my room," I say with a nod. "I always perform a protective chant before I go to sleep in a new place. It won't have worn off yet, so that will be the safest place."

The amount of relief that crosses their faces is enough to make me laugh out loud. Unless you count the conversation I had with Birdie last night, there's been nothing done inside that room worth note. The only chanting I did was counting sheep while I fell asleep.

"Thank you, Madame Eleanor," Sid says with real feeling. She reaches over and squeezes my hand. It has the effect of tilting the candelabra and covering my fingers with cascading hot wax, which instantly hardens. "Oh, dear. I'm sorry about that. I'm sorry about all of it, actually. When I wrote to Nicholas asking for help, I didn't think—"

Another bolt of lightning zigzags across the gray sky. Sid's jump is less pronounced this time, but there's no doubt that she's feeling uneasy. "I didn't think it would be like *this*," she says, her voice barely above a whisper.

"I did," I reply. I feel a bit like Elspeth, with her hearty cheer and maternal clucking, but what else can I do? Sid might be a beautiful, wealthy woman with a literal castle at her feet, but I'm starting to realize that she has all the fortitude of a caterpillar. "Dealing with supernatural entities was always going to be a bit dark, you know. If it were all puppies and rainbows, anyone could do it. Believe me when I say this is nothing compared to some of the cases I've seen."

I hand her the candelabra before she can ask me to elaborate. Some of the cases I've seen would make her blood curdle.

"After you," I say with a gesture toward the doorway. "I'm just going to grab the table salt before I go. For extra protection."

Sid and Ashley accept this as a perfectly rational way to conduct business and head out the main door, allowing it to swing shut behind them. Salt won't protect us against anything but garden slugs and low blood pressure, but what they don't know won't hurt them.

"Salt won't be enough to protect us from Gloriana's Curse," Birdie says, repeating my thoughts almost verbatim. "Nor will your chant. What else do you have?"

I turn to look at her. She hasn't moved from her spot at the head of the table, where she stands like a statue presiding over the ruins of our meal.

"What else do I have?" I echo, blinking. There's a chance that Ashley and Sid are still near enough to overhear, so I answer with, "There were all kinds of supplies in my bags—sage smudging sticks and the like—but who knows where those have gone."

She snorts. "Sage smudging sticks? Do you have any idea what we're dealing with?"

To be perfectly frank, no, I don't. Nor am I unduly worried. Curses are, in my experience, nothing more than a guilty conscience working overtime. I once cured the village butcher by making him take a fresh roast to the neighbor whose tulips he drove over with his delivery truck. I *told* him that it was the blood of animal sacrifice that countered the curse, but I suspect it had more to do with the Sunday dinner the family enjoyed at his expense.

"I'm hoping that Sid and Ashley will tell me about it as soon as we're safely huddled in my room," I say. "Which we should probably do soon, or they'll think we've been swallowed by the evil entities plaguing the house."

Birdie doesn't move. "But you knew."

"Is that a no? You don't have to come with me. I can handle it on my own."

"Gold coins," she says. "Last night you mentioned gold coins. You knew what the heirlooms were."

It had been my intention to abandon Birdie to her mystical hysterics, but something about the serious note in her voice stops me in my tracks. She's no longer speaking in that foretelling, melodious way. She sounds, well, *human*.

"I *guessed* what the heirlooms were," I counter. A pang of uneasiness settles in the pit of my stomach, since it wasn't my guess so much as Winnie's, but I do my best to ignore it. "Let's call it a strong feeling and leave it at that."

"I don't believe you. No one could have guessed that." There's nothing of a question in this remark. It's not an accusation, either, but I still don't like it—mostly because she's right. There's nothing natural about the way I came by my information.

Just like there was nothing natural about my vision of Harvey's death.

Partially to cover my discomfiture, and partly because I'm starting to grow weary of all this tiptoeing around, I turn to her with both a question *and* an accusation.

"It doesn't matter what you believe, because it's the truth," I say. "But I have the oddest presentiment that you were expecting the heirlooms to be something else. Diamonds, perhaps? A stamp collection worth a ridiculous sum that the family, in their gratitude, would have no choice but to share with you?"

My attempt at unsettling her falls flat. Her attempt at unsettling *me*, however, is much more successful.

"Someone in this house is going to die," she says. Once again, she seems to be speaking from a normal place—a human place—and she looks almost defeated as the words leave her mouth. She seems much older and less imposing than she did a few minutes ago. Even her eyebrows look droopy. "No good can come of searching for those heirlooms, Madame Eleanor. You already know that. You felt it the moment we stepped onto this island."

It's not my custom to fidget or squirm or do any of those things that unconsciously reveal my inner workings, but I find myself picking at the hardened wax on my hand. From this angle, it appears to have formed a sinister sneer in the center of my palm—a sneer that's warning me, mocking me.

I crush my hand around it, cracking the wax to pieces. I don't believe in reading candle drippings any more than I do tea leaves. In fact, *not* believing in things is what makes me ideally suited to a job like this one.

"No good can come of leaving those poor people to their fears, either," I say as I send wax crumbles to the ground. "Not when they've already suffered so much loss. Come on, Birdie. There's no such thing as curses. You know that as well as I do."

The speed with which she resumes her earlier posture is almost ludicrous. Before I can do more than blink, she's standing rigid and domineering once again. Even her feather, which had been showing signs of wilting, pops back up to its former glory. "I know nothing of the sort. I can see now why Glenn wanted me to be here. Someone is going to have to protect this house—protect this family. *You* obviously have no idea what you're up against."

On the contrary, I'm starting to develop a very good idea of the obstacles in my path. Or, I should say, the *obstacle* in my path.

She's about five foot ten, dripping in jewels and feathers, and has snatched the salt cellar from the table before I have a chance to realize what she's doing.

Chapter 6

"Protect this hearth and defend this reign. Dispel all evil and malign each bane." Birdie lifts the salt cellar to her lips and blows, sending a spray of crystals all over the floor of my bedroom. "In safety's honor and security's name."

She uses the scoop in the salt cellar to dump a line across the doorway. Ashley and Sid watch, fascinated, as she does the same around the windows and the fireplace hearth. I can practically see their fear melting away, their uneasiness ebbing with each mess Birdie makes. It doesn't occur to any of them that I'm going to have to clean that up later. If there's one thing I've learned in my years of visiting other people's houses, it's that as much as they love the spectacle of protective measures, they don't love walking barefoot on salt in the weeks and months to follow.

To be fair, it's a good chant. Rhymes always go over well with clients, and the fact that we're standing in a dark, heavily brocaded room lit by candle and firelight only adds to the ambience. Birdie couldn't have created a more fitting environment had she set it up herself.

Then again, she *might* have set it up herself. I'm not saying she can control the weather, but there is a chance she can control the questionable infrastructure that keeps this island running. I'm not putting anything past that woman.

"There. That should keep us protected for another hour, at the very least." She sets the salt down and seats herself in the same wingback chair from last night. She looks as much at home now as she did then. "Between dear Ella's little spell and my more powerful invocation, no spirit will be able to break through."

I'd like to ask why Birdie's nonsense is any more powerful than my own, but that would only be giving her what she wants. There's no doubt in my mind that she has an answer ready—and that it's designed to make me look as small as possible.

Instead, I install myself with my back to the door, standing guard over the room and ensuring that I can watch for any tricks Birdie might be inclined to play. "Now that we're all wrapped up in safety's honor, why don't you start from the beginning?" I say.

Sid and Ashley share another one of those worried looks, but Sid eventually nods and lowers herself to the bed. I didn't make it up after I awoke this morning, but it's as tight and tidy as if it belongs in a hospital. Elspeth must have been through here while we were at breakfast.

"If you've already heard of the curse, there's not much to tell." Sid waits until Ashley installs himself by the fireplace before continuing. He leans an elbow on the mantel but is careful not to dislodge the salt. "It's been part of our family history for as long as I can remember—centuries, in fact."

Birdie nods as if this makes perfect sense. Which, considering that she already knows what Sid is talking about, is probably true. I'm the only person in the room who's never heard of

Gloriana or the havoc she seems to have wreaked upon this family.

Sid plucks at an invisible string on the blood-red bedspread. "Of course, it sounds outrageous to anyone hearing it for the first time, but you have to remember that we grew up with these stories, were reared by them. Every Stewart is. It's the price we pay for all this."

The *all this* is encapsulated with a grand sweep of Sid's arm. It covers the entirety of my room and the valuables contained within it. At first appraisal, I'd put the furniture alone at no less than ten thousand dollars. I can't imagine what the entire estate must be worth.

Or, rather, I *can* imagine it. That's the problem. If I can accurately sum up this family's value at a glance, then Birdie can, too. There's a fortune to be made here, and I don't just mean in finding the missing family heirlooms.

"Curses aren't written in stone," I say, determined that no one will be making any fortunes under my watch. I was called here to help Nicholas's friend as a favor, and that's precisely what I plan to do. The line between me and Birdie White might be a thin one, but it's a line all the same. "In blood sometimes and, in your case, gold, but they're not irreversible. I take it to understand that this Gloriana of yours put a curse on some coins that belong to your family?"

"She's not *our* Gloriana," Ashley says with what I detect is a note of lofty disdain. It's followed almost immediately by another of his quotations. "'That greatest Gloriana . . . that greatest Glorious Queene of Faerie lond.'"

Although I'm starting to get the feeling that Ashley is much better read than I am, I recognize the line from Edmund Spenser's most famous work. If I remember my reading of *The Faerie Queene* correctly, Gloriana is used to refer to no less a personage than Queen Elizabeth I.

"Wait—this curse was put on your family by Queen Elizabeth?" I ask. I pause only to cast a glance between the siblings before speaking again. "As in *the* Queen Elizabeth? The one with the big white ruff and lead poisoning?"

My irreverence isn't appreciated. I cough and attempt to put on an appropriately sober mien, but the damage has already been done. Once upon a time, I was exceptional at playing this game, at pretending to be serious about the idea of laying imaginary ghosts to rest. But that was before Winnie showed me that *real* ghosts aren't all that emotionally invested in the living.

"I'm sorry. I don't mean to be rude. It's just that I've never worked with so . . . illustrious a spirit before. My most famous ghost to date has been a man said to have once shaken hands with JFK."

"I've worked with such ghosts," Birdie says. Birdie *lies*, I should say, but I can't confess to being surprised. She's the exact sort of person who would claim to have connected with the most famous English monarch in history. She and the queen probably have regular chats about imprisoning their enemies and the best methods to get beheading bloodstains out of silk. "And the queen's not the one who put the curse on the gold. It was cursed when it was given to her. I have that correct, yes?"

This question is directed at Sid, who nods both her agreement and appreciation at finding at least *one* of her mediums to be sympathetic.

"No one knows where the curse first came from," Sid says. "Some claim it was a spell put on the gold by a priest who sold his soul to the devil. Others say it was the blood of the men who died while mining it. All we know for sure is that the ship that first brought the treasure to England crashed and sank when it was only a few klicks from shore."

"Every man, woman, and child on board died at sea," Ashley adds. "The only thing they were able to recover was the gold."

I nod my head in understanding, since that's obviously what's expected of me. What I think—but don't dare add—is that a great number of ships crashed and sank in the glory days of Elizabethan seafaring. And considering how many of those were carrying pillaged Spanish gold at the time, I imagine that recovery of the cargo was prioritized over saving lives.

Unfortunately, as much as it would help them to hear this, rational discourse is obviously off the table.

"The gold was a worth a fortune, even back then," Sid says. "But every time the chest was opened, something terrible happened. Ships sank. Battles were lost. Entire families were torn apart. Eventually, the queen had no choice but to get rid of it. It was too risky to keep, even riskier to spend. She put it on the next ship out of England."

Now it's Birdie's turn to fall into quotation. " 'He who looks upon Gloriana's Burden will suffer and repent.' "

Sid nods eagerly and pushes back a lock of hair that's come loose from her careful chignon. "You *have* heard of it."

Birdie scoffs and casts a very obvious look at me. "Every good medium makes it her business to know such things. If it's cursed, haunted, or possessed, I know of its existence. What I don't understand, however, is how the gold came to be in your family's possession. I thought it disappeared after it was stolen by pirates."

"It was," Sid says. She speaks like that's the final word on the subject, as if the mention of pirates is the clincher to an argument no one knew we were having. "*We* stole it."

What happens next will forever cause me to feel a pang of equal parts anguish and embarrassment. I'm not, by both personal and professional necessity, a jumpy person. I've been known to chase down criminals and chastise ghosts to their faces. I can watch a horror movie from start to finish without covering my eyes. But when a voice from the doorway says, "Oh, dear. Have you been spilling the family secrets without me?" I have no choice but to turn around.

That's when I scream.

It's mostly the fault of poor lighting. The room is visible enough, what with the curtains thrown open and the fire flickering in the grate, but the hallway is as dark and gloomy as any interior castle passage without electricity can be. The man standing in the doorway is equally dark. He's dressed in a long black overcoat that reaches all the way down to his toes. His boots are black, his hands are encased in black gloves, and even his hair, which clings in damp curls to his head, appears to be of a deep, rich midnight.

However, none of that is what causes my lamentable lack of restraint. *That*, unfortunately, comes from the black eyepatch covering his right eye. It's so rare that pirates manifest in front of me while they're under discussion that I'm taken completely by surprise.

"Otis!" Sid's shriek is equal to my own, but hers takes on a much more rapturous guise. It's accompanied by her springing to her feet and greeting the man with outstretched arms. "We had no idea you were coming."

Otis accepts this greeting with a warm embrace, but his eyes—or eye, I should say—meets mine over Sid's head. "So I apprehend."

An embarrassed heat flushes my cheeks, but I'm not able to apologize or explain, since his gaze moves smoothly over the rest of the room. He pauses at Ashley to give a brief nod, but the sight of Birdie causes him to drop his arms from around Sid's shoulders and blink.

"I see you went through with that psychic business, after all," he says in a tone as dry as his overcoat is wet. "I warned you what would happen, but you two never listen. Now see what's come of it. You'll excuse my plain speaking, ma'am, but you look like you eat children straight out of the oven."

For the second time in as many minutes, I'm betrayed by my inability to control myself. Instead of screaming, however, I outright laugh. Never has a woman been so accurately summarized in such a brief space of time.

Although Birdie doesn't go so far as to join in my laughter, she takes no offense. "People are often scared of what they don't understand," she says in her magnanimous way. She lifts one of her ring-bedecked hands and holds it out to the newcomer, her palm down as if expecting a papal kiss. With an indifference I can't help but admire, Otis draws forward, dragging the line of salt everywhere, and gives her hand a perfunctory shake.

I find less to admire in the way he turns his attention to me. In any other man, the dark clothes and eyepatch could easily be taken as an affectation, but I doubt that's the case here. He seems almost born to them.

"*That* one's purpose is clear, but I can't quite make you out. You look like a magician's assistant, but I don't see any need to cut damsels in half out here in the middle of the ocean." He taps his deeply cleft chin in consideration. "Let me see . . . Vaudeville comedienne? Burlesque dancer at a G-rated club?"

"Otis!" Sid cries in a voice that contains more laughter than chagrin. "I'm so sorry, Madame Eleanor. Don't believe a word out of Otis's mouth. He never means any of the things he says."

"I doubt my lies are the ones you should apologize for," he says in a show of shrewd understanding. "Well, Ashley? Aren't you glad to see me amongst all this female sentimentality?"

"Hullo, Otis," Ashley says. The words are almost wrung out of him, as is the hand he grudgingly holds out. "It's good to see you again."

"No, it's not. You wish I'd shipwrecked on my way here. But you know I'll take any excuse I can get to pull my boat out, and Uncle Glenn wouldn't have wanted you searching for the family fortune without me." He turns to me with a sardonically lifted brow. "Never count a pirate out of a treasure hunt. Have you checked the safe yet?"

This Otis person—a cousin to Sid and Ashley, by his own admission—is by no means an attractive man. His facial features are over-large and distinguished by a scar that escapes from both the top and bottom of his eyepatch in a gnarled twist. The curled locks of his hair are so tight they look recently permed, and the sneering way he's treated everyone in this room except Sid indicates a cynical disposition.

I like him immensely.

"Of course we checked the safe," Ashley says, crossing his arms with all the petulance of a boy half his age. "And the library. And Father's study. *And* everywhere else that springs to the mind of anyone who's not an idiot, so you can stop looking at me like that."

"Well, now. That's cast me down, hasn't it?" Otis asks in a purely rhetorical spirit. "When you very well know this is the only way I *can* look."

Another laugh is startled out of me. I'm about to apologize for my lack of decorum—really, it's highly unprofessional to keep breaking out like this—but Birdie beats me to it.

"I'm sorry that you've found us in this state," she says, gesturing to the glimmering darkness and broken line of salt over the doorway. "It's not an ideal place to hold a session, but the spirits are displeased at our intrusion into this household. *Gloriana* is displeased."

"Well, if it comes to that, I'm not too keen on it myself," Otis says, unruffled.

He strips his gloves from his hands, handing them to Sid before continuing to unpeel the other layers from his personage. He's not, as the bulk of his overcoat suggests, a very large man. Small and lithe, he looks more like a shadowy version of Ashley than a big, scary pirate. Even the clothes he has on under the coat, a gray turtleneck and well-cut slacks, are somewhat disappointing. Only the eyepatch and gnarled scar remain.

"I wish you would have called me before you let these charlatans into the house," Otis says. With a nod at me, he adds, "No offense, of course."

"Oh, none taken," I reply, amused. He's not the first man to call me a charlatan, and I doubt he'll be last. Even Nicholas, in his more ironical moods, has been known to throw the term about.

Birdie, however, doesn't take this remark as well as she did the aspersion on her appearance. I could almost swear the feather on her head ruffles up in protest. "I hardly think you're a fit judge on matters of the afterlife," she says with a sharp sniff. "We were in the middle of discussing the nature of your family's troubles when you so rudely barged in."

"By all means, don't let me stop you," he replies. He tosses his wet coat onto the foot of my bed, heedless of what it will mean when I slip between the sheets later. I don't take that to heart, either. If he arrived via his own private boat, that means we have at least one exit route available to us. I'm prepared to overlook quite a bit for that.

After a quick glance around the room, Otis settles himself on the wide frame of the window. Once again unaware of how his feet scuff the line of salt as he crosses over it, he seats himself amidst the scattered crystals. "Perhaps I can help condense the story. Let's see . . . The queen had gold. The queen had death. Our forebearer, with a profound lack of insight, ransacked the ship meant to free the sovereignty of its burden. Then *we* had gold and *we* had death. A rather neat transaction, don't you think?"

"Otis, don't," Sid pleads.

He doesn't heed her. With the sneer firmly in place again, he fixes his gaze on Birdie's profile, which is being held in stiff disapproval. I can almost find it in my heart to pity her. She wouldn't like being upstaged by anyone, but for a man like this to barrel in and wrest her from her perch must be too much.

"Dear old Great, Great, Great, Great, Great—honestly, I don't know how great he was, nor do I care—Grandpa Stewart was a pirate, you understand. Don't look so shocked; it was de rigueur for Hebrideans to plunder English ships in those days. How else do you think we came by all this wealth?"

I'd assumed it was through the systematic disenfranchisement of the masses, as per the usual custom, but that works, too. Enmity between the Scottish and the English has been the cause of many worse crimes than piracy.

"Alas," he adds with a mock sigh. "*I* might look the part of a villainous rogue, but the acclaim goes to him."

"At least he had manners," Ashley mutters.

"A matter of pure conjecture. For all we know, he ate with the same knife he used to clean his toenails. Come to think of it, he probably did. Most of them did back then."

This proves too much for Sid. "Otis!" she cries in a voice of real disapproval. "You can't have heard what's happened, or you wouldn't talk like that."

"Fiend seize it. What is it now? Banshees screeching in the night? Ghostly fingers tapping on the windows?" He hooks a thumb at Birdie. "That one looks like she could set up a good holler if she put her mind to it, and as for the fingers, you know as well as I do that it's nothing more than the rain going sideways over the ocean."

Sid casts a scared look at me, which I interpret to mean that she can't bring herself to divulge the news of the most recent death in the family.

"It's regarding Harvey Renault, your uncle's solicitor," I say as gently as I can. "He passed away while taking a train up here."

To do him credit, Otis looks genuinely shocked at this piece of news. The sneer dies on his lips, and he doesn't move a single muscle, not even to wipe away a drop of water that's trickled from his damp hair down the side of his nose.

"Harvey Renault died?" he echoes.

Sid nods, her expression grim. "We got a call from the train station late last night. No one has been able to give us much in the way of information, but from what they're saying, it sounds as though he had a—"

"Heart attack," Otis finishes for her.

Ashley whirls on his cousin. "You knew? You knew what happened, and you still came in here laughing at the curse and acting as though you don't have a care in the world?"

"Of course I didn't know he died. But Harvey was eighty, if he was a day, and he's had two heart attacks already. It can hardly have come as a surprise." Otis glances around the room, taking each face in its turn. His sneer returns. "Or, rather, it *should* hardly have come as a surprise. But I can see I was grossly mistaken in thinking I'd encounter wisdom in this house. You, the Burlesque Bambi one—"

"My name is Eleanor Wilde," I interrupt. "*Madame* Eleanor Wilde."

He ignores this. "You look like a woman of sense. Is it possible—just possible—that an older man with a weak heart might succumb to his ailment for no other reason than that's how nature works? Not because of a centuries-old curse placed on a pile of gold that no one in this room has laid eyes on in decades?"

His question puts me in a difficult position. On the one hand, I absolutely agree with him. It *is* possible that Harvey died of natural causes, especially in light of this new information about his heart condition. On the other hand, I resent the implication that I look like a *woman of sense*.

I look mysterious. I look all-seeing. I look like someone who's going to lay a curse to rest even if it means I have to pretend to believe in it first.

"The secrets of this world aren't so easily explained," I say in a tone that sounds alarmingly like Birdie's. I nod toward the candelabra. "Already, the elements are wreaking havoc on our setting, drawing upon the wrath of nature to—"

"Oh, for the Lord's sake." Otis throws up his hands and jerks himself from the window seat. "I'm not going to sit here and listen to this. I have better things to do."

"Where are you going?" Sid asks as Otis scoops up his overcoat and gloves. They leave a large, damp imprint behind. "You can't go, Otis. Not now. We need you."

Otis's expression, which had been turning decidedly wrathful, softens as it lands on his cousin. His voice, however, remains resolute. "I'm going to fix the generator," he says, and shoves his arms into the coat. Turning the collar up around his throat and tugging the gloves back on, he once again regains his piratical air. "As much fun as it is to tell ghost stories in the dark, there's no way I'm living in this house for the next week without any power. Some of us would like to eat and bathe like normal human beings."

This eminently sensible plan finds favor with me, but I don't dare say so out loud.

"The next week?" Sid asks hopefully. "Does this mean you'll be making a long stay?"

"No," he says, and heads out the door. "It means that's how much time I'm giving myself to get rid of your houseguests. Any longer than that, and I'm likely to start putting my own curses on this place."

"Well," Birdie says in a comprehensive manner. She watches as the door swings to a close, the latch clicking triumphantly behind Otis. "That man is going to have a very negative impact on the energy of this place."

"Yes, but I believe he's going to have a very positive impact on the *electricity* of this place," I counter. "For that, I'm willing to forgive him. What boat was he talking about, by the way? I thought McGee was the only regular transportation."

"Oh, Otis has his own vessel for work. He's always coming and going." Sid worries her lower lip between her teeth. "During the warm season, it's mostly going, but he doesn't take anyone out this time of year. He does boat tours. He's sometimes hired to do private excursions and fishing expeditions, but it's mostly families up on holiday during the summer."

I can't imagine that's a particularly well-paying profession, especially considering how little he must have to do during the winter, but I don't say anything out loud. To be honest, I find Otis's presence here a decidedly helpful one. He's too perceptive, brusque to the point of rudeness, and he left a huge wet patch on my bed, but if anyone is going to prevent Birdie from becoming overly confident, it's a man willing to take the wind out of her sails by slicing them right down the center.

"Not everyone has the same sensitivity about these sorts of things," I say. "Nicholas himself is a skeptic, but I find it doesn't limit me in the least. There will continue to be magic and miracles regardless of whether or not men like them believe."

Sid accepts this with a nod and seats herself on the bed once again, unconcerned with the damp that must be seeping into her skirt. "You're right—of course you're right. Otis doesn't like to admit it, but Father's death affected him quite severely. Near the end, he was closer to him than either of us. Well, he'd have to be, wouldn't he?" She blinks up at me, a tear catching in one corner of her eye. "Ashley and I don't live here, and we didn't come out to visit as often as we should have."

I'm quick to interpret her real meaning. "He was alone when he died."

Sid nods, shaking the tear free. "It's not always easy for us to make the trip, especially this time of year. But Otis has a beautiful little house on Barra. He stops by more than anyone."

I nod and tuck this tidbit away, along with the information about his tour-boat business. Proximity and access to this island might mean nothing . . . or it might mean everything. Especially since it seems Otis can slip in and out with no one in the castle being any the wiser.

Not to be outdone, Birdie makes her own pronouncement. "He has a tragedy in his history, that man. A terrible accident, a tortured past."

Well, obviously. That's a fairly safe bet, considering the state of his scarred face, but I wasn't going to say so. Not yet, at any rate.

"Oh, yes," Sid agrees wanly. "Otis's life hasn't been an easy one."

"He's an orphan."

This is a new one to me—but, again, completely within the realm of possibility. A close relationship with an uncle hints at a lack of direct parental influence, and a man with a personality as abrasive as that one is most likely hiding some mommy and daddy issues. Even the most inexperienced con artist—I'm sorry, *medium*—could tell that much.

"You can see all that?" Ashley asks. "After just one meeting?"

Birdie's answer to this is to fall into a trance-like state that forces me to take my tongue between my teeth. She's still in that stupid red chair, sitting like Queen Elizabeth herself holding an audience. It's not that I begrudge her this opportunity to show off; it's that she's doing it before I've had a chance. I'm not 100 percent sure of her game just yet, but there's no denying that she's trying to outplay me. Outplay me, outperform me, and out-psychic me.

The worst part is, she's succeeding at it. I could almost curse Nicholas—yes, *curse* him—for foisting this job on me with all of twelve hours' advance warning. There's no denying that Birdie has done her homework. She knows about the Stewart family, about this house, about Gloriana's curse . . . and about me.

I, on the other hand, am like a puppy just beginning to snuffle her way about. An extra day of research would have gone a long way in helping me make a more convincing show of things.

"His pain runs deep," Birdie says, her eyes closed and her fingers fluttering in front of her. I'm not sure what she's supposed to be doing, but it's effective. Her hands look as though they're holding something sinister at bay. "It extends beyond this castle . . . and beyond this world. A wife lost. A future blighted. And worst of all, a child never born."

Her eyes pop open again. They bear the dazed, unfixed look of someone awakening from a deep sleep. I assume she's working too hard keeping them focused on nothing to see Sid and Ashley's reaction, but it doesn't matter. Her words have struck home.

"Madame Eleanor," Sid says weakly, one arm extended in my direction. Her whole body shakes like a blancmange, her face devoid of color. Even when her hand finds mine and clutches it, she continues shaking. "She can't know that. How can she know that? Otis doesn't talk about that accident with *anyone*. The boat, the storm . . ."

I don't know how Birdie has all this information about Otis any more than I know how she predicted Harvey's death. The one thing I *do* know is that she's seriously starting to tick me off.

"It was to be a baby girl," Birdie adds in her deep, musical voice. "Colleen."

Sid visibly blanches, her grip on my hand tightening to the point where I can no longer feel my fingers. "Please make her stop," she says, her voice barely above a whisper. "I can't bear to hear any more."

This is a task I'm more than happy to perform. "Birdie," I call sharply. When this doesn't appear to affect her, I disentangle my hand from Sid's. Snapping my fingers, I try again. "Birdie, you're scaring Sid and Ashley. Stop this at once."

I know she hears me, because a *ghost* of a smile flickers on her lips before it disappears again. "That was Gloriana's doing, too," she says. "Gloriana is particularly drawn to children."

"Enough." I stalk over to where Birdie is sitting and kick the leg of her chair. The wood is so solid that it doesn't move her, but at least she gives a start of surprise. "If you can't find anything productive to say, then kindly keep your thoughts to yourself. We're not here to tell these people what they already know. We're here to find a trove of gold coins, and that's it. All you're doing right now is making a scene."

I have a dozen other things to say to her—all of them sharp, most of them antagonistic—but Ashley speaks up before I have a chance to utter any.

"She's right," he says. Like Sid, he's taken this last bit of information to heart. His face has grown pale and his expression taut, the silent film star at his most forlorn. "It's always children who suffer the most."

Naturally, Birdie finds this an ideal opportunity to be ghastly. "Children will continue to suffer," she says. "Until Gloriana is appeased, the descendants of the Stewart line will fall victim to her wrath. No child is too young, no babe too innocent."

As far as I'm concerned, this is the final straw. I've done a lot of things in my life that I'm not proud of, but cursing *children* isn't one of them.

"Birdie, if you don't snap out of your trance this instant, I'm going to call on the power of the Great Goddess to remove you from this room." I kick the leg of her chair again and lower my voice to a whisper only she can hear. "And if that doesn't work, I'm going to call on the power of Otis Stewart to lend me his aid instead. I'll tell him exactly what you just said and how you said it. You decide which approach you think is more likely to succeed."

My words strike home. Birdie's posture becomes less rigid, her eyes once again fixed on the world around her.

I turn to face Sid and Ashley. "*Now*. I know you've been through a lot, but I'd really appreciate it if you continued your story. The sooner I can get to work locating this treasure of yours, the sooner we can lay all this to rest." I take a deep breath but a short one, fearful that to pause for even a second will give Birdie an opportunity to get going again. "I take it that your family's piratical history included the theft of Gloriana's, uh, Burden? At which the point the curse transferred itself to you?"

"What? Oh, yes. Yes, that was it exactly." It takes Sid a moment to return to the topic at hand, but she makes an admirable show of corralling her thoughts. "It was soon discovered that the only way to prevent the curse from killing everything and everyone was to hide it—to protect it. The gold can't be spent or invested, can't be placed in a museum or even in a bank for safekeeping. We're only allowed to be its caretakers. Nothing more."

It sounds like a terrible waste of gold to me, but I'm willing to play along. *For now.*

"Otis said that no one has seen it in decades. Is that true?"

Sid shoots her brother a scared, anxious look. When she speaks, her voice is hollow. "Yes. Ashley and I saw it years ago, but only once."

"Once was enough," Ashley says bitterly.

Although I don't have any of Birdie's insider information, I'm able to put the pieces of this conversation into a neatly fitted puzzle. I may not have been fed Otis's tragic backstory or told about the pregnant wife he seems to have lost in a boating accident. I might not know where Glenn Stewart kept his best wine reserves or the entirety of every curse and haunting that has ever plagued the United Kingdom. What I do know, however, is what it's like to lose everything that matters in one awful, catastrophic swoop.

"How did she die?" I ask, my voice slightly cracking. "Your mother?"

There's no surprise in either Sid's or Ashley's expression. Whether because Birdie has inured them to the mysteries of the sixth sense, or they simply don't have enough in them to care anymore, all they bear is heavy resignation.

"Pancreatic cancer," Sid says. She hugs the post of the bed as if to brace herself. "It hit violently and suddenly. She passed within a month of her diagnosis."

I nod my understanding and refrain from offering the token sympathies that rise to my lips. My own mother passed away when I was eighteen, taken in the car accident that also robbed me of my sister, Winnie. Words did little to help me then, and they're equally useless now.

Unless, of course, they're coming from Winnie herself.

"How old were you at the time?" I ask instead.

Ashley answers for them both. "Sid was thirteen. I was twelve. We were both old enough to have outgrown looking for buried treasure, but we were home on school holiday and bored to tears."

"We thought it would be fun," Sid adds. "An adventure."

"Some adventure," Ashley sniffs.

Sid looks to me as if for absolution. "We were so young," she explains. "And we figured it would be a game—just make-believe, you know? We'd grown up hearing about the curse, but we didn't actually *believe* it."

Ashley gives up his position near the fireplace and begins pacing the room. His steps are long and firm—at direct odds with the lithe, boyish lines of him. "We knew right away what we had done," he says. "Father never blamed us for her illness or her death, but he vowed that no one would ever find the treasure again—not that either of us looked for it after that. We learned our lesson the first time."

Sid sags against the bedpost. "And that was it, really. We knew the coins were hidden somewhere on Airgead Island, because Father told us it was too dangerous to keep them anywhere else. As long as they stay isolated here, the world is safe from the curse. It's our duty—our *burden*—to continue to watch over them. It's the only way to keep it from hurting people."

I do some rapid mental calculations. Queen Elizabeth I died in the early sixteen hundreds, which means they've been sitting on this curse for well over four hundred years. I've worked with some old ghosts in my day, but never anything like this. Four centuries is an awfully long time for fear to hold fast, for one family to bear the weight of keeping superstition alive. It's also a long time for no one to cash in on a treasure that sounds to be worth a small fortune. Surely even cursed gold could be melted down and repurposed for general resale?

"It would have been fine like that," Ashley says. He takes another long-strided turn about the room. "It could have stayed hidden forever. It *should* have stayed hidden forever."

I don't want to interrupt the flow of the story by asking questions, so it's just as well that Sid takes any remaining guesswork out of it. She catches my eye. "As he got older, Father started to develop fears about what would happen to the gold once he died," she explains. "Ashley and I, we don't . . . It's so far to come and so inconvenient to travel. It's no wonder he started to get strange notions in his head."

Ashley chuffs a bitter laugh. "You mean it's no wonder that someone started *putting* strange notions in his head."

Sid frowns. "We don't know that for sure, Ashley. It's only a guess." To me, she adds, "A few weeks before he died, Father announced that he'd come up with an ideal hiding place. We tried to talk him out of moving it, and I thought we'd succeeded, only—"

"—only he drowned," Ashley finishes for her. His lips form

a flat line. "A man born and reared on the sea, who lived his entire life with one foot on land and another in a boat, drowned in all of six inches of water in the bathtub."

"Ashley . . ."

"What? It's the truth. If the gold was still here, then none of this would have happened. But it did happen. It *is* happening." He turns to me, his eyes glittering in the candlelight. "Someone took it. It's the only explanation I can think of. Whoever convinced Father to move the gold must have been watching to see where he put it. They're out there somewhere—selling it, spending it—and we're the ones paying the price."

Sid, apparently, is done arguing. She sighs and takes her lower lip between her teeth.

"And until we have it back, we're all at risk." Ashley glances around the room, his gaze pausing meaningfully on each face. "We have to find it and bring it back to the island, or one of us will be next."

As much as I love a melodrama playing out before my eyes, I take umbrage at that last part. "No one is going to die," I say with a stern warning look at Birdie lest she take it into her head to start doomsaying again. "For one thing, I'm here, and I have yet to lose a single client. For another . . ."

For another, it's starting to feel as though what we're dealing with is less like a centuries-old curse and more like a modern-day murderer. I wasn't here when Glenn Stewart died, obviously, and I haven't had a chance to scrounge up his autopsy report, but I'd be mightily interested to know the details of that final bath of his.

Like Otis pointed out, I'm a woman of sense. That sense is telling me that however fun it is to weave tales of ancient curses and threats of death hanging overhead, the much more likely possibility is that someone decided they wanted that gold for themselves—and that they'd stop at nothing to get their hands on it. It wouldn't be enough to convince Glenn to move the treasure and pillage the new hiding space; if they wanted to get away with the crime, then Glenn couldn't be around to put two and two together afterward.

However, I can hardly say any of this out loud. Not only am I working on pure conjecture at this point, but I doubt there's any way I'll be able to convince this family that their underlying problem is plain, ordinary greed. They've given this curse so much power over their lives, allowed it to dictate so many of their actions, that it's become a self-fulfilling prophecy. One of us could sprain an ankle on a slippery rock, and these two would most likely assume it was caused by ancient supernatural powers instead of the fallibility of human joints.

"For another," I say, thinking quickly, "an entire month passed between your father's death and Harvey's. However powerful this curse is, it's not a fast-moving one. We have plenty of time before we need to start worrying."

As if on cue, the lightning outside cracks once again, this time followed closely by a boom of angry thunder. Since we're already without power, there's not much the elements can do to harm us, but that doesn't stop Sid and Ashley from falling prey to their worst fears.

I catch Birdie's eye over the top of Sid's swooning head. *Do something*, I mentally will her. *Say something.* All the calm wisdom I can muster isn't going to help if Birdie sits there pretending like I'm the only person in the room who understands the true state of affairs around here. She's intelligent—and perceptive—enough to have reached the same conclusion as me.

In fact, there's something about the tilt to her head, the way she allows our eyes to meet and hold, that makes me think she shares my suspicions about Glenn's *real* fate.

"You two are absolutely right," Birdie says as she rises to her feet. She places herself in front of the now-sputtering candelabra, which has the effect of silhouetting the drapes of her figure in a perfectly ghoulish way. "The sooner we find that gold, the better it will be for all of us."

That's not quite what I had in mind, but Birdie's speech has the effect of drawing Sid's attention, so I consider it a plus.

But then she speaks again. "It's not a good idea to let Gloriana flitter about this castle for much longer. If we don't get a handle on her soon, there's no telling what horrors she'll unleash."

It's all I can do not to heave a despairing sigh. I really wish Birdie would stop inventing additional ghosts for us to conjure up. We're only on the first day, but between Glenn, Gloriana, and Harvey, she's promised a total of three spirits. I have no idea how many special effects she can come up with on the fly, but until I get my hands on my own belongings, there's no way I can keep that kind of pace.

Sid turns to her with the first look of hope she's shown since we entered this room. "So you can do it?" she asks. "You can talk to Father and ask him what happened to the treasure?"

Birdie lifts her chin. "It won't be easy, especially now that I know what it is we're up against, but I'll be able to contact him. You have my word on that. When Birdie White comes to your aid, you can rest assured that the outcome will be a happy one."

Now that the guarantee has been offered and accepted— which, by the way, is a terrible practice in a business like this one—Ashley loses some of his fear. It's replaced by a look of interest.

"How *did* you know to come to our aid?" he asks. "Sid wrote to Nicholas, asking him to send Madame Eleanor, but no one else knows of our troubles. If she didn't bring you . . . ?"

Not even a pointed question like this has the ability to discompose Birdie.

"Your father visited me in a dream," she says in her musically intoned, dramatic way. "I was called to support you—and dear Ella, of course—in your hour of need. How else would I have known to be on that particular train at that particular time?"

Dear Ella has some questions of her own on that subject, but she knows better than to ask them. If Birdie didn't out-and-out lie in response, she'd most likely spin it into some tale designed to make me look like a fool.

"How, indeed?" I echo. Birdie might be beating me at my own game, but I'm not ready to admit defeat just yet. I turn my attention to Sid. "If it's not too much trouble, I'd like to start with a tour of the castle and the island grounds to get my bearings. Birdie, you're more than welcome to come along, but I imagine you're already familiar with the layout."

In fact, I wouldn't put it past her to have memorized the blueprints weeks ago.

To her credit, Birdie doesn't take any umbrage at my words. She merely bestows a magnanimous smile on me before turning an even more magnanimous one on Sid and Ashley. "By all means, take dear Ella on her tour," she says. "I'm sure this is all a bit new and unusual for her. I'm going to reach out to my spirit guide and see if he has any insight."

It's all I can do to keep myself from groaning out loud. That makes four spirits now. *Four.*

"Your spirit guide?" Sid echoes.

"Oh, yes. Montague is always communicative in situations like this. He adores family entanglements. In fact, he helped me connect Lady Gainsborough with her grandmother just last month. You may have read about it in the papers."

This commentary appears to impress the company. I don't know if it's the noble name-dropping that does it, or if it's the confidence with which she utters it, but Birdie White knows her audience.

"Oh, my," Sid murmurs. "And what, exactly, will this Montague do?"

In this, as in all things, Birdie has an answer ready. "All spirit guides are different. Some are the ghosts of those who have gone before us; others are heavenly beings. My Montague is one of the former. He's good at seeking out information and connecting me with people and services in the great hereafter."

"Like a helpful hotel concierge," I agree in bland innocence.

Birdie doesn't miss my sarcasm. She turns to me with her brows soaring high. "Exactly so. What did you say the name of your spirit guide is, dear? Or don't you have one?"

It doesn't behoove me to rise to the bait. I'm better than that—better, I'm almost certain, than Bridget Wimpole-White. It makes me odiously self-consequential to say that, I know, but it's true. If I can't out-medium this woman, with her tired tricks and overdrawn sentiments, then I'm not worthy of the title bestowed on me by the powers that be.

"I do have one, actually," I say. "And like your Montague, she falls into the first category."

Any triumph I might feel at getting the best of Bridie is flattened by the voice that immediately fills my ears. *Ellie, don't,* Winnie says. *This isn't a good idea.*

I know it isn't, and I wish I had the strength of character not to give in, but what can I say? I'm only human, after all.

"Her name is Winnie."

Birdie's eyebrows disappear into her hairline. "Winnie?" she echoes. "How quaint."

Even though I know I should stop there, refuse to fall any deeper into this hole of my own making, I don't. There's something about the way she's playing Sid and Ashley—the way she's *using* them—that makes me acutely uncomfortable. I know it's not the most honorable work in the world, feigning a connection with the great beyond for personal gain, but I've always believed that my services have real value.

I can help this family, I'm sure of it. If not to find the gold, then at least to break the idea that it wields some kind of supernatural power over them, to prove to them that the tragedies that have recently befallen them are of human—not ghostly—origin.

And Winnie is going to help me.

"It's short for Winifred," I say tightly. "Winifred Wilde. She's my sister. Or, rather, she *was* my sister. She died last year."

I can tell that this news takes Birdie by surprise. Unless I'm very much mistaken, it also impresses her. Her brows come back down. "A family connection," she muses. "How unusual."

She wants to say more on the subject, but Sid—either with profound insight or with a desire to get on with her day—forestalls her. "I'd love to take you around myself, Madame Eleanor, but I've got to see Elspeth about the menus for the rest of the week. Ashley, could you . . . ?"

"I'm going to head out and help Otis with the generator." He shakes his head and sighs in a way that alerts the entire room that another quote is imminent. " 'Let us be men, not monkeys minding machines.' "

No one seems to have anything to say in the face of such damping commentary, so I step into the breach. "Don't worry about it. Winnie is all the company I need. I'm sure she'll point out anything worth note. Maybe she can even recruit Montague to lend a helping hand."

I half expect my sister to reply with something sharp and scathing, but she has no more to add to the conversation. Either that, or she's not happy with the way I'm handling things. To be honest, I'm not altogether pleased about it myself. So far, this case isn't at all what I expected. Nicholas isn't here, I have two complete fools for clients, Birdie is plaguing the life out of me, and there's a very real possibility of murder hanging overhead.

Some women might be daunted by such a prospect, but I refuse to be one of them.

"Make you sure you take some extra candles, Madame Eleanor," Sid says with a wavering smile. "We wouldn't want you to get lost along the way."

"I won't," I promise. And even if I do, I don't mind this opportunity to poke around on my own. I hardly expect to stumble on the treasure or a murder clue during my first look around, but some things in this world are more valuable than gold.

Information, for example.

And, now that I think about it, my bags.

Chapter 7

By the time I'm done going over the castle and its grounds, I'm tempted to send a wire to Vivian asking her to send me that metal detector she suggested from the start.

Castles are, by their nature, full of winding stairways and walled-up cubbies, with closets shoved into any available crawlspace and rooms closed off due to centuries of disrepair. In fact, it's one of my favorite things about them. I love the twists and turns that can only be found in architecture that's several hundred years old.

This castle takes that idea to a whole new level . . . and then multiplies it. Not content with a haphazard construction of stairways that lead nowhere, dumbwaiters that haven't worked in two hundred years, and—in one alarming instance—a door that opens up onto nothing but a sheer drop to the ocean below, the Stewarts are *collectors*. The gilded room from last night turns out to be just one of many such opulent, over-whelming displays in the castle. Thanks either to their piratical past or to the simple pride and greed of acquisition, every room is stuffed to the ceiling with artifacts. I've looked behind the heads of numerous animals killed in African safaris, inside curio cupboards brimming with exquisite Chinese figurines, and underneath rugs that look as though they were once trod by maharajas of centuries past. With the exception of Antarctica, no continent is lacking representation inside the Stewart castle walls.

In other words, the places to hide a pile of gold number in the thousands, with hundreds more in the rocky outcroppings and coves that dot the island's exterior. If the treasure is hidden here somewhere—a thing that isn't guaranteed—then it won't be found by merely narrowing down the likeliest places and making an educated guess.

I'm not as daunted by this prospect as it seems. In fact, I'm rather pleased to find this task to be more complicated than expected, if only because Birdie will be facing the same obstacles as me.

There's no way she's going to figure out what happened to that gold first. This is a case that requires skill and finesse. This is a case that needs me to dig into the intricacies of Glenn's life and death. This is a case that—

"Ahoy! Who goes thar?"

At the sound of a voice, I whirl where I stand. I've since given up on the interior and am standing on a platform up a long, rocky path from the castle itself. At one point, it must have been used as a way to view ships as they came in from the ocean. A bronze telescope is bolted to the rocks at one end of the platform, but it isn't able to pierce the swirling gray mist in the distance. I'd been hoping a bird's-eye view would help me get a feeling for my surroundings, but I mostly just feel dizzy.

The feeling doesn't abate when the voice sounds again. "Blow the man down!"

I whirl again, unable to tell where it hails from. This isn't the smartest move in the world, since I'm wearing T-strap heels on a damp and uneven stone path. Fortunately, there's a handrail screwed into the rock wall to my right. I realize why it's there when my foot gives way underneath me and I almost plunge off the edge of my vantage point.

"Lucifer's touch!" I curse as I grip the handrail so tight I can feel a splinter working into my palm. I manage to keep myself from slipping off the edge, but it's a much closer thing than I care to admit.

I can think of few worse fates than to die in the middle of this investigation. Birdie would probably have me conjured up by morning, making me say and do all sorts of nonsensical things.

"Who said that?" I ask as I plant my feet once again on the ground and look for the owner of the voice. There doesn't seem to be anyone on the path leading to the platform, but that doesn't mean much considering the recent turn of events. For all I know, it's old Glenn Stewart himself materializing for a chat. "Who's there?"

"Shiver me timbers!" the voice replies.

My heart has resumed a normal beating pattern by this time, and no ghostly figure has appeared through the mist, so I'm able to make a more accurate assessment of the situation. Or as accurate as I'm able to get, anyway.

"Avast, ye landlubbers?" I call back with a hint of a question.

There's a pause and a scuffle before a head appears over the edge of the platform. It's a small and scruffy head, and it appears to be boasting an eyepatch over its right eye in a way that looks alarmingly like Otis's. Neither the boy's impaired vision nor the fact that the rocks are almost cliff-like in that direction seem to be slowing him down.

"I'll give ye no quarter," he warns as he scampers up over the edge and plants himself in front of me.

My knowledge of pirate lingo now at an end, I have to make do with an "Aye, aye, captain" and wait for him to speak.

Although I don't have children of my own, my recent experience as the village freak has turned me into something of an expert. I'd gauge this boy's age to be around eight. His brown hair is incredibly dirty, but then, so is the rest of him. He's not wearing nearly enough layers to protect him against the mist and mizzling rain, and what he does have on is more like loosely jointed rags than actual clothing. Only a blue scarf tied around his waist looks to have been manufactured in this century.

He looks, I'm forced to admit, very much like an actual pirate. Or a cabin boy, at any rate.

"Oh, dear. Are you a ghost?" I ask, blinking down at him.

He doesn't seem to take this question amiss. He blinks back at me. "No. Are you?"

"Not to my knowledge," I admit. "But ghosts sometimes don't realize they're dead until someone points it out to them. Can you see me?"

The boy's one visible eye narrows. "Yes."

"Can you hear me?"

"Yes."

I hold out a hand. "Can you feel me?"

He hesitates a moment before dashing a grubby finger out and poking my palm. Any anxiety he might feel melts away the moment he makes contact. "Yes."

I shrug. "Then I guess we're both alive and well." Now that he's drawn a little closer, my gaze is caught once again by the flash of blue around his waist. The scarf is damp and muddied, which is no surprise, given the state of the rest of him, but I could almost swear the sheen on it signals pashmina.

I know this because I own a scarf exactly like that. Or rather, I *used* to until my bags disappeared. I always travel with a full rainbow of scarves at my disposal.

"You're a boy," I say, a light suddenly dawning. I don't mean that a light literally dawns, since the clouds overhead have formed a barrier against any and all heavenly bodies, but certain pieces of the puzzle are starting to click into place. When McGee said that the boys were going to grab my bags, he meant actual *boys*. I cast a glance around. "There must be another one of you around here somewhere."

A second head pops up in the exact spot where the first one appeared. If I hadn't already ascertained for myself that these are no ghostly apparitions, I might have started to question my sanity. He's one hundred percent identical to the other boy, from the scruffy hair to the ragged clothes and the eyepatch over the right eye. He even has one of my scarves tied around his waist, though this one is red rather than blue.

My *favorite* red. I have a nail polish and lipstick in the exact same shade. They go incredibly well with my liquid eyeliner— a thing these two boys seem to have discovered for themselves, if those inexpert rings around their eyes are any indication.

That solves one of the mysteries around here, at least.

"How on earth did the two of you get up here?" I demand as I pick my way carefully to the platform's edge and peer down. We're at a dizzying height, level with the tallest tower of the castle, and it looks to me as though the way down is nothing but rocks and treachery. There's not even a rope that they might have feasibly scrambled up.

"We climbed, o'course," the red one says.

The blue one elbows him.

"I mean, we *walked*," the red one says hastily. "On the path. Just like you."

"I don't believe it. I didn't see you as I came up. You *must* be ghosts."

They both grin to reveal not-so-twin smiles. Red has a full mouth of pearly whites, but Blue's smile is made crooked by the absence of one of his front teeth. "There's no such thing as ghosts," Blue informs me.

"Or witches," Red says, but not without a dubious look at my attire.

"Or curses?" I suggest before I can stop myself. Interrogating small children—even small children who stole my bags—isn't my normal way of doing things, but these two seem to know what they're about. Anyone who scaled a rock wall as steep as that one can stand up to a few questions about what's going on inside this castle.

They share a look, brown eye meeting like. Red turns a shoulder on me. "We're not 'fraid of the curse," he says, but with a wariness that indicates he might not be quite as brave as he'd like me to think.

"We're not 'fraid of witches, either," Blue claims. Of the two boys, he seems to be the ringleader. His chin comes up at a tilt. "Leastaways, not a witch like *you*."

"But t'other one . . ." Red begins, but he meets his brother's eye again and clamps his mouth shut.

I'm trying to decide how to best broach the subject of my missing luggage when Blue flips up his eyepatch. The organ underneath is perfectly sound, though he blinks at the sudden change in light. "D'you know any spells for removing teeth?" he asks.

I blink, too, but only at the quick change of subject. That's another thing I've learned about children over the past few months—they don't hesitate to say exactly what's on their minds at any given moment. It's what makes them such valuable allies in situations like these. As long as Sid and Ashley are bound by their fears and superstitions, I can't trust a word out of their mouths. Otis might prove a better source of information, but I doubt he's going to make anything easy. I haven't gotten much of a read on Elspeth yet, but she doesn't strike me as the sort of woman to be hoarding information on the gold's whereabouts.

And since I'm not likely to see Harvey again unless Birdie manifests him over dinner, I'm going to have to forge new paths.

"I thought you said you don't believe in witches."

"I don't," Red says.

"Me either," Blue agrees. He adds, after a brief pause, "But d'you know any?"

I hold up my hand and begin ticking off fingers. "I can remove warts. I can remove curses. I can remove bad energy. Teeth, however, are outside my jurisdiction. Have you thought about seeing a dentist?"

The boys don't seem to appreciate my attempt at a joke. Red looks slightly relieved, but Blue falls into a deep scowl.

"I told you she wouldn't be able to do it," Red says.

Blue heaves a sigh and squares his little shoulders. "It'll hafta be the doorknob, then."

Red's eye shows a tendency to spring from its socket at this. He swallows heavily and runs his tongue over the unbroken line of his teeth. It's that gesture, more than the perplexing conversation, that brings enlightenment. With the exception of my beautiful pashminas, these boys are completely identical. They look the same, they walk the same, and they talk the same. Having grown up as a non-identical triplet to Winnie and Liam, being the exact mirror image of my siblings isn't something I ever aspired to.

With these two, it's clearly otherwise. Blue is the only one to have lost a front tooth and, until Red screws up the courage to tie his face to a doorknob, is likely to remain that way.

"Twins are very powerful forces in witchcraft, you know," I say, struggling to subdue my grin at Red's predicament. In my particular sibling trio, I was more of a Blue than a Red, creating havoc and mayhem everywhere I went, but I can understand Red's reservations. "The duality of nature, the binding of souls—that sort of thing."

They both nod as if this makes perfect sense.

"Although there's no magic that can remove teeth, there are ways you can use your twin power to help move nature on her course." With one glance at Red's stricken look, I hasten to add,

"No doorknobs or strings, I promise. It's more of a kind of incantation—"

I'm unable to finish proffering my not-so-expert advice. Even though I don't hear a sound, Blue's attention snaps on something a few inches above my left shoulder. He must not care for what he sees, since he loses no time in turning around and darting back the way he came.

And, yes, by that I mean the cliff. Every instinct I have warns me to catch hold of his collar—or, you know, his scarf—and hold him fast. No good can come of anyone plunging off the side of those rocks in a hurry, especially since Red follows closely in his wake. But although I'm in decent shape, I'm no match for a pair of eight-year-olds who could easily pass for mountain goats. Before I realize what's happening, they've dashed over the edge and out of sight.

I turn to find myself facing Otis. Other than a slight twist to his lips that could just as easily be a sneer as a smile, there's no sign that he noticed my recent company—or if he did, he has no interest in small, thieving children in desperate need of adult supervision.

"I hate to interrupt you while you're communing with the elements, but you're wanted inside." He hooks a thumb over his shoulder. "There's been an incident."

"An incident?" I don't have to look at my watch to know that it's only been a few hours since the last one. "Already?"

Otis must share my sentiments, because his lips decide on the smile. "I'm afraid so. It's the one with the eyebrows."

"Oh, for the love of Beelzebub. What's she done now?"

"You mean, other than tell Elspeth that she doesn't have a lifeline on her palm and should therefore be dead already? Or quote Edgar Allan Poe at Ashley in an attempt to outdo him? Oh, not much. She's currently having a fit of the hysterics in the wine cellar. A delightful woman, to be sure."

I pinch the bridge of my nose, but it doesn't help in keeping an encroaching headache at bay. There's not enough gold in the world to make up for this kind of trouble. I don't care if the lost crown jewels are buried with it.

"You'll forgive my saying so, but you have odd taste in friends."

I rearrange my paisley scarf around my shoulders and take a deep breath. It does much to fortify me for the trials ahead. "Birdie White is *not* my friend."

"Coworker?" he guesses. "Associate? The evil sorceress who taught you everything you know?"

I don't allow my laugh to escape. "As hard as I'm sure it is to believe, I met that woman for the first time yesterday. She attached herself to me on the train, and I haven't yet been able to shake her."

"I should rather think not. I don't know how much experience you have with unwanted houseguests, but women like that are only removed by force. Well, force or death. Perhaps we'll get lucky and the curse will take her next."

We've started down the rocky path back to the castle, but our steps are dawdling. Not, as I first suspect, because of how difficult the way is, but because Otis seems to want a private word with me as much as I want one with him.

"You don't believe in the curse or that your uncle died because of it," I say, making no attempt to hide my sentiments on this subject. Experience has taught me that it'll be the fastest way to get him to open up. "You think Sid is sentimental and soft, and Ashley a fool."

"Ashley *is* a fool."

I wholeheartedly agree but am not about to say so. Especially since I consider Otis just as much of a fool—only of a different type. He belongs to the class of people who never learned that it's much easier to catch flies with honey than a battering ram.

"Men with a poetical turn of mind often appear that way on

the outside. His head and his heart are searching for somewhere they can comfortably coexist. It's not an easy place to find."

Otis scoffs with so much scorn that he sounds exactly like, well, a battering ram. "I can tell you exactly where to find it. In the halls of academia. A more overblown, self-aggrandizing, pompous set of persons—"

I place a hand to my temple. "You are not a scholar. I can see it so clearly."

Despite himself, Otis laughs. It's a promising start, but he cuts it short and immediately turns sober. "Neither is my cousin, despite what he may have told you. Uncle Glenn sunk tens of thousands of dollars into that precious university of his, but it never did the least use. They want nothing to do with him or the drivel he writes."

Since I haven't heard any verse from Ashley that doesn't come from a long-dead poet's pen, I maintain my silence. I have every expectation that Otis will continue on in this vein, spilling family secrets in his bitter, straightforward way, but it seems I've underestimated my foe.

He gives a short laugh. "He didn't tell you anything about it, did he? And since you can no more read minds than I can, you had no idea. Well, well."

It's my intention to defend both my honor and my professional abilities, but Otis continues before I can come up with the most efficient way to do it. "You know, you're going to have to make some drastic improvements if you intend to beat that other one."

We've reached the bottom of the path by this time. The doorway to the castle is a large wooden portal. The bright, well-fitted slats look similar to the ones on the hidden stairway leading up from the docks. For all that this castle is an old one, the family has done an incredible job making sure it stays up to date.

An incredible, *expensive* job. That sort of upkeep can't be easy to maintain over the course of four hundred years.

"Beat her?" I ask.

"I had a feeling you two were evenly matched, but that was before she took it into her head to start screaming fit to cave the roofs in."

It had been my intention to pull open the door and lose no time in making my way to the scene inside, but at this I pause, my hand on the knob.

"Unfortunately, she's managed to get both Sid and Elspeth in hysterics with her. Not for her this slow wasting of time in making a survey of the island. Surely you've figured out by now that you're not going to find any gold here. What do you think of it?"

Of the island, I don't think much. It's too big for me to search by myself, too difficult to navigate in weather like this, and far too remote for my peace of mind. I'd have been better off trying to find hidden treasure in a place like Barra. It might be a hundred times the size of this island, but at least I wouldn't be battling so many unknowns.

Of Otis Stewart's belief that there's no gold to be had, however, I think plenty. Either he knows more about this business than he's letting on or, well, he knows more about this business than he's letting on. Come to think of it, that sweater he's wearing looks to be cashmere. That seems like an awfully nice wardrobe for someone who drives a tour boat around a place that sees maybe fifteen visitors a year.

"I think the island is excessive," I say, deciding to repeat my sentiments from last night. It seems like the safest approach while I'm standing near so many cliffs with a man I neither know nor trust. "I understand why the Stewarts of pirates past might have wanted to live in a castle in the middle of an ocean with nothing but the stars to keep them company, but sitting out here on a gilded rock protecting a cursed treasure in this day and age is ludicrous. We've put men on the moon and mapped the entire human genome, yet we still hold fast to the idea that a hex put on an inanimate object half a millennium ago wields unfathomable power. Believe me when I say that the only thing condemning your family to a life of misery is themselves."

"Bravo, Madame Eleanor," he says, using my name for the first time. It doesn't appear to bring him any joy. "I wonder why can't you march inside and say all that to my cousins?"

"Because, Otis Stewart," I say, returning the gesture syllable for syllable. Like the game I'm playing with Birdie White, I'm rapidly coming to learn the rules of this one, too. "You've spent the past—what?—thirty or so years of your life trying to reason with these people, but it doesn't seem to have done you the least bit of good. I'm guessing you're not the first one to try, either. Harvey Renault, for example, must have done his best to get your uncle to strengthen his grip on reality once or twice in their long friendship."

Otis's glance is sharp. "What makes you say that?"

"Well, for one, he embarked on a long and tedious train journey—and with his health—to ensure that I wouldn't be left alone to influence the Stewarts with my evil, superstitious ways."

Otis's burgeoning sneer confirms me in this theory, so I keep going. My next move is a bold one, but I'm sure enough of my ground by now that I don't falter. I've dealt with enough skeptics in my lifetime to know how to handle them. Some of them, like my own dear Nicholas and the honorable police inspector Peter Piper, view me with reluctant respect. They might not believe most of what I do and say, but they know I get results—and that results are the most important thing. Others, like Otis Stewart, would gladly see me tied up, tossed into the ocean, and laid to eternal rest with the fishes.

I'll let you guess which type I prefer.

"For another, he called to warn you of what was intended," I say. There's no wobble in my voice, no sign of discomposure as I hold my gaze steady with his. "He asked you to join him at this castle, to take part in these proceedings by his side. He hoped that between the pair of you, you could force Sid and Ashley to realize how ridiculous all of this is. But that, unfortunately, was where the pair of you took a misstep."

"Oh?" he asks, his voice dangerous. That slice of steel, that sharp note that's meant to reduce me in size, tells me that all my theories are correct—and that he's not happy about it. "Is this where you tell me that if he'd heeded the curse, he might still be with us today?"

"No. It's where I tell you that although you might not think much of my tactics, I promise you that I'll be able to bring peace to this household much faster using my methods than you will be using yours. You've done it your way, and it hasn't made any difference. A man is dead—no, *two* men are dead—and you aren't anywhere nearer a resolution now than you were before. Don't you think it's time to try a different approach?"

For a long, drawn-out moment, I think I've gotten through to him. We're still standing on the threshold to the castle, my hand paused on the doorknob. The only sounds I hear are the lashings of the ocean and the steady thud-thud of my heart. Otis can't move past me unless he physically forces his way in through the door, throws me into the ocean, or answers my challenge.

The last one wins out.

"My opinion on your presence in this house is unchanged," he says tightly. "But I'll repeat what I said before . . . If you want to succeed, you're going to have to find a way to beat that other one first."

I barely manage to subdue my groan in time. *Birdie.* By now, her hysterics have probably become a three-ring circus—a three-ring circus where she's the ringleader, acrobat, and elephant all in one.

"Birdie White isn't my enemy," I say with a convincing show of truthfulness.

"No?" he asks with a sardonic lift to his scarred eyebrow. "Forgive me if I don't take comfort from that. You obviously don't think I'm your enemy, either, but I'll warn you right now that I am."

Truth be told, I *do* think Otis will do whatever he can to thwart me in my efforts. Concerning how far those efforts will take him, however, I'm still uncertain. I don't *think* he'll resort to murder, but there's no denying that the deaths of both Glenn and Harvey are clouded with suspicion.

"As strange as you may find this to believe, I'm only here to help," I say, and pull open the door. A blast of warm air swirls around us, but neither of us heeds it. We're too busy locking horns. "I took this job because Nicholas asked me to, and that's all there is to it. There's no ulterior motive, no dark deed undergirding my purpose."

Otis doesn't seem to buy it. "How odd that Nicholas isn't here to back that claim up," he says. "You'd think he'd be moving heaven and earth to be by your side."

Since these are sentiments I share, there's little I can do to counter them. "He will be," I say, more in a show of optimism than actual belief. Whatever spell Birdie cast to keep him away seems to have been successful. Either that, or his business is turning out to be more difficult than he anticipated. Since Birdie's spell casting is no more real than mine is, I'm leaning toward the latter. "And until that time, you're just going to have to trust me."

From the glowering look Otis gives me, it's obvious he'd rather fling himself from the nearest parapet, but I don't mind. As little as Otis Stewart trusts me, there's one thing I can promise for sure: I trust him a lot less.

Chapter 8

After separating ways with Otis, I lose no time in heading to the wine cellar.

It's not, as the name suggests, located in a cellar of any kind. Birdie had been correct when she pointed out the lack of an underground infrastructure on this island. Whether because of the movements of the tide or because it would be incredibly difficult to drill into all this rock, the castle is lacking in those damp, dark places where wine, hidden treasure, and the bodies of their enemies would normally be stored.

Instead, I find myself walking through a glass-paned door into an interior room in the main wing. Floor-to-ceiling wood shelves cover almost every square inch of wall space the room contains. They're filled with bottles that are older than I am and worth much more. Otis and Ashley were unsuccessful with the generator, so the room is plummeted into the same darkness seeping through the rest of the castle, but I imagine that's a point in the wine's favor. A point *not* in the wine's favor, however, is the fact that Birdie is yanking bottles at random and flinging them around her in a shattered arc of alcohol and broken glass.

Sid heralds my arrival as she would a savior. She practically falls on my neck the moment I walk through the door.

"Oh, Madame Eleanor, please make her stop," she begs, her whole body aflutter. "I know it's only wine, and most of it is insured, but she's in *such* a state."

I can see that for myself. Not content with the smashing of wine bottles, Birdie is also muttering to herself in a low, gravelly voice that I can only assume is meant either to be her guide Montague or Glenn Stewart speaking through her.

"Hey, now—not that one!" Ashley makes a leaping grab for a particularly weathered bottle Birdie is preparing to smash at her feet. He makes it in time, but just barely, almost losing his balance in the process. I can hardly blame him for it; all that wine does make it a touch slippery. "She's made it to the French vintages. Please, Madame Eleanor. *Do* something."

Considering that Birdie White stands half a foot taller than me and outweighs me by an entire case of all this wine, I'm not sure what he expects me to do. I'm already starting to feel giddy from the overpowering scent of spirits.

Still, I feel somewhat responsible for her presence here. My supernatural senses tell me that nothing short of throwing her off that train would have prevented her from eventually making her way to Airgead Island on her own, but I *did* make things easier by letting her travel with me. I can at least save the family's burgundy.

"Birdie!" I call, my voice sharp.

To my lack of surprise, she ignores me and continues tearing through the bottles. I've been known to break a few myself in the name of spiritualism, but this is taking things too far.

"Birdie, can you please stop that for two minutes so we can sweep up some of this broken glass? You can get back to your destructive trance once it's less of a hazard."

She turns toward me with such awful deliberation that I shiver where I stand. The room isn't the least bit cold, but there's something about her expression that would strike fear into the most stalwart of hearts. It's too dark for me to make out the details, which might perhaps account for the terror I feel. Her features aren't human so much as *human-like*. I'm not sure how else to describe them. Instead of eyes, she has two black holes. Her mouth is a blood-red slash, her nostrils flaring and wide. Even her eyebrows, which normally make me giggle, have taken on ominous proportions.

"You dare to interfere with Gloriana?" she asks in that low, croaking voice. "You dare to intrude in matters you cannot possibly understand?"

"Yes, I do," I say, though not without a *little* quiver of fear. I don't know what she's done to make herself look like that, but her special effects are nothing short of fantastic. "It's been a trying day, and you're wasting perfectly good wine."

The nostrils flare wider. "What do I care for wine?"

"You cared quite a bit for it last night, if I recall correctly." I clap in an effort to bring us both to our senses. "Let's go, Birdie. Enough is enough."

"I will not stop for him. I will not stop for you. You will feel my fiery wrath before I'm through."

Her recitation calls to mind some of Ashley's worst poetical turns. "Yes, yes. You don't like green eggs and ham, either. I'm familiar with the tale."

My flippancy elicits nothing but a shriek of dismay from Sid. She clutches at my arm with a strength belied by her fragile, wispy air. "Please, Madame Eleanor. Don't you know a . . . chant that will call her back to us? She must be inside there somewhere."

With an inward sigh, I realize that the only way I'm going to end this charade is by becoming one of the players. With a nod toward the Stewart siblings, I take a deep breath and draw closer to my target.

I know, in my heart of hearts, that the woman I'm approaching is just that—a woman. A very skilled woman, yes, and a woman who clearly knows how to get the most out of a crowd, but she's still flesh and blood, like me. She's still a sneaky, conniving fake medium, like me.

It's important to bear that in mind, especially when she lifts an entire magnum of wine and brandishes it over her head like a club.

"Hguone si hguone," I murmur, my voice pitched low to match hers. *"Uoy deen ot llihc."*

The recitation isn't my best work, but it's what happens when I don't have time to plan ahead. Rock songs played backward have been known to frighten soft-hearted parents into believing their children possessed of the devil; words spoken backward have a similar effect.

"Lla sgniht ni noitaredom," I add, lest she think I'm trying to cut her off at the source. It's true, too—all things should be done in moderation. Theatrics like this are acceptable when it comes time for the grand finale, but we haven't had an opportunity to lay the groundwork first. I need to talk with the family members and Elspeth one-on-one. I need to learn more about the mysterious circumstances surrounding Glenn's death. I need to talk to someone about the way Harvey died and whether or not Birdie had any contact with him on the train before she made her way to my side.

However, none of this is going to happen if I have to rush in and do damage control every time Birdie decides she's been too long without the spotlight.

Since my backward chanting seems to have soothed not just the spectators in the room but Birdie, too, I decide it's safe to take a more proactive approach. With my arms outstretched to protect me from any wine bottles that might become airborne in the next few seconds, I draw forward and place my hands on

Birdie's shoulders. The moment I make contact, it feels as though I've plunged my hands into the frigid ocean, numbing them all the way to the wrist.

I draw my hands away as if I've touched fire rather than ice. Humans can't be that temperature and still be alive. I'm sure of it.

"Birdie?" I ask, more cautiously this time. "Are you all right?"

If she answers me, which I doubt, I don't register her remark. It's at that moment I notice what she's doing. The abandon with which she's been tearing through the wine isn't as reckless as it seems. In fact, she has a clear destination in mind. Each bottle and rack she's gone through has brought her one step closer to a small cubby inset into the back wall.

"Quick—Sid, Ashley—one of you get me a candle."

Neither sibling is willing to get that close to Birdie, even though she's no longer thrashing about. I'm forced to make do with the flashlight function on my cell phone, even though I'd prefer to conserve what little battery I have left until I manage to discover what those little boys did with my luggage. I hold up the bright beam of light, which glistens on the broken glass and spilled wine in a kaleidoscope of brilliance, to reveal a small black box sitting in the cubby.

Sid's gasp is all I need to know what I'm looking at.

The gold. Birdie found it. In less than twenty-four hours and with nothing more to go on than a spirit guide and a few apocryphal family tales, she's located the cause of all this misery. If I thought her work brilliant before, it's nothing compared to the downright magnificence of this latest development.

I'm nudged not-so-gently aside by Sid, whose fear of Birdie's antics is now displaced in favor of her find.

"Not yet—" Birdie flings up her arm, her voice returned to normal. I dare to make a quick sweep of my phone's light over her face, but there's no sign of any stage makeup or other prosthetics that would have made her look so terrifyingly haggard. I know, without quite understanding how, that if I were to touch her, her body temperature would be back to normal, too.

Birdie winces at the bright light but doesn't chastise me. "Let me ensure there's no spell trap on the box before we lift it out."

I open my mouth to suggest that it's a little late—and a little silly—to worry about spell traps, but I keep my thoughts to myself. I might not be willing to assign Birdie the powers of clairvoyance, but *something* strange is going on here. Yes, she was in this wine cellar last night, by her own admission, but she can't have planted the box herself, since the shelves are literally built into the wall. There's more at play here than mere trickery.

I should know. Trickery has been my stock-in-trade for years.

Birdie delivers a quick chant that I could almost *swear* is "I found it first" backward and waves her hands over the box before stepping aside to allow Sid access.

"I can't believe this." Sid drops to a crouch, looking like a child in front of the worst Christmas present of all time. Her hands hover over but don't reach for the hinged lid. "Ashley, what do we do now?"

"*Not* open it, that's for sure," he says with more decision than he's shown thus far. He brushes past me, his feet crunch-crunching on the broken glass, to squat by his sister's side. He glances back over his shoulder at me. "Didn't you say you could break the curse?"

I *can*, but not yet. That's another reason I'd like to take Birdie soundly to task. She's allowed us no time to build up a sense of mastery over the curse, no opportunity to create the kind of spectacle that could lay this specter to rest for good. These sorts of things need to be established slowly and carefully, allowed to simmer alongside the family's trust.

"It'll take some time, but it can be done," I promise.

Ashely nods and reaches for the brass handles on either side of the box. They're the only ornamentation save for a small clasp on the lid. Although Sid draws in a sharp breath as he makes contact, she allows him to hoist the burden.

A thing he does *far* too easily, if you ask me. I can't say that I've often held a small fortune's worth of gold in my hands, but gold isn't exactly a light metal.

"As long as we don't open the box, we'll be fine," Ashley says, more to allay his own fears than any Birdie and I might harbor. "No harm can come if the gold remains unseen."

Sid nods her agreement. "We'll have to find a new hiding place. I've been thinking about what Otis said, about the safe. Perhaps we should keep it there until we can come to some sort of arrangement—"

I'm still debating whether or not to point out the obvious when Birdie does it for me.

"The gold isn't in there," she announces in her favorite doomsaying voice. She's careful not to meet my eyes. "Gloriana played a trick on you—on us all. You should have known better than to trust her."

They should have also known better than to trust Birdie, but at this newest burst of insight, Ashley is so startled that the box falls from his hands. For a long, slow-motion moment, I'm afraid Sid is going to make a dive across the field of broken glass, but it hits the floor before she starts moving. There's a short, splintering sound as the box cracks at the corner, followed by the thud of the lid falling open on its side.

As if by—yes, I'll say it—magic, a single gold coin rolls out. We watch, transfixed, as it turns, spins, and eventually settles flat against the wine-spattered tile.

The coin itself reinforces everything the Stewarts have told me about the cursed gold. Its date is obviously not of recent origin. The rough cut of it, the raised cross on the surface, and the dull color bear out the story of a fortune that's been sitting untouched for centuries. If it's a fake, it's a good one—so good, in fact, that Ashley and Sid don't even think to question its authenticity.

"Good God, don't touch it!" Sid cries as Ashley makes a move to pluck it from the wreckage. Her voice wavers on the edge of hysteria. "What does this mean? Where's the rest of it?"

"It's just as I suspected," Ashley says. He's standing half-hunched, his fingers hovering over the gold coin but not making contact. "Someone took it. Someone knew Father hid it here and then stole it. That's why all this is happening to us now."

"Is that true, Birdie? Madame Eleanor?" Sid looks back and forth between us. "It's really gone?"

As was the case when we arrived at the castle last night—and, indeed, at breakfast this morning—Birdie is content to stand back and allow me to smooth the edges. Like so many things about the woman, this habit is starting to annoy me. How convenient it is for her to make profound statements and grand gestures and then leave me to deal with the mess that's left behind.

"That would appear to be the case," I say. Since we can hardly leave the gold coin on the floor—and because no one else seems willing to touch it—I palm it as though it means no more to me than a quarter dropped at the laundromat. The cross stamped on the surface is crude but beautiful. I run my thumb over it to find it much smoother than it looks. "How many of these would you say are supposed to be in the box?"

Neither Stewart sibling answers me, so I look to Birdie.

"Several thousand, according to most reports," she says.

I nod a quick thanks for the information, though I'm not sure what I'm supposed to do with it. What I *do* know is that gold in such a quantity would be heavy, difficult to transport, and even more difficult to sell. What I *don't* know is, well, everything else.

I don't know where the rest of the gold is, I don't know who has it, and most important, I don't know what Birdie is playing at by uncovering it in this way.

I tuck the coin in my bra, since this dress doesn't have any pockets and I'm not so crass as to shove it in my shoe. "I'll hold on to this," I say. Lest anyone think I'm about to add theft to my list of sins, I add, "Gold is a powerful spiritual conductor even when it isn't cursed. When it is, it's practically a talisman. As long as I keep this on my person, the curse will have to go through me before it strikes anyone else. Right, Birdie?"

As before, Birdie is content to let me have my way. She nods once.

"So what happens now?" Sid asks, beginning to wilt. She seems exhausted by the day's events, barely able to hold up her head in the face of so much turmoil.

"You're going to head to your room and take a nap," I command. Considering how much work Elspeth must have to do to keep a place of this size clean and running on her own, I add, "Ashley, if you could find a broom and mop, we can get started clearing this away."

"I?" He blinks at me, startled. "But 'few tasks are more like the torture of Sisyphus than housework, with its endless repetition.'"

Tell that to poor Elspeth, I think. Since quotes seem to be the only way Ashley is capable of communicating, I reply with, "Manual labor is the privilege of the enlightened."

His brow furrows as he seeks to place my piece of wisdom in the annals of literary history. Since I just this moment made it up, I imagine his brow will remain like that for the foreseeable future.

"A nap," Sid echoes weakly. She passes a pale hand over her even paler forehead. "Yes. I think I would like to lie down for a bit, if you don't think it too rude of me to leave you on your own again."

Ashley notices his sister's waning state and immediately offers his aid. "I'll help you to your room. I'm sorry, Madame Eleanor, but she won't want to be alone at a time like this."

As true as that may be, what I *really* suspect is that Ashley is avoiding something—and I don't mean the menial task of housework. This makes the second time he's hastened away when faced with the prospect of some one-on-one Eleanor Wilde time. Once, and I'm willing to look the other way. Twice, and my suspicions are roused.

"Of course," I say sweetly. "I'll come find you just as soon as I confer with my colleague here."

Ashely nods, but there's a twitch to his mustache that indicates he's not excited at the prospect of our future meeting.

"And don't worry," I say as they begin to head toward the door. I give the coin in my bosom a pat. "I'll draw the negative energies toward me for as long as I'm able. That should give you enough time to rest and rally your resources before we take the next step."

After an interlude like the one we've just experienced, the thing I want most in the world is a moment to collect myself—to think. Things are happening too quickly, and too far out of my control, for me to even pretend that I have answers.

I want to search this wine cellar. I want to examine that box more closely. I want to lock everyone in their rooms and tell them to sit still long enough for me to make some real headway in finding the missing gold.

Birdie knows this, of course. She knew it last night when she wouldn't let me out of my room to search the castle, and she knows it now by refusing to leave the wine cellar. In fact, if there's one thing that's been popping up with painful regularity, it's that she knows too much.

So that's where I decide to start.

"How did you know it was in here?" I ask as I whirl to face her. "Who's been feeding you information?"

There's just enough light in the room for me to make out Birdie's smug smile. "I told you already. My Montague. He was able to contact Gloriana straightaway."

I'm not buying it. "Your spirit guide has a direct link to the former queen of England?"

"Your sister doesn't?"

The quick way Birdie replies does little to endear her to me. If she had any idea how much I treasure those moments with Winnie, how fleeting and precious every second of contact is, she wouldn't use her as a way to bait me.

"I don't know," I reply with complete honesty. It seems as though *one* of us should. Otherwise, we're just going to keep tiptoeing around half-truths until one of us gives up. "She might. I'm rarely able to get a good hold on her. She's usually the one to contact me, not the other way around."

At this confession, some of Birdie's smugness drops. An expression of genuine interest seems to take over . . . if anything about this woman *can* be genuine.

"How interesting. Under what conditions?" Without waiting for me to answer, she rushes on to add, "On the train, you seemed to go outside yourself for a moment. You didn't move, not even to breathe. Was she talking to you then? Telling you about the shoes and the red seats?"

I have no way of answering that, since I don't know. I *think* it was Winnie who sent me that vision of Harvey's death, but I can't be sure. She tried so hard to prevent me from pushing forward, warned me against what I was about to see. It was almost as though she was protecting me from it instead.

"You don't know how to control it, do you?" Birdie asks suddenly. "No one has ever showed you how."

"What?" That one syllable is all I can utter. It's more of an exhaled breath than a word, the air punched from my chest.

"I can help you, if you'd like. There are ways to strengthen the bond between the two of you."

In that moment, I want so badly to believe her. Opportunities to meet other mediums—fake or otherwise—are incredibly rare. If there's even a sliver of a chance that Birdie White is the real thing, then I should be doing everything in my power to learn from her. I don't understand what's happening to me, and I don't have any way to find out. On a good day, my brother thinks I'm a few sandwiches short of a picnic. Nicholas humors me, but with the jaundiced eye of a man who's been around the world a few times. And the one person I know who has actual spiritual leanings, a witch in my home village, deals more in spells than spiritualism.

I want to understand. I want to trust. I want to *learn*.

"My private readings typically run at a thousand pounds an hour, but I'd be willing to sit down with you for free the first session," Birdie says. "As a courtesy between professionals."

My hope dies before it has a chance to do anything but flicker, leaving a strong aftertaste of bile in my mouth. This woman knows no more about contacting the spirits than I do. What she *does* know, however, is how to leverage a broken woman's emotions.

"Thank you, but I'll be fine," I say, my jaw so tight it feels close to cracking. "She's usually more communicative than this, but I don't have my cats with me right now. Winnie is always more active in an animal's presence. She uses them to strengthen her hold on this world."

I realize my mistake the moment the words leave my lips. Birdie visibly brightens, her whole body rising as though moving up a flagpole. "A witch's familiar?" she asks, mostly to herself. "Yes. *Yes*. Why didn't I think of that . . . ?"

"It's not that big of a deal," I'm quick to say. "I don't even know that having Beast around helps draw Winnie closer to me. It's just a working theory I have. Forget I said anything."

"I'll mention it to Montague," Birdie promises. "He might have some ideas about how we can use it to our advantage. You were wise to mention it."

Hearing those words spoken aloud—and in Birdie's self-satisfied way—reinforces everything I've come to suspect about this woman. Professionally speaking, I can only admire what she's doing. She's using my emotions to exploit my weaknesses. She's planting a seed of hope in a place where I desperately want it to thrive. There's no better—or faster—way to manipulate a person than that.

Personally speaking, I'm terrified of what will happen if we continue under the same roof. A few more days of this and I'm going to start twittering and fluttering like Sid every time Birdie enters the room.

Since Birdie shows every sign of wanting to continue this conversation, I decide the time is right to make my escape. She hasn't provided any information about finding that box, and I have no idea how she managed to make herself feel so cold when I touched her, but I don't dare stay in this room in my current state.

Logic, not emotion, is the way to the bottom of this.

Evidence, not a conversation with the dead, is how you find the answers to a man's mysterious death.

I'm halfway out the door before Birdie makes any attempt to stop me. "By the way, Madame Eleanor," she calls as though the balance between us hasn't just fallen decidedly in her favor. "I'm curious. What do you plan to do with that coin?"

I pause on the threshold, the press of gold against my skin suddenly the only sensation I have. "I don't know yet," I say truthfully. "Why? Do you want it?"

Her eyes grow wide, and she shakes her head with a vehemence that seems all too convincing. "Not I. I warned you already how powerful this curse is. There's no spell in my playbook that would make me willing to risk it."

"Not even if Montague promises to protect you?"

Birdie barely manages to repress a shudder. "No, my dear."

"Not even if *I* promise to protect you?"

She hesitates, almost as though she's considering the offer. In the end, she only shakes her head. "Not even then. Though, to be fair, I might take up the offer if your Winnie were to make it."

Chapter 9

The Stewarts abandon me to my fate for the rest of the day.

In the name of fairness, it *could* be that they're afraid of being nearby while I carry that gold coin nestled against my bosom, but I'm not feeling particularly fair. Both Ashley and Otis must know I want a word with them, and, anticipating that I'd lose no time in seeking them out, have gone into hiding. Conversely, Sid is sound asleep in her bed, and looks so tired and pale that I don't have the heart to wake her.

"Elspeth it is," I say with determined cheer. "Feel free to join me in questioning her, Winnie. I have a feeling I'm going to need all the help I can get."

Winnie doesn't respond. Like the rest of the inhabitants of this house, she seems only interested in being mysterious and disinterested, unwilling to help me do any actual work. Then again, she could just be mad at me for being so stupid as to give all our secrets away to Birdie. I'm none too delighted about it myself.

Locating Elspeth isn't a difficult task. As I anticipated, she's been left holding the broom—literally. The door to the wine

cellar is propped open, the rich, tangy scent of age-old fermen-
tation mixing with citrus-based cleansers to make an interesting
and not altogether unpleasant aroma.

"Can I help?" I ask as I approach the door. In yet another
burst of practical common sense, Elspeth has set up a large
framed mirror that leans against the opposite hallway wall. It's
perfectly angled to catch the light from a nearby window and
cast it into the room. The light's not as bright as an actual bulb
would be, but her setup does facilitate the task of locating all
those broken pieces of glass.

"If you've a mind to it, I could use the hands." Elspeth holds
out a large black garbage bag. "I shouldn't put a guest to work,
but my back's not what it used to be."

Although I'd already decided that her common sense made
her a woman to admire, I like her even more for her easy acceptance of my offer. Taking the bag, I begin to pluck the larger
pieces of glass from the floor and toss them in.

"That generator must go out quite a bit," I say with a pointed
look at her mirror. "Either that or you've been here since before electricity was invented."

She pauses to grin at me. Her cheeks push up into twin roses.
"Now, how am I to take that, so young and spry as I am?"

I grin back. "The generator, then. I thought as much."

"It's none so bad. The young Stewarts don't care for it when
the lights go out, but old Mr. Stewart—that's our Glenn—liked
the peace and quiet." She shrugs and starts sweeping a wet pile
of glass toward the center of the floor. "Come to that, so do I.
It's more work, but nothing forces folks to slow down like a return to their roots."

"I like it, too," I admit. At Elspeth's lifted brows, I add, "I
own an old thatched cottage that's practically falling down
around me. I can't imagine living anywhere else."

"Nor I," she says simply. She pauses a moment to lean on her broom. I suspect she's not looking at the destroyed remains of the wine cellar so much as the structure around it, this ancient old castle so meticulously and carefully maintained—and, if the current state of affairs is any indication, by her hands alone.

I recognize the moment for the opportunity it is. "What happens to you now, if you don't mind my asking? Are Sid and Ashley likely to keep you on as housekeeper, or will they make alternate arrangements?"

"Oh, I'm not going anywhere. Airgead Island will always need a keeper." There's a pride in her voice that's similar to how the Stewarts discuss the unquestionable authority of the curse. It's almost as though they take perverse pleasure in being set in their ways—as if life, this far from civilization, is required to bear a heavy cost. "Glenn was kind enough to put that in his will. I have tenancy for life."

This is the first time anyone has directly addressed Glenn Stewart's death, and I'm not about to let it go to waste.

"That *was* kind of him," I agree. "Everything else goes to his children, I presume? The property, the money . . . the gold?"

"Aye. It's all very straightforward. The Stewarts have always been careful about that. No mistakes, no surprises."

I'm not sure how much to believe her. My instinct says she's telling the truth, since the details surrounding Glenn's death bear out her tale. He died alone and under mysterious circumstances, but no official inquest has been made. No one is stoking the police into action, and no one is trying to pin a murder on anyone else in an attempt to take everything. I've been around this kind of situation enough to know that the authorities are quick to jump on anything that smacks of greed.

Then again, there's also the small matter of the family solicitor dying under similarly mysterious circumstances—and right after he sent Otis here to counteract the evil influences of a medium. That means Harvey knew something was going on with the gold—that it needed, at all costs, to be protected.

But protected from what—or from *whom*—I'm unwilling to say.

"Is it true that you and the other medium found a piece of the gold?" Elspeth asks, almost as though her train of thought matches my own. "Right here in this very room?"

"Yes. Would you like to see it?"

"Oh, not me. I've seen it before. Not"—she's quick to add—"recently, but years back, before dear Katherine passed away. I didn't much care for it then, and I certainly don't care for it now. But if you wouldn't mind giving my grandsons a peek, they'd be right glad of it. They're keen on everything to do with pirates."

Yet another mystery appears to have solved itself for me.

"Your grandsons?" I echo. "Let me guess. Twin boys? About eight years old and wearing eyepatches? Able to scale impossible cliffs?"

Elspeth beams in a way that's as old as time itself. "Aye, that's them. Ferguson and Jaime. They got sent down from school again last week."

"Again?" I can't help but laugh. "Is that a common thing with them?"

Elspeth sighs, but she hasn't lost any of the light in her eyes. "Dear me, yes. Every other week, it seems. My daughter and her husband are having a holiday in Spain, so Sid said I was more than welcome to bring them here. They've spent many a summer here, so it's no matter. I made sure they'd be a help to me around the castle—and so they have been, fetching things for me and doing odd jobs."

Tell that to my luggage, I think. What I say, however, is, "Are you sure that's safe? What with all this bother about the curse?"

She catches my gaze and holds it. In that moment, I can see everything that's in her thoughts—not through supernatural means, but because there's no mistaking a rational woman's logic.

"It's not my business to tell you how to get on," Elspeth says carefully, "and I wouldn't upset dear Sid for the world, but the sooner you can lay that nonsense to rest, the better it will be for everyone in this house."

"You don't believe in it?"

She doesn't answer me right away—and when she finally does, it's in a roundabout, noncommittal way that would do any fake medium proud. "There's folks hereabouts that'll tell you not to take a fishing boat out if you pass a minister on the way to the docks, and there's them that will always sail sunwise around an island before they land. But my husband has been sailing these waters for longer than any living man, and he doesn't hold by any of it."

"McGee is your husband?" I ask, delighted by this new development.

"Aye, and before you ask, he's never seen a mermaid nor a kelpie on his rounds, neither."

I'd like to grin my appreciation at such a picture, but this isn't the moment for levity. Elspeth might not be aware of it, but in this short talk, she's provided me with more information than the rest of the Stewarts combined.

"If you don't believe in the curse, then what do you make of Glenn's death?" I ask. "You were the only one here when it happened, weren't you? Do you believe it was an accident?"

For the first time, Elspeth appears her age. It comes in a flash as the light from the mirror gleams brighter. I assume the beam is caused by the sun breaking through a cloud, but there's no denying that the timing is good. She leans on her broom as though suddenly *feeling* her age, too.

"I'm no doctor, Madame Eleanor."

"I know. But in your opinion? He drowned in the bathtub, didn't he? Was there anything out of the ordinary about that evening, something about the circumstances that didn't feel right to you?"

She hesitates in a way that indicates wariness—not of confiding her thoughts in *me*, but of confiding them in anyone. "I called Dr. Fulstead to come out straightaway," she says, both answering and not answering my real question. "He did all he could, but it was no use. Poor Glenn was already gone."

There are several follow-up questions I'd like to ask to this, but there's no way for me to do so without rousing Elspeth's suspicions. I'm not supposed to be here to investigate a death; I'm here to contact a ghost.

"His spirit is caught between worlds," I say in a belated attempt to return to my ostensible purpose. I doubt Elspeth buys it, but at least I can pretend I'm doing my job. "That's common when a death is extraordinarily gruesome or caused by malicious means."

"Well, it wasn't gruesome, if that's what you're asking. Right peaceful he looked, and to be honest, I've seen no sign of his spirit lingering on." She straightens herself from the task of sweeping and glances around the room. Now that most of the glass has been cleaned up, the spilled wine looks like a patch of glistening blood.

Even that doesn't have the power to scare her.

"Well, that's much better, isn't it? Thanks for your help, but I can take it from here. A good scrubbing'll have this floor as good as new." It's a kind but firm dismissal, and I recognize my cue to leave. Still, I can't go without asking one last question.

"If I needed to get to Barra, is there a way to contact your husband and have him make a special trip? If I needed some supplies, I mean? Or does he really only come once a week?"

She eyes me as though seeing straight through to my real meaning. "Is this about your luggage?"

It's not, but it's as convenient an excuse as any. What I'd really like to do is visit the medical authorities on the island, to ask questions of this Dr. Fulstead without anyone on Airgead Island being the wiser.

Lying isn't necessary, however, when she offers me an easy—yet impossible—solution. "If you want to head out this evening, Otis is the man to ask," she says. "Next to my man, he's the best sailor in these parts. He could run you up and back within the hour."

I have no doubt that he could. Since he would also see right through my pretense of hitting up the local shops, I don't plan to take up Elspeth's suggestion. The less that man knows of my suspicions, the better.

"Good to know, thanks," I say.

Since I've gotten all I can out of Elspeth without giving myself away, I take my polite leave. I pass the mirror as I go, my view into the wine cellar as clear as if I were still standing inside. If Elspeth had been paying attention, I'm sure she would see me watching her. As her attention is fixed on the now-empty cubby, however, she doesn't notice.

I, on the other hand, notice plenty.

With a sigh and a shake of her head, Elspeth falls to her knees and reaches her hand inside the hole. I hold my breath, half expecting her to pull out another black box or a pouch of gold coins that we somehow missed, but all she does is feel around before returning empty-handed.

Her face is averted, so I have no way of knowing what her expression is at that exact moment, but I'd have given much to find out. Is she sad not to have found sudden riches? Worried that the rest of the gold is still out there somewhere?

Or relieved that there isn't enough evidence in that cubby for a conviction?

The evening is ideal for conjuring ghosts.

The electricity is still on the blink, casting every corner into shadowy relief. The wind is howling against the sea-battered stones of the castle with such force that it rattles the windowpanes. And the mood is one of fear and trepidation, the curse hanging ominously overhead.

In all my years of ghost hunting, I couldn't have chosen a more ideal time to fabricate a specter. As I enter the gilded drawing room, which looks even more decadent with the candles flickering in the chandelier, I'm prepared to mystify and awe doing just that. There might even be a spring in my step—I'm feeling that good about the entertainment I have planned.

"Are you wearing the curtain rings from your bedroom as jewelry?" Ashley demands before I make it more than two steps inside the room. He pulls himself away from the window, where he'd been staring poetically out to sea, to peer closer at my face. "And is that ash around your eyes?"

I halt, all my excitement deflating like a helium balloon three days out. It's easy for Ashley, in a rich, plum-colored sweater and polka-dot ascot, to point out the deficiencies of my wardrobe, but what else could I do? Embellishing my tired velvet dress with rows of jangling bracelets up my arms and dabbing a little residue from the fireplace on my eyelids was supposed to make me look resourceful, not ridiculous.

"I, uh . . ." I cast around in my mind for an explanation. The truth is that I spent the rest of my afternoon unsuccessfully tracking down Ferguson and Jaime. Wherever it is they hide themselves—and the suitcases they steal—it's not an easily accessible location. I have the horridest suspicion it's at the bottom of that cliff. "Until my luggage is found, I'm afraid I don't have many—"

BOOM!

There's no need for me to continue my feeble explanation—a thing I'm grateful for until the boom sounds again, this time accompanied by a tinkling shatter of glass.

BOOM! CRASH!

Ashley and I lock eyes. My instinct is to rush into the next room, from which the sounds seem to be emanating, but he flings up a hand to hold me back. "I wouldn't go in there if I were you," he warns.

"In where?" I ask. "Isn't that a library of some kind?"

He nods. "It is—or rather *was*—Father's study. He loved sitting in there. 'Study is the bane of boyhood, the oil of youth—'"

It's my turn to fling a hand. "Yes, yes. I'm sure there are dozens of sayings related to the subject, and that you know them all by heart, but we should go see what that is. It sounds dangerous."

As if in agreement, a shout sounds, furious and low. Instead of taking alarm, Ashley merely pokes a finger into his ear and twists. "I wouldn't recommend it."

My interest is seriously piqued by this time, but I'm torn between whatever mayhem is causing all that noise in the next room and the fact that I'm finally alone with Ashley—and that he seems to be in a receptive mood. I hesitate.

"What exactly is happening over there?" I ask.

"Birdie is giving Otis a reading. It's not going well, if you can't tell from the noise. I left once she started talking to his dead wife."

In that moment, I make my decision. Lowering myself into the nearest chair, I turn my attention to Ashley, ignoring the sounds of the altercation reaching its pitch. "Then it would be rude of me to interrupt. I'm sure Birdie has a handle on things."

Ashley grins. It's the first time he's let his erudite façade slip, and it makes him infinitely more attractive. Not *physically* attractive, but literally. I'm much more drawn to him now than I have been since my arrival. He looks young and boyish in a way that reminds me strongly of my own brother.

"Scared, Madame Eleanor?"

BOOM! CRASH! THUMP! That last one sounds like a book hitting the wall not too far from where I sit.

"Terrified," I admit. "What on earth made Otis agree to sit down with her?"

"I don't think he's in there willingly. When I slipped out, she was getting ready to bar the only exit with a chair. She's a braver woman than I. There aren't many people willing to tackle Otis in one of his black rages. *I'm* certainly not."

" 'There was a laughing devil in his sneer,' " I quote from *The Corsair*, unable to help myself. Doing so only opens the door to Ashley spouting more poems at me, but it's an apt line. Otis is a quintessential Byronic hero if ever I've met one. "Will he hurt her?"

Ashley shrugs and turns his face away. As an answer, it's not very helpful, but I accept it. Birdie is a grown woman who ostensibly knows what she's doing. If she wants to poke at a man's raw, gaping wound like that, then she's going to have to accept the consequences.

THUMP!

And the books thrown at her head.

"Does he get those rages often?" I ask. Since I'm supposed to be the woman with all the answers, I add, "His aura is muddled, so I can't get a good read on him. It often happens that way when someone suffers a severe emotional trauma. The man he used to be and the man he is now are at odds with one another."

Ashley's head tilts toward me. I recognize the gesture the same way a fisherman knows when his catch is nibbling on the line. He's not hooked yet, but with a little deft handling, he will be.

"You're also muddled, but not to the same degree. Your mother's death . . ." I shake my head when his expression doesn't do more than flicker. "No, not that. Your trauma came later and much more subtly."

"You can see that?"

No, but I can see that he's warming to the topic—and to me. There's a tense expectation about the way he's holding himself, as if he wants to let himself be drawn into my sphere but hasn't yet decided whether or not it's safe.

"A man like Otis wears his darkness for all to see. A man like you, on the other hand, keeps it locked tight inside." It's time to clinch this thing. Drawing on yet another Byron quote, my supply of which is rapidly reaching its limits, I adopt a sad smile and add, "'Those that know the most must mourn the deepest.'"

It works. By this time, Ashley is facing me, his mustache twitching with interest. "You're not at all like Birdie, are you?"

A shout and a thud cause us both to jump. With a guilty flush at my cowardice in avoiding that room—and at the sad realization that Birdie and I are much more similar than Ashley will ever understand—I shake my head. "She's a very powerful medium, and having her here can only strengthen my own ability to seek answers, but no. She's a woman of action, of purpose. You and I, on the other hand, like to take our time with things. We're thinkers. Philosophers."

He nods, clearly pleased at this portrait of himself. I might also add that he's incredibly vain and far too willing to foist his burdens onto someone else's shoulders, but I don't. Vain, burden-foisting men rarely like to have those attributes pointed out to them.

"It's not easy, is it?" I ask with a cluck of sympathy. "Feeling so much and hiding it all away?"

He nods again, his eyes taking on the glaze of a man in rapt contemplation of himself.

"Especially when your father was the exact opposite." Since Birdie has proven to be all-seeing in practically every instance so far, I steal some of her wisdom. "He had more power than was good for him. More money than was good for him, too. A man like that can only value the things he can see and touch.

Your home is filled to the brim with expensive goods, but words, poetry, *beauty* . . ."

As I hope, Ashley is all the way caught by now. He nods at each word, his body leaning closer and closer toward mine.

"He never understood my work," he says eagerly. "He never even tried. All those years I spent writing, all that time I dedicated to my art—did he ever ask to read it? Even once?"

I don't say anything, hopeful that we're only starting to scratch the surface of Ashley's strained relationship with his father. I don't *think* he's about to confess to murder, but stranger things have happened. With an encouraging nod, I gesture for him to continue.

And immediately regret it.

"Will *you* read it?" He whisks a hand into his back pocket and extracts a leather-bound volume that's far too thick for my peace of mind. "You seem to understand literature—better than anyone else under this roof, at all events. You could take it to bed with you tonight. I think you'll enjoy it. Look at this passage I wrote about my father: 'Oh, noble brow, heavy under the weight of familial ignominy . . .' "

It's all I can do not to run screaming into the next room. I'd rather take my chances with an angry pirate exacting vengeance for his deceased wife than listen to Ashley quote his poetry at me.

"Thank you for the offer, but—"

"I have a room full of these," he adds with a sad sigh. "I gave a signed copy to Harvey, but no one else seems to want one."

Mention of the solicitor's name has me rethinking my stance. "Harvey was a poetry lover?"

Ashley's answer is as evasive as his gaze. "He handled all the publication details for me, so it was the least I could do. Percy Shelley paid to have his first book published, you know. Lots of the Romantics did back in the day."

I *do* know that, actually. I also know that Ashley is unwittingly reinforcing everything Otis told me about his scholarly ambitions and the precious university his father poured a small fortune into. I have no idea how much it costs to have one's work published in a volume as beautifully bound and gilded as the book Ashley is holding out to me, but I can't imagine it's cheap. If Harvey was privy to the publication details, then he was aware of the financial details, too.

That kind of knowledge can be dangerous when there's a missing fortune on the line.

"Thank you." I accept the book with more eagerness than I would have a few minutes earlier. It won't fit as neatly into my brassiere as the coin did, but I can still add it to my growing pile of clues. I'm not sure yet what everything in the pile means, but there's no denying that this family is a complex—and un-happy—one.

"And you'll tell me what you think?" Ashley asks with what appears to be genuine earnestness. "Honestly?"

It's a heavy price to pay, but I agree with a nod. I open my mouth to add a lie about what a slow reader I am, but we're interrupted by a splintering sound that's so loud, it's no longer possible for us to pretend that Birdie has a handle on things in the next room.

"Oh, dear," Ashley murmurs. "That can't be good. We should probably check on them."

I couldn't agree more. And since it turns out Ashley isn't the sort to run headlong into danger if there's literally anyone else to do it for him, I'm forced to lead the way.

This I do quickly and with the full expectation of finding the library to be in a state equal to that of the wine cellar. Imagine my surprise when, instead of bookshelves strewn about and couches upended on their sides, I walk in to see Birdie sitting at a desk in the darkness, a single broken lamp tipped on its side next to her.

"What on earth—?" I step into the room and cast a quick

glance around, searching for a sign of Otis or something else that would have been capable of making all that noise. A rhinoceros, for example.

Neither of these things is in evidence. Instead, Birdie pivots her chair toward me to reveal a serene smile and her carefully arched brows. "Ah, there you are, dear Ella. I was wondering what could be keeping you when so much paranormal activity was afoot."

"I didn't realize you required assistance," I reply somewhat drily. That *dear Ella* tells me that her speech is meant more for Ashley's ears than mine. "You should have called out if you wanted me."

"I did."

"I'm afraid I didn't hear you. Perhaps all the crashing and booming covered the sound of your cries."

"But I didn't call out with words. I summoned you, but you couldn't be reached. Are you feeling blocked? You feel blocked to me."

I don't dignify this with a response. I'm not meant to. Birdie has clearly been sitting here awaiting an audience—and I, in my foolishness, rushed in to provide her with one. "Where did Otis go?" I ask, fairly confident this is the line she's expecting.

I'm not wrong.

"Poor Otis." She heaves a monumental sigh and stabs a finger at the floor next to her. "He broke that lamp."

"I'm surprised he didn't hit you over the head with it. It's what you deserve."

Although the room isn't nearly bright enough for me to make out the details of Birdie's expression, I could almost swear that her eyes glint with appreciation.

"His wife asked me to reach out to him," she responds primly. "It's not my place to deny the spirits. I am merely their vessel."

For those of you keeping track at home, Otis's wife now makes the fifth spirit Birdie has communicated with. *Five.*

Ashley provides the next line in our little farce. "If he only broke one lamp, what was making that noise?"

I'm similarly curious as to the source of all that distress. A good recording and a few well-timed thumps on the wall can go a long way in faking a disturbance, but Birdie has just as little access to her luggage as I do to mine. I know this for a fact because the patchouli scent is almost entirely absent from her person by this time.

"Your father."

I bite back a groan. *Of course* it was.

"F-father?" Ashley takes a huge step backward, almost colliding with me in the process. He darts a nervous look around the room, as if expecting his sire's ghostly apparition to appear in the corner.

To be perfectly honest, I wouldn't be surprised if some sort of entity *did* materialize—not a ghost, obviously, but a cheesecloth dangling from a string or an aerosol spray hitting baking powder at just the right angle. These tricks, however, don't appear to be in Birdie's repertoire.

"He's here? Now? Did you ask him where the gold is?"

I could kiss Ashley for getting right to the heart of the matter, even if it is incredibly suspicious. Anyone who's confronted with the great beyond and can only think to ask about money has some strange priorities. Doesn't he want to know about what happens in the afterlife? The possibility of God's existence? Or, at the very least, what caused his father's death in the first place?

"I didn't have to ask," Birdie replies. "He already knows why I'm here."

I won't say it. I won't play into her hand.

Ashley, bless him, does it for me. "*And?*" he demands. "Where is it?"

Birdie rises from her chair. Her movement is fluid and grace-ful, though I hear the crack of her knees before she reaches a full standing position. In a more sentimental mood, I might say the sound is like that of wooden parts clacking together, her puppet strings being tugged and pulled.

My mood takes a turn in that exact direction when Birdie lifts her finger and points it at me. "Only Madame Eleanor knows. Only Madame Eleanor can find it."

It should be a moment for triumph. Birdie is basically admit-ting she has no idea where the gold is or even where to look next. Her only lead must have been the wine cellar. Now that the hand has been played—and lost—she needs me to help di-rect her next actions.

Unfortunately, triumph is the last thing I'm feeling.

"Seriously?" I put my hands on my hips. "You're making it *my* sole responsibility now?"

"The ways of the dead are not for me—or you—to ques-tion." Birdie smiles at Ashley. "Your father has told me that he'll communicate with dear Ella or with no one. The fate of the gold and of your family are now in her hands."

I shake my head in warning, but Birdie doesn't pay me any attention.

"He's taken an odd liking to her, our Glenn. He always did have an eye for a pretty face."

My face is none too pretty as I hold back the torrent of emo-tions this speech is eliciting, but Ashley glances over and de-cides the epithet is close enough to count. He also decides he's had enough of our company for one evening and makes good his escape. He lingers only enough to ask, "How much longer do you think it will take, Madame Eleanor?"

"Lifting a curse is a tricky business," I say through clenched teeth. "These things can't be rushed."

The answer isn't a helpful one, but Ashley is forced to accept it. He expresses his hope that I'll enjoy his poems before heading on his way.

I'm deciding how best to tell Birdie what I think of her tactics when she beats me to it. "You really ought to be doing more to find the gold, you know. The longer we stay here, the more dangerous the curse becomes."

I throw my hands up. "I'm so sorry. I wasn't aware I was disappointing you."

"I'm not disappointed. Just curious." She tilts her head to one side, a thoughtful purse to her lips. "What do you intend to do next?"

"Well, I *was* going to try and fabricate a ghost, but that's probably out now that you've enraged Otis and used up all the spooky sound effects. What was it? A recording? A crash box? I've been thinking about making one, but I don't know how to steal a bunch of plates without Elspeth finding out."

Birdie blinks at me. "A crash box?"

I'm not fooled by that innocent stare. Even beginning theater students are familiar with the basics of stagecraft. Shaking or dropping a box filled with broken glass and porcelain is the easiest—and cleanest—way to create crashing sounds in the distance.

"What do you want, Birdie?" I ask, suddenly exhausted with it all—the pretense and the doublespeak, this idea that either one of us believes in any of this for real. I sag against the nearest bookshelf, dislodging several large tomes. "Is it the gold? Is it to show off? To win? Because I can tell you right now, you're winning. You're winning big-time."

Tell her it's not safe, Winnie says. *Tell her she knows too much.*

I close my eyes and sigh. The last thing I'm going to tell Birdie White is that she has more insight than is good for her. Her ego is big enough as it is.

"That's her, isn't it?" Birdie says before I have a chance to share my sister's otherworldly wisdom. "Just now. Your spirit guide was talking to you, wasn't she?"

I'm back to standing straight and being alert in no time. "What? You can tell?"

Birdie nods and draws so close that her face is practically pressed up against mine. She peers into my eyeballs, but not in the way of a medium pretending to see something deep within my irises. This is more of a medical check, as if she wants to make sure I'm taking all my vitamins.

"How does it work?" she asks. "Do you hear her? See her? Feel her?"

"I, um. I don't know exactly. I hear her, I guess. But it's not an external sound. It's more like she exists inside my head."

"What did she say?"

I can't think of any logical reason to lie. Besides, Birdie did say that she might be able to help me hone my powers. I mean, I don't believe her, obviously, but it's not as if I have any other options.

"That I should tell you it's not safe. That you know too much."

She jerks back. "Too much? She said that?"

"Yes. Does it mean something to you?"

Birdie doesn't answer. Instead, she puts her face next to my eyeballs again. Her breath is hot and smells of seawater. "What else does she know? About me? About the curse?"

I shake my head. "I told you. It doesn't work like that. She comes to me, not the other way around. It doesn't do any good to ask her questions. She won't answer them unless she wants to."

Birdie's response to this is to pull me into an embrace. She's far too tall and gaunt to be a good hugger—it's all angles and the thin press of her bosom. Her elbow even manages to wedge between us, which seems anatomically impossible.

"There, there," she says.

"Um. I'm okay, Birdie. There's no need—"

"You poor dear. You miss her, don't you? Your sister?"

I don't know how to explain that I *don't* miss her—or, rather, that I miss her less now than I did when she spent ten years in a coma. During that entire decade, I could see her and touch her and brush her hair, but I couldn't reach her. Not in any way that mattered.

Now that she's gone, however, I get direct access to her soul.

I try to pull out of Birdie's embrace, but she's much stronger than she looks. She holds me there a moment, soothing and patting, before finally putting her hands on my shoulders and pushing me back.

"You'll tell me if she contacts you again?" Birdie asks. All the kindly solicitude seems to have left her, returning her once again to a woman I neither know nor trust. "We won't accomplish anything unless we're totally honest with one another. Gloriana is too powerful for one woman alone."

Wait a minute. "I thought you said I'm the only one who can find the gold. You basically told Ashley that the rest of this is on me."

"I'll make you a spagyric tincture." She nods once. "To strengthen your abilities."

"I don't want a spagyric tincture."

"And we'll see if there are any amethysts in the house for you to put under your pillow. Perhaps that will call Winnie to your dreams."

"Now see here, Birdie. You can't just barge in like this and—"

But she can. She totally can.

"I don't know why you're wasting your breath. In fact, I don't know what you've been doing with yourself this whole time. So far, I've done all the heavy lifting. Are you even *trying* to help this family? What kind of a medium are you?"

I'm so bewildered by this sudden attack that Birdie manages to slip past me and out the door without answering a single one of my questions. Nor do I have a chance to defend my honor even though I have an answer at the ready.

I'm the kind of medium who knows that answers lie not in the mysterious, but the banal. In understanding people and their relationships. In asking questions and listening to the answers behind the answers.

I glance down at the book of poems in my hand and groan.

In reading two hundred pages of poetry before bed on the off chance that Ashley knows something more than he's letting on.

Chapter 10

The only good thing to come out of Ashley's book of poetry is my discovery of the cavern.

Strictly speaking, it's more of an alcove than an actual cavern, a rocky indentation at the bottom of the cliff so favored by Elspeth's grandsons—and, in his younger days, by Ashley himself. Apparently, this place had a profound effect on his childhood. There were no fewer than thirteen poems dedicated to "slipshod, slapping susurrations of the sea against the shore."

As there was also a lengthy description of the winding path that leads to it, I was able to find my way down here without assistance. And, I need not add, without letting the twins know that I was about to descend on their privacy. Two less gracious hosts I have yet to meet in my lifetime.

"Just say it. I promise it won't hurt." I settle onto the damp rocks along one side of the cavern, careful to protect my velvet dress from the seaweed residue that coats every visible surface. A cursory glance around the cavern reveals it to be a trove of boyhood treasures—rocks and cracked shells, driftwood and my two filthy pashminas—but my luggage isn't anywhere to be seen. If they're hiding it somewhere in here, it's not visible to the naked eye.

"Lily-livered landlubber," Red says.

I nod and smile my encouragement. A used rope spool has been set up between us to serve as a table, but I don't dare touch it. I saw a crab scuttle out from underneath it not too long ago. I'm horrified to think of what else might be living inside.

"Now try another one. Lex Luther loves lollipops."

Red looks doubtful at this, but when he glances up to find his brother nodding his encouragement, he gives in. "Lex Luther loves lollipops," he recites. His words echo inside the rocky inlet, making him sound much older than his eight years.

"One more," I urge. "The lion licked his lips and laughed."

This, apparently, is taking things too far. Red crosses his arms and refuses to indulge me. "That doesn't sound like a real spell. You're just making up nursery rhymes."

He's not wrong, but I can hardly admit it. I'm already a trespasser in their secret hideaway, an adult interloper guaranteed to ruin their fun. To admit my tactics would be to get myself permanently banished.

"Where do you think nursery rhymes came from in the first place? They're nothing more than ancient witches' spells that have been passed down through the ages. 'Ring Around the Rosie'—you know that one, right?"

Both boys are interested enough to nod.

"It's about the bubonic plague. The 'ring around the rosie' is code for the rash that breaks out when you get infected. The 'pocket full of posies' is an herbal remedy. And when they all fall down—well, you know what that means."

Since they don't hazard a guess, I go through the motions of a terrible and gruesome death before slumping into a heap onto the ground—seaweed slime and all. As I expect, this pantomime of death delights the boys more than it should, given the recent history of events inside this castle.

"No way," Blue breathes. Of the two of them, he naturally finds this macabre tale most suited to his taste. "So it's a spell?"

"In a way, yes." I gather my dead and scattered limbs and resume my seated—and now damp—position. "It might be best if you think of it like a special kind of chant."

"And if I sing it at someone, they'll die? Of the plague?"

"Well, no. Spells don't really work that way."

"You mean they don't work at all," Red says with a jut of his lower lip. "I knew it was fake. My tooth'll never come out just by saying all that daft stuff."

Blue doesn't seem the least dismayed by this—a fact that's explained when he extracts a string from out of his pocket and whips it over his head. "You know what that means . . ."

"It means that neither one of you is a certified practitioner of the dark arts," I say sternly. I have no doubt that if I said the word, Blue would willingly—and happily—extract every one of his brother's teeth by force. "And my incantations *will* work. If you practice them all day every day, your tooth will be barely holding on by the end of the week. Word of a witch."

This isn't as far-fetched as it seems. I might not know much about the magical removal of teeth—or, admittedly, the forcible removal of teeth—but I do know how the mechanics of linguistics work. Those repeated l-sounds will push Red's tongue against his front teeth and loosen them naturally. Like I told Nicholas, all my spells come with a side of science.

Unfortunately, little boys seem much less impressed with my knowledge base.

"A whole week?" cries Blue, giving the string another whip over his head. "That's forever!"

I recall feeling much the same way when I was eight years old. Every day was an adventure, each week an eternity. Now that I'm an adult, I know better. Time is practically whizzing by, and unless I do something about this curse soon, Birdie is going to take it into her head to do something drastic. Theatrics, hysterics, *murder*—I'm not putting anything past her.

With this in mind, I smile at Red in hopes of furthering this interview along. "Keep saying the chants," I tell him. "By this time tomorrow, you'll start to feel how loose that tooth is becoming."

"Fine," he agrees glumly. "I s'pose it can't hurt."

I wink at him. "Not as much as yanking it out with a door, at any rate." Without waiting for the boys to respond, I adjust my position so that my hands are clasped and resting on the spool table. "Now. It's time for your payment. No chant or spell comes without a heavy price."

The boys exchange a wary but excited glance. My lips twitch as I struggle to suppress a smile. They obviously think I'm going to exact a pound of flesh or the handover of their firstborn children.

"What do you want from us?" Blue asks, his eyes alight with possibility.

Red is more circumspect. "Will we have to tell Nanna?"

I pass a finger over my lips. "This one should stay between us. What I'm going to ask you for is a very special artifact—a talisman of sorts."

"But we don't have any talismans," Red says.

"We don't know what a talisman is," Blue corrects him.

The liars. They have oodles of talismans. Talismans and bundles of sage and a backup phone battery. Not to mention my toothbrush and clean underwear. Since to ask for such earthly belongings will only cause me to lose what little credibility I have with them, I plan to ask for items of strict necessity—in this case, my favorite white scarf and a small motion detector I plan to plant outside Birdie's bedroom door.

"What I require is one object of great value and one of great beauty."

"We don't have those, either," Blue says quickly. He shoots his brother a dampening glare. "We're kids."

"Yes, but you're *twins*," I remind him. "Remember how powerful I told you twins could be?"

Blue isn't buying it. "This doesn't seem like a fair trade," he protests. "All you did was tell us some stupid old nursery rhymes."

"Yeah," Red chimes in. "T'other one gave us—"

He claps his hands over his mouth before he can divulge what Birdie gave him, but it doesn't matter. He's been made, and he knows it. So does his brother. Blue shows every sign of wanting to remonstrate with his brother, but he's too smart to do it in front of me.

"What did she give you?" I ask. Without her luggage, Birdie has about as many resources as I do, so I hazard a few guesses. "Money? Snacks? Oh! She told you how to curse your enemies, didn't she?"

From the guilty yet excited flush that rises in their cheeks at that last one, I know I'm on the right track. Trust Birdie to know exactly what would appeal to two mischievous scamps like these.

"When did you talk to her?" I ask.

Their eyes shift toward each other in mute solidarity.

"What did she want from you?"

They cross their arms and glare at me from under mulish brows. I think fast.

"Well, at least tell me whether or not she remembered to teach you the knot of invisibility."

That one gets them. Well, it gets Red. Blue isn't about to give himself away so easily. I heave a sigh and focus my attention on the child most likely to spill his secrets. "Of course she didn't tell you about the knot," I say. "Forget I said anything. It's too powerful for beginners. Now that I think about it, the talismans are probably too much for you, too."

I rise to my feet and make as if to leave, confident in the trap I've set. The boys are wise enough to suspect a trick, but it's not often that a pair of witches comes their way.

I'm almost to the mouth of the cavern before Red calls to me.

"Wait, Madame Eleanor!"

His brother hisses his displeasure, but Red's hand is touching my arm before he can be stopped. I turn to find a solemn face peering up at me. "Do you really know how to make us invisible?" he asks.

"Of course not," I say with complete truthfulness. "Invisibility is impossible."

"But you said you could!"

"I lied. I'm just an ordinary human woman. How could I make anyone disappear?"

"But—" Red takes his lower lip between his unbroken line of teeth. "That would be smashing."

I allow a mysterious smile to touch my lips. "It would be, indeed."

Confident that I've given them enough to mull over for a few hours before I try them again, I prepare to make my departure. To my surprise, Red's hand touches my arm once more.

"We do have *one* talisman," he confides.

Only one? In addition to my clothes and toiletries, my bags also contained a spell book full of nonsense, another spell book that contained a list of all known poisons and their side effects, fake elixirs by the dozen, and the cosmetics the boys are now applying with an even heavier hand than before. I have no idea what they plan to do with the half of it.

"Oh?" I ask in a show of disinterest.

"Jaime, *don't*," Blue warns.

At the sound of Red's—no, Jaime's—actual name, I realize I'm dealing with a serious matter. Thus far, the boys have been careful not to divulge which one of them is which. I imagine having different names is as painful a source of discrepancy as Jaime's full mouth of teeth. Now I know: Jaime is Red, the reasonable one, and Ferguson is Blue, the one I need to watch out for.

"But we could be invisible," Jaime pleads. "Think of what we could do to Headmaster Grimsby if we're invisible. The fire rocks, Ferg. The *frogs*."

I have no idea what either of those things indicates, but Headmaster Grimsby has my sympathies.

"I'll let you pull out my tooth any way you want," Jaime says, and goes through a series of finger motions that must indicate their secret handshake. "Brother's oath."

Ferguson repeats the motions, though reluctantly. "Fine. You can give it to her. But not for *keeps*," he adds to me.

"I wouldn't dare," I say, my interest now high enough to overlook the fact that I'm going to have to somehow manufacture their twin invisibility after this. A dark piece of cloth and some shadow tricks might do it.

The boys give me their backs, deep in a conversation I'm sure I'm not supposed to overhear. It contains several swear words, some Gaelic I can't understand, and a few giggles. None of these fill me with much in the way of optimism, but when the boys turn around to face me once again, optimism is the last thing I care about.

Triumphant and not a little proud, Jaime reaches into his pocket and pulls out a coin for my inspection.

A *gold* coin.

"Where did you get this?" I snatch it out of his hand. The weight and size of the coin are identical to the one I already have. The cross is as crudely stamped, the gold as burnished. As is the case with the one I'm carrying nestled inside my brassiere, something about it strikes me as off. I don't know what it is, but it has something to do with how smooth it is to the touch. It *looks* pocked and damaged with age, but when I run my thumb over the surface, there are none of the expected bumps or ridges.

"Boys, I need you to tell me where you got this. Did you find it? Are there more somewhere on this island?"

In my alarm and eagerness, I seem to have forgotten my role as the cool witch. Authority—especially boring adult authority—has a way of bringing the shutters down over juvenile eyes. Bribing them with promises of even greater witchcraft *might* work, but this is too important to leave to chance. I should have known that two boys who would unhesitatingly steal and hide two strangers' luggage might also have located that gold long before the rest of us even started looking. Kids always know the best hiding spots inside any house.

"Well?" I close my fist around the coin. "Are you going to tell me, or do we need to take this to your grandmother?"

My threat does little to move them. Without a word, the two boys align themselves side by side, nothing but belligerence in their identical, pirate-patched faces.

"We're not afraid of Nanna," Ferguson says.

"We're not afraid of witches," Jaime adds.

"We're not afraid of curs—"

"Yes, yes, I know. You're not afraid of anything. You're the epitome of bravery, fearful of nothing and no one." A sudden, devious thought flashes in my mind. "Except, I think, for Otis."

The flicker of fear in their eyes is unmistakable, so I press on. "How would you feel if I decided to tell *him* about this? Nanna might not scare you, and you might laugh in the face of the curse, but I don't think he'd be so quick to understand. Do you?"

I don't get an answer right away. The boys do their best to hold my gaze, to remain stoic and unblinking in the face of such a threat, but it's to no avail. Like being able to throw my voice and perform simple sleight of hand, teaching myself to win staring contests was an early part of my medium training.

Ferguson is the first to look away. "I told you," he mutters. "You can't trust any of 'em."

Jaime gulps, but his concerns are of a different variety. "Does this mean you aren't going to teach us how to be invisible?"

"Why don't you tell me where you got this gold, and then we'll see." I feel a bit like a traitor, going back on my promise like this, but some things are more important than salvaging my reputation in front of a pair of eight-year-olds. Laying a murderous curse to rest is one of them. "I know it makes me no fun, and that you're regretting letting me into your secret clubhouse, but this is important. I know it, you know it, and Otis knows it."

I'd hoped that mentioning Otis again would hasten the spilling of the secrets, but Jaime looks down at his feet and kicks at a large rock.

"Hey," I say softly. "I won't really tell him. Not if you don't want me to. You just have to show me where you found this gold."

Jaime kicks harder. "Do you promise?"

"Witch's honor." I make the motion of an X over my chest. "This will stay strictly between us."

Ferguson looks as though he'd like to stop his brother, his face growing pinched and white, but Jaime, for all his sweet disposition, is made of sterner stuff.

"It was on his boat," Jaime says, his voice barely above a whisper.

At first, I think I must have misheard. "I'm sorry?"

"His boat." Jaime is louder this time, but not by much. "We aren't supposed to go on it, and he'll be right miffed if he finds out."

My heart leaps to my throat. The feeling is so sudden, so

constricting, that I have to bolt to my feet to untangle what's happening to my innards. "You found the gold on the boat? *Otis's* boat?"

Jaime nods. That small gesture confirms everything I've suspected since Otis first appeared at the castle—as well as a few more suspicions that just now occur to me. I already know that Otis's clothes are too good for a tour boat operator and that he's the only person on this island—with the exception of McGee—who has the ability to come and go at will. He also could have arrived with plenty of time to knock out that generator. For all I know, he was even on that train with us.

He admitted as much to me already—he's here at Harvey's instigation, and came only to ensure that no one takes advantage of Sid and Ashley's foolishness for personal gain.

Or to ensure that the only one taking advantage of them is him.

"You two stay here," I command. "Or, better yet, go help your grandmother up at the castle. Don't let her out of your sight, mind?"

The edge of fear in my voice should have been enough to send them scurrying off in search of a responsible adult, but it seems to have the opposite effect. Jaime straightens until he's a good two inches taller; Ferguson shakes his head with a resolution rarely seen in adults four times his age.

"Do you want us to show you the place?" Ferguson asks.

I'd like to see the location, yes, but I hardly want these two to accompany me. "Just tell me where to look, and I'm sure I can find it."

I might as well have not spoken for all the heed they pay me.

"Jaime'll be lookout," Ferguson says decisively. "I'll show you the broken window we used. You aren't a very big lady. You'll fit. Won't she, Jamie?"

Jaime nods and kicks his heels like a sailor receiving his shipping orders. "Aye, aye. On the ready." When he sees the anxiety

I'm unable to hide, he adds, "It's all right, Madame Eleanor. I'm a super lookout. I'll climb to the top of the mast and call like this if anyone's coming."

He proceeds to make a series of soft whoops. Aviary species native to the Outer Hebrides are unknown to me, but he sounds very similar to the small gray birds I've seen perched overlooking the ocean. Like Birdie, these children are rapidly putting me to shame with their ability to outshine me.

I shouldn't accept their help, I know. If Otis has the missing gold coins on his boat, then there's only one conclusion: he's a thief and possibly a murderer and undoubtedly a man to be feared. The smart thing would be to get everyone on this island to safety.

Which, considering that his boat is the only way on or off, presents a bit of a problem. Or, considering your perspective, *a lot* of a problem. I need to confirm that the gold is there before I start calling in specialty evacuation helicopters or whatever else is used when the threat of death is hanging overhead.

"Fine." I give in, but not before raising a finger in warning. "But if you see any sign of Otis, even in the distance, you two will clear out and leave me to deal with him, understand?"

"But Madame Eleanor—"

"Please, Madame Eleanor—"

I firm my position, both physically and mentally. "It's non-negotiable, I'm afraid. I want your solemn oath that you won't put yourselves at risk, or I'll march up to the castle and tell everyone where you got this coin."

It's with extreme reluctance that they agree, but they do eventually come around, our pact sealed with spit-covered handshakes that are as disgusting as they sound. The promise thus made, Ferguson loses no time in dashing out the cavern opening. Jaime is equally keen, but he's nice enough to stay back and keep me company as we wend our way along the water's edge. If I were of Ashely's turn of mind, I might take note of how the feeble, misty sky mirrors the slate-colored water, or how the damp air seeps so deeply that it penetrates my bones, but I'm not. It's gloomy and wet, and that's all I need to say about it.

The dock where Otis's tour boat sits gently rocking back and forth is the same one where McGee originally dropped us off. Whereas McGee's vessel had looked as though one strong gale would smash it to pieces, Otis has put time and money into the maintenance of his watercraft. It's also kitschy as all get-out. He's obviously leaned in to the idea of his family heritage and his eyepatch. A bright red YE OLDE PIRATE TOURS is painted onto the side of the hull, along with the traditional image of the Jolly Roger. Old fishing nets are affixed at random to the outer walls of the main cabin, and the planks have been falsely weathered to give the appearance of antiquity.

Under any other circumstances, I'd have been delighted at such incongruity—at a fierce, angry, possibly murderous man who would willingly captain such a tacky vessel. Unfortunately, I'm far too aware of how visible we are from the castle. My room doesn't overlook the docks, but most of the living spaces do. It would be very easy for Otis—or, indeed, for anyone—to peek out and see what we're up to.

As if sensing this, Jaime scrambles away to secure his lookout perch. I have no idea how he manages it, but within a few seconds, he's hoisted himself up to the top of a swaying pole about ten feet above our heads.

"Okay, Ferguson," I say in a needlessly quiet voice. I can barely hear myself above the incessant slap of the waves, but stealth seems like our best bet. "How do we get into the main cabin?"

"It's this window," he says. He leads me around to the starboard side of the boat, where a plank leads the way on board. No sooner do we make it up than I'm hit anew with the pirate-themed décor. Plastic skulls are affixed to the outer walls of the cabin like macabre handholds, each one linked with a plastic chain meant to look like shackles. To complete the picture, a large, fake cannon sits underneath the ledge of a round port-hole-style window. None of this seems the least bit historically accurate, but that doesn't bother Ferguson. He clamors on top of the cannon and fiddles with the latch of the window for all of five seconds before it swings open. I have no idea how he and his brother managed to find the one broken latch in what looks to be about three dozen such windows, but I can't say I'm sur-prised they put in the effort.

"I'll go first," he says before I have a chance to stop him. He slithers his body through the hole and lands with a thump on the other side. I almost shriek when his head pops back up, his gap-toothed smile brimming. "Come on, Madame Eleanor. I'll help you."

I am not now nor have I ever been a large woman. My size and youthful appearance have always been something of a detriment, since it's difficult to instill awe and respect in some-one when you look more like a babysitter than a woman who will banish your home of evil entities. In this instance, I can only be grateful. My head makes it through the hole without fuss, and my shoulders lodge less than I expect them to, but my hips only slip through thanks to the grace of God, a hefty tug from Ferguson, and the rending tear of my dress as it catches on the frame.

"Next time, we'll use butter," he informs me as I fall from the window to the floor, mournfully noting a large rip along my hem. "Butter'll slide you through anywhere."

"Next time, you can just undo the lock and let me in that way," I say with a nod toward the cabin door. A very obvious bolt makes it easy to get in and out.

Ferguson's wide grin informs me that such a notion had oc-curred to him, only to be discarded in the name of adventure.

"Let's make this quick," I say, mistrusting that grin.

I stand and make a quick survey of my surroundings. The

cabin isn't overly large, but it is much more technologically up to date than the fake props would lead me to believe. Even the oversized wooden steering wheel can't make up for the screens, buttons, and multiple mechanical devices that indicate the real driving system.

"Where did you find the gold?" I ask, my heart sinking at all the possible hiding spaces. "Inside a hidden panel? Tucked inside a false wall? Stowed away under the floorboards?"

"No, it was right there," Ferguson says. He nods toward a treasure chest in one corner of the cabin. It looks like a movie-prop version of a treasure chest—which, as I draw closer, turns out to be exactly what it is. I've seen similar Styrofoam coolers being carried by families at the beach. This one has been painted to look like aged wood grain, but there's no mistaking that squeak as I lift the lid.

"Uh . . . Ferguson?" I glance over my shoulder at the boy. He's stationed himself with both hands on the steering wheel, his imagination taking him over the seven seas and back again. "You're saying the coin came from this exact chest?"

"Yup." He joins me and stabs his finger at the bounty contained within it. "See? Otis has a million of 'em. Jewels, too, and rings, and if you look really deep, some rubber rats. We put one in the toe of Nanna's shoe once. You should have heard her scream."

His assessment is an accurate one. There are—if not millions—several hundred gold coins inside the chest. However, like the chest itself, they're nothing but props. Plastic, from the look and feel of them, though of a high-enough quality that it's understandable the boys got them confused with the real deal. I plunge a hand in and let the coins slide through my fingers. As he said, a few plastic rings and fake rubies are also scattered amongst the booty. I don't go deep enough to find any rats, but I take his word for it that they're there.

"Ferguson, are you *sure* this is where you got the coin?"

He nods. "Jamie picked it. He liked that one best because of the plus sign on it—he's keen on maths, but I think it's dead boring. I wanted this one."

Predictably, the coin he holds up bears a gruesome skull and crossbones.

"If you're gonna keep the maths one, I'll take this," he says as he tucks the coin in his pocket. With an anxious glance at the chest, he adds, "You don't think Otis will be able to tell?"

I have no idea what Otis is or isn't capable of, nor do I know what I'm supposed to do next. There's no doubt in my mind that Ferguson and Jaime are telling the truth about where they got the coin—nothing would be served by their lies, and they're much more interested in the excitement of having it rather than its value.

I take a minute to rifle through the chest in hopes that I'll find another real coin—or, better yet, a false bottom that leads to a trove of them—but I don't find anything out of the ordinary. Even the rubber rat I eventually extract leaves me unmoved.

"Ferguson—" I begin, but am cut short by the telltale sound of a bird whooping in the distance.

Both Ferguson and I freeze.

I hold my breath, hoping the sound will turn out to be nothing more than an *actual* bird coming close to mate or eat or do whatever it is that keeps them busy all day, but it sounds again. It's much more urgent the second time around.

"Go," I say, pushing the lid of the chest back down. I press so hard that the Styrofoam splits, but there's no time to worry about that now. "Out the window and back to the castle, just as I said. Take Jaime and make sure no one sees you."

"But, Madame Eleanor," he protests, "how will you fit if I don't push you?"

"I'll find a way," I promise. When the bird call sounds for a third time, I put my hands on Ferguson's back and propel him toward the porthole. "I mean it, Ferguson. Get your brother to safety, and don't tell anyone where you've been."

He doesn't, as I'd hoped, immediately dash to safety. He gets one small leg out the window before turning to me with a look that I could almost swear is relief. "You're scared of him, too, aren't you?" he asks.

I think of Otis and the gruff, angry way he navigates the world—of how he overreacted when Birdie mentioned his wife— and nod. Yes, it's fair to say that I'm scared of Otis, though it's more for the boys' sake than my own right now.

Ferguson must see some of this, because his eyes grow wide and he loses no time in scrambling the rest of the way out of the window.

I have no idea how much time I have to evacuate the premises. My fight-or-flight instinct has always leaned strongly toward the flight side of things, but that window looks even smaller from the inside than it did from the outside. It's one thing to be caught trespassing on a man's boat in a torn dress and with two gold coins secreted in my bosom. It's another to be caught dangling halfway through a porthole window, unable to move in either direction.

Fight it will have to be.

Waiting only until I'm sure the boys have had time to make it to safety, I unlock the latch on the main door and steel myself for the confrontation to follow.

Then I steel myself again. And I steel myself some more.

When a full sixty seconds have passed and there's no sign of an angry pirate at the door, I start to wonder if Jaime had been mistaken and made the bird call preemptively. There's been plenty of time for me to hide myself away or sneak along the water's edge, and all I've done is stand here like a fool waiting for evil to befall me.

Which, as it turns out, is exactly what I've done.

In this instance, evil *literally* befalls me. It strikes as a blow to the back of my head, sudden and sharp and wholly unexpected. I see nothing but a flash of black and the sudden burst of stars that follow before I fall in a heap next to that fake chest full of even faker treasure.

Chapter 11

I awake with a roaring headache, a mouth that feels stuffed with cotton wool, and ghostly feline apparitions at my feet.

"Beast?" I blink at the image of my cat sitting at the end of my bed. It's not unusual for a woman suffering from a head injury to experience blurred vision, but it does seem highly unlikely for that vision to take the shape of a black cat.

Or—wait—*two* black cats.

"Freddie?" Despite the pain splitting my head in two, I jerk to a seated position. While most black cats look similar to one another, the smaller kitten is unmistakably my own. The white tips on her ears and a small kink at the neat point of her tail could belong to no other. "How is this possible? Am I dead? Are *you*?"

A low chuckle at my bedside draws my attention. It also pulls my head in that direction, which is a mistake for a lot of reasons, not least of which is that I shouldn't be making so many sudden movements in my condition.

"Your cats are very much alive, though I'm not ashamed to admit that it was a near-run thing. As it turns out, they don't

much care for air travel. Or for being put forcibly into a crate."
Nicholas extends his arm, his shirtsleeve rolled to expose his
sinewy forearm. Several bright red scratches adorn that well-
sculpted limb. "The feline temperament leaves much to be de-
sired. I've always preferred the simple obedience of a dog."

These words are calculated to get a reaction out of me, I
know. Unfortunately, I find myself unable to rise to the task.
Gratitude and the percussive ache of my head are bringing me
much too close to tears for that. I reach out and grasp the hand
being held out to me instead.

"It's about time you got here," I say as I lower myself back
to my pillow. A sore spot on the back of my skull throbs in
protest. "I can't believe you abandoned me like this. Actually,
I *can* believe it. That's the worst part. I should have known
better."

"Oh, dear." A softer, female voice sounds from the other side
of the bed. I'm too weary to turn my neck again, but I recognize it as Sid. "It's all my fault. I'm so dreadfully sorry,
Nicholas. I wouldn't have had this happen to her for the world.
You must believe me."

"Of course I believe you," he says, and in a much kinder
voice than he used with me. "I should have warned you that
Eleanor is prone to getting herself knocked over the head.
Something about her compels people to violence. I can't imagine what it is."

If I had the energy, I'd lose no time in telling Nicholas that if
he continues in this vein, *he's* the one in danger of being on the
receiving end of violence. As it is, I can only accept the warm,
purring bundle he places gently on my lap. Beast would never
lower herself to cuddle—and in front of an audience, no less—
but Freddie has always been a sweetheart.

"What time is it?" I ask. My bedroom is just as dark now as
it's been the entire time I've been on this dratted island, but the
light from the window seems to indicate it's still daytime. "Or
am I better off asking what day it is?"

"I think you should take her home," Sid says as though I haven't spoken. "It's too dangerous for her to continue her work. It's too dangerous for any of you. I don't know why I thought *I*, of all my family, could defeat the curse."

"Nonsense," Nicholas replies, once again in that kind voice. "For all we know, she slipped and knocked herself out on the steering wheel."

Mention of the steering wheel brings all the events leading up to my incapacitation rushing back to me. The boat, the gold, the boys. *Otis.*

"Ferguson and Jaime," I say, once again jolting into an upright position. My head swims with the sudden movement, but I close my eyes and will the sensation to abate. "Where are they? Are they all right?"

"Yes, they're fine. The last I saw, they were downstairs playing jackstraws with Otis and Ashley."

"Otis?" This time, my jolt is strong enough that Freddie lifts her head and mewls a protest. Nicholas also releases a murmur, his hand checking me before I can leap out of bed. "But—"

Sid releases a sound somewhere between a sigh and a laugh. "Oh, dear. He was afraid you might assume that he was the one who attacked you, since you were on his boat when it happened. But it wasn't him, Madame Eleanor, on my honor."

Sid's honor isn't something I value all that much, but I can't think of a polite way to say so. Nicholas steps into the breach. "Of course it wasn't," he soothes. "You were with him at the time. And Ashley and Elspeth were down in the kitchen—everyone safe and accounted for. It's as I said. She must have slipped."

There's no mistaking his firm tone in that last bit. I notice that Birdie is conspicuously absent from the list, but since I know all too well that it's fruitless to oppose my will to Nicholas's when I'm in anything but full fighting mode, I smile weakly and continue stroking Freddie.

"Yes," I murmur. "That *is* what happened, now that I'm

thinking more clearly. All that rain and seawater—it's a wonder I've made it on two legs this long. I'm so sorry to have put everyone out."

Nicholas releases a breath that's tinged on the edges with approval, but Sid isn't so easily won over.

"But I don't understand," she says. "What were you doing on Otis's boat in the first place? And how—?"

As much as my head hurts right now, it doesn't pain me nearly as much as what I have to do next. I know for a fact that I was struck by an outside force—by human hands wishing to do me harm. This idea is borne out when I take a deep breath and feel nothing swelling up in my bosom except air. The two gold coins are no longer safely nestled where I kept them. Someone must have taken them while I was unconscious.

Someone who purposefully hit me. Someone who didn't like how close I was getting to the truth.

"The curse," I moan, lifting a feeble hand to my brow. Freddie doesn't approve of this action and paws at my arm, but this isn't a moment for playing with kittens. I'll make it up to her later. "I was called to the boat, drawn to its presence. As soon as I set foot on board, I knew it was a trap—that Gloriana had forced me on board."

I happen to think this a fairly good piece of acting, particularly since I'm feeling none too spry, but for the first time, Sid displays an intelligent—if not particularly well-timed—burst of common sense.

"If you knew it was a trap, why did you stay?" she asks. "Why didn't you run for help?"

I'm not looking at Nicholas, so I can't see his expression, but his silence communicates plenty. It's an *amused* silence—the kind that's waiting to see how I plan to wriggle my way out of this one.

Good thing I happen to be exceptional at wriggling.

"Something . . . grabbed me. Something sinister, something

not of this world." As if just now recalling the painful interlude, I reach down to finger the edges of my dress. The tear sustained as I wedged through the porthole window is still there. "Look. This is where it pulled me. Its claws rent through the fabric."

Sid releases a sound halfway between a moan and a shriek. I'd feel bad for adding to her already monumental fears, but this is her fault for asking sensible questions in the first place.

"I tried to escape, struggled to get free, but someone—something—was on the boat with me." The shudder that moves through me isn't entirely faked. I was facing the door when I was struck over the head, which means whoever hit me had to have been hiding on board the entire time. Either that, or there's an access point the boys don't know about. "That's all I remember. I was attacked from behind, and my world went black."

The sound Sid makes is a full-fledged wail this time. The high pitch of it is agony to my already throbbing head, and I wince. Nicholas must see it because he rises smoothly to his feet and puts an arm around the sufferer. At that small bit of contact, every part of Sid wilts against him. She's like a flower folding against the elements—the one plant this island of rock and sea can grow.

"I knew it," Sid murmurs, her arms wrapping around Nicholas's neck as if he's her sole means of strength and support. "We'll never be free of this thing. We're doomed to suffer like this forever."

I watch, somewhat detached, as Nicholas sets out to calm his friend. Nothing about his low, soothing murmurs or the way he leads her out of the room is the least bit romantic. It's more like watching a man care for his grandmother than anything else, his steps slowed to match hers and an expression of kind—if pained—resignation on his face.

In other words, there's no reason for a girlfriend to feel jeal-

ous. And I don't—not really, not in any way that's a recogniz-
able part of that emotion. It's just that I've never seen him like
that with *anyone* before. He treats his mother with amused respect. He treats his niece with amused affection. Me, well, I get
a little of both.

And that's exactly how you like it, Winnie reminds me.

My hand curls automatically around Freddie. I take comfort
from that small, purring bundle of fur and the larger, not-
purring Beast casually grooming herself at my feet. I have no
idea how Nicholas knew I needed my cats, but I'm more grateful than I can express. I never realized before how much I rely
on them, how much stability they bring.

As I also need to start figuring out what happened to me on
that boat, I lose no time in swinging my legs over the side of the
bed and testing my physical capabilities. Although I'm shaky
and my head is likely to ache for a few days, I'm able to stand
on my own two feet.

Unlike Sid, I always have been.

After setting Freddie down next to her mother, I make a survey of my injuries. A lump the size of a ping-pong ball behind
my ear indicates the source of my distress, but there's no sign of
blood or broken skin, which is good. Whoever hit me was either experienced enough to know exactly how hard to clobber
a woman to incapacitate but not kill her, or they got lucky. My
hair is a nest of tangled curls and half-done braids, and my velvet dress is now little more than a rag, but all my body parts are
intact and fully functioning, so I'm calling it a win. In fact, the
only thing that truly alarms me are the missing coins. I sweep a
hand inside my dress in hopes of finding that they've merely
settled somewhere else on my person, but to no avail.

"Do I dare ask what you're doing?" Nicholas slips into the
room so quietly he might as well be a ghost, but I've passed the
stage of being alarmed by anything that happens inside this
house.

"Please tell me you heard the clunking of two gold coins inside my bosom and took it upon yourself to safeguard them."

He raises a brow.

It's with a heavy sigh that I say, "I assume that's a no."

"I'm afraid so. Would you like me to make a more thorough search of your person? I'm willing to do whatever is necessary to find them."

I hold up a hand to prevent him from stalking to my side and making good that threat. There are too many thoughts jumbling around inside my cracked head, so many vague ideas flitting around without anything to anchor them. As easy—and delightful—as it would be to forget these for a few minutes in the arms of a man like Nicholas, I refuse to be distracted.

"Do you know who found me on the boat?" I ask. "And who brought me up to the house? Also, what day *is* it? This place is so dark all the time, it's like living inside a cave."

Nicholas's expression is neutral, which I take to mean he's disappointed not to be invited to manhandle me. He does, however, hold up one elegant hand and start ticking off answers. "Yes, I do know who found you—it was me. I'm also the one who brought you up to the house. And it's still Tuesday. You've been unconscious for the better part of the afternoon, but that's not surprising considering the size of the bump on your head."

"You found me?" I echo.

"Yes. I was brought to Airgead Island in the company of a delightful old man named McGee. When he pulled up to the dock, the first thing he noticed was that the door to the cabin on the tour bout was open. He suspected his grandsons were up to no good, but I knew better."

I look a question at him.

"*You* were the one up to no good," he explains. "McGee obviously doesn't know that a troublesome pair of eight-year-olds has nothing on you when you're in the middle of a case."

As this is uttered with a chuckle and a lurking smile, I take it as a compliment.

"And there were no coins on me at that point? Well, I guess that's my answer. Whoever hit me definitely took them. I wonder if that was why I was attacked, or if they were afraid I was getting close to something else. Please tell me you searched the boat while you were on it."

"Alas, no. I felt that the woman passed out on the floor was of more immediate concern. Your cats, too." Since stroking me is out of the question, he pets Beast instead. Although that cat refuses to let me show her any affection, she turns her head into Nicholas's hand with haughty pleasure. "I think it was the noise of the airplane they objected to the most. I have no idea how we'll get them back. If you wanted them with you, you should have brought them on the train in the first place."

I blink at him. "But I don't want them."

Freddie turns to me with such a look of wide-eyed betrayal, I immediately contradict myself and set out to soothe her. I use every term of feline endearment that comes to mind, aware the entire time that Nicholas is watching me with a twisted smile.

"I had no idea you were so eloquent," he murmurs as soon as Freddie is back to a full purr. "What does a man have to do to earn the same regard, I wonder?"

"Don't," I warn him with a raised finger. "You're straying from the topic."

"Which is?"

I hold a hand to my head and sit on the bed. For once, this move isn't intended to inspire awe in my audience. Everything still feels so fuzzy and muddled that I close my eyes in an attempt to corral my thoughts.

The mattress sinks, and I feel the heat of Nicholas settling next to me. To his credit, he doesn't speak or move or do anything to interrupt my thought processes. It's one of my favorite things about him, to be honest. He's an unreliable travel companion, he has a tendency to revert to levity at the worst possible moments, and he could have had the decency to search that dratted boat while he had the chance, but he has his virtues. His unquestioning willingness to sit back and let me conduct my affairs in my own way and my own time is one of them.

"The treasure is real, that much I know is true," I say, more to myself than to him. "I've seen the coins, and if they're a sample of the rest, they're worth more money than I'll see in my lifetime. If that's not a motive for all this, then I don't know what is. The curse *isn't* real, that much I know, too. It was a person who hit me over the head, not a ghost or a dead monarch. That same person most likely killed Glenn Stewart and maybe Harvey Renault, too. You heard about Harvey?"

I open my eyes and wait until Nicholas nods before continuing. That's another great thing about him—he makes it a point to gather as much information in as unobtrusive a way as possible. In the brief time he's been here, he'll have amassed almost as much information as I have.

"What I don't know, however, is whether or not Birdie is real. My gut reaction is no, but she has more information about this place and its people than she's letting on."

"Yes, I gathered as much from your first message," Nicholas says. "By the by, I'd appreciate it if you hold me excused from having purposefully sent her on the train with you. I'd never heard of the woman until you mentioned her name."

"Well, she's heard of you, so watch what you say around her. Why *did* you send me by train, anyway? She claims responsibility for it all—says she magically waved her wand to take you away on business and arrange the seating on the train to her satisfaction."

"Unless she can personally control the Minister of Education, I don't see how that's possible." He pauses, as though conversations revolving around high-ranking government officials is an everyday occurrence. Which, in his world, it is. "And

I didn't think sending you on the train would be such an issue. Sid assured me it's a very comfortable ride."

I seriously doubt that Sid has ever lowered herself to travel in anything but first class, but I don't mention it.

"If I'd have known . . ." Nicholas's voice trails off, his brows knitted in worry. "I thought you could use the extra time to your advantage."

"I did use it to my advantage," I reply with a shake of my head. "Just not as well as Birdie. She's *good*, Nicholas—really good. Better than me, and you know I don't suffer from low self-esteem."

He grins, the deep lines of his face lightening momentarily. "Don't you? I never would have guessed."

I bump him with my hip, feeling much easier now that I've had my say. One thing, however, is niggling at me.

"And what do you mean by *my first message?*" I ask. As far as I can remember, I only sent him the one. I've been trying to eke out my phone's battery life as much as possible, since I have no way of recharging it. "I didn't send you a second one after you failed to acknowledge the first. I know better than to level at the moon."

He stares at me for a moment before reaching into his pocket. Extracting his cell phone, he pushes a few buttons before holding it out to me. My image pops up on one side of the screen, a candid photo of me squishing a reluctant Beast up to my face, accompanied by a text I have no recollection of sending.

I need you, Nicholas. Bring the cats. XOXO

"Um." I lift the phone out of his hand and study it more carefully, as though I might be able to peer through the screen to the computer code below. "I didn't send that."

"So I'm beginning to gather."

"I would *never* send you hugs and kisses via text."

"That should have been my first clue."

"And using someone's full name like that is weird."

"Agreed."

"But the cats were a good idea." I pause and give Freddie a pat. "I missed them."

"A sentiment that does you justice. It's only a pity *my* presence doesn't affect you so strongly."

I realize my mistake at once. Nicholas obviously hightailed it here on the mistaken belief that I couldn't live another day without him—and then arrived to find me unconscious. He'd never let on that he feels anything more than the mildest alarm for my safety, but there's no denying that being in any way tied to me is a trial.

"My poor darling," I say, reaching for him. "Did you dash all this way to come to my rescue?"

"I *did* rescue you," he points out. He also takes the hand I'm holding out, twining his fingers through mine. "As I also requested you come up here in the first place and then abandoned you, I imagine that makes us equal. I'm sorry, Eleanor. I had no idea it was going to be like this. When Sid said she needed a medium to communicate with the ghost of her father, I thought it would be fun for you. Not . . ."

I squeeze his fingers. "I know. Murder wasn't my first guess, either."

"Are you certain that's what it was?"

As certain as a person can be without a medical report or a firsthand examination of the body, yes. "I can't prove it, obviously, but it's not looking good. There's too much going on around here that doesn't make sense. Even this text is suspicious—who sent it? How did they access my phone without me knowing about it? And why did they want you here?"

"That settles it." He drops my hand and turns to face me, his shoulders square and a look of determination rendering his expression even more attractive than usual. "What do you need me to do?"

Freddie responds for me with a plaintive mewl and a butt of

her head against my hand. She blinks expectantly up at me, as though she's sure I have all the answers. Now that I think about it, Nicholas is looking at me a bit like that, too. And Sid. And Ashley. And the twins. Even Birdie seems to think I know much more about this curse than I'm letting on.

Birdie. Of course.

"Let me see your phone again." I hold out my hand and study the text anew. It's short and to the point, designed to get results with the least amount of communication possible. Anyone with quick, light hands and an ulterior motive could have lifted my phone from my person and sent it—especially if that *anyone* gave me an odd, awkwardly long hug in the library last night. The time and date of the incoming text confirm it. "Blast that woman. I should have known better. This is just like her."

"That woman?" Nicholas echoes.

"Bridget Wimpole-White. My nemesis. The Wicked Witch to my Glinda. The Voldemort to my Harry Potter. The—"

His lips twitch. "The one with the eyebrows."

"Exactly. I don't know what she wants with a couple of cats, but she's not getting her hands on my babies." I ignore the way that *babies* makes his lips twitch even more. "Okay, here's what I need from you: you're going to become Birdie's biggest fan."

"Oh, dear. Why do I get the feeling I'm going to regret this?"

"You believe every word out of her mouth, got it? Every nonsensical vision she sees, every piece of your aura she reads—I don't care how demeaning it is. You think *my* brand of mysticism is garbage, but you buy wholesale into the garbage she sells and can only wait with bated breath to hear more."

He sighs, his breath not the least bit bated. "Are you sure I can't just buy you a new chest of gold that we can pass off as the real deal? There's still enough time for us to scrap this whole ghost thing and go to Malta."

I point a warning finger at him. "I mean it, Nicholas. It's the least you can do after everything you've put me through. I need you to get close to her. Watch her every movement. See if she does anything suspicious. And if she gets anywhere near these cats, protect them with your life."

"Aye, aye, captain," he says with a salute that would do Ferguson and Jaime proud.

At the thought of Ferguson and Jaime, another idea occurs to me. This one makes me even more upset than all the rest.

"Lucifer's touch!" I cry.

Nicholas's brow raises.

"Can you *believe* the gall of that woman? She texted you and tricked you into bringing my cats, but it didn't even occur to her that I might want clean clothes, too."

"This line reveals your love life," Birdie says. She's sitting across a chessboard from Nicholas, his large palm held upward in hers. Her fingers trace one of the many lines that cover the hands of every human being in the world—none of them linked to premonitions of the past, present, or future. "See how it's broken in the middle? You'll suffer a romantic loss, but not for long."

Nicholas's eyes meet mine across the gilded salon. Now that we're sitting in this room lit only by candles, I realize the true value of all that gold plating. It's almost bright enough for us to converse like human beings.

"That doesn't sound good," he murmurs. "I hope she's not carried off by a head injury."

Birdie tsks and yanks Nicholas's hand closer to her face. "Yes, and see this one that intersects the love line? That's your friendship line. Your second romantic interlude will be someone you know, someone who's already dear to you."

It's not the most subtle palm reading I've ever witnessed—or, indeed, performed—but I have to give the woman credit where it's due. She obviously read the relationships in this room and is doing her best to leverage them to her advantage. If I'm not mistaken, her goal is to inspire me with jealousy for my hostess, to create a gnashing envy that distracts me from her own villainous deeds.

Well, too bad. I can read relationships, too. Sid is like a beautiful orchid—fragile and exotic, but useless unless she has someone stronger to attach herself to. I was that person until Nicholas arrived; now he can take his turn, and welcome to it. It'll free me up to focus on more important things.

In this instance, I mean Otis. I don't know what pressure Sid brought to bear on him to put him in a conciliatory mood, but he's seated next to me, sipping his after-dinner coffee and casually petting Freddie. The kitten, unable to distinguish between friend and foe, took to him immediately.

It almost makes me believe in his innocence. Freddie might not be as worldly-wise as Beast, but I don't think she'd be purring that loud on the lap of a murderer. At least, I *hope* she wouldn't. Discretion is a necessary attribute in our line of work— a thing that Beast, sitting queenly and alone near the fireplace, seems to have perfected.

"Is this the part where you ask me to give you my palm so you can take a turn?" Otis turns to me, his tone only slightly drawling. "I should warn you that Birdie already tried, and it didn't end well."

He shows me his palm. Even in the low lighting, I can see the raised, twisted contour of a scar bisecting his hand. It obscures any and all other lines that might have once provided insight into his soul.

"There are several on my legs, a rather large one on my side, and the one that took my eye, too, if it helps," he says. "I'm a gnarled maze of the man I used to be."

I refuse to allow him to lead me down that path. I have no doubt that's exactly what he did with Birdie, resulting in their explosive argument. It's a good tactic for those who are trying

to hide something; by going on the offensive, Otis is able to ensure that he controls the flow of information.

"I don't read palms," I say flatly. It's a lie, of course, but
what the Stewarts don't know won't hurt them.

"You can't read palms?" he echoes. "By your own admission, you also can't read auras. Nor can you conjure up my
uncle or, it seems, find where he hid his gold. Forgive me for
asking, but what *can* you do? Other than breaking onto people's boats and falling and hitting your head?"

I don't dare look around the room, but I know everyone's
eyes are on me. The lull of conversation has all but stopped, the
sound of Freddie's contended purrs growing loud in its absence. I'm tempted to show off a little—the result, no doubt, of
Nicholas sitting on the other side of the room and the challenge
glittering in Otis's eye—but I don't.

"In some cases, nothing," I admit. "I don't always control
my gift. There are times when I hear nothing but silence, and
then there are times when—"

"—the ghost 'is beating on the door,'" Ashley interrupts.
"There's no need to explain. *I* know."

I smile my agreement. For once, Ashley's quote is apt. And,
bless him, brief.

"To be fair, we may see more activity now that my cats are
here. They seem to strengthen my powers, but . . ." I trail off,
my head whipping around to where Birdie and Nicholas are
holding their palm reading. It had been my intention to point
out that I don't control my cats any more than I do my sister,
but a sudden flash hits me—not a vision, but a memory.

Me, confessing to Birdie that having my familiars around me
helps boost my abilities. Me, immediately regretting that confession for fear that she'd figure out how to use it against me.
Except . . .

She glances up long enough to catch my eye. There's nothing
about her expression to give her away—not even a quirk of

those frightful eyebrows—but I could almost swear that an understanding passes between us. Like a current, it jolts in my limbs and makes my fingertips twitch.

She did this. She did this on purpose. She did this on purpose to . . . help me?

There's no time for me to explore this unprecedented idea further. Our cozy gathering is interrupted by a knock at the door and the soft footfall of Elspeth making her way into the room. She's not, as I first suspect, bringing dessert to tempt our dainty appetites. On the contrary, the two figures she's dragging aren't the least bit sweet, though they do look contrite and recently scrubbed. Each one is being held by the scruff of the neck and presented like a pair of puppies recently caught rolling in the mud.

"Now, be gracious and say 'good night' to the company," Elspeth says with a gentle shake of each one.

"Hullo," says the one on the left.

" 'Night," says the one on the right.

Since the two boys are in matching blue pajamas and neither one shows the least inclination to smile, I'm unsure which is which. Even their hangdog expressions are identical.

"They wanted to come in to apologize for their role in this afternoon's episode," Elspeth says. "Making up that story about finding gold on Otis's boat and luring Madame Eleanor out there to do a mischief. It's not a nice way to treat a guest, and so they know it."

I blink. This is a new spin on events, and one that's not wholly out of the realm of possibility. True, the boys had a real coin in their possession, but considering how many of those seem to be floating around hereabouts, there's a good chance they came across it naturally. From there, it would have been easy for them to feed me that tale about Otis's boat, to abandon me on the inside and even to knock me on the head from behind.

The boy on the left kicks at a fraying bit of carpet and looks up at me. They aren't wearing their eyepatches, and there's such a stricken sincerity in his eyes that I immediately recognize him as Jaime.

"What do you say, boys?" Elspeth prods.

Neither one of them answers her until she gives them another shake.

"Sorry," they mutter in unison. Ferguson goes so far as to add that he knew from the start that all grown-ups are rotten, but Jaime doesn't chime in. He's still looking at me in that earnest, oddly expressive way. He gives a slight shake of his head and makes a move as if to speak, but their grandmother prevents it.

"I'm ever so sorry, Madame Eleanor," she says. "They *do* have manners, and they *have* been raised to use them."

"Of course they have," Sid says warmly, her smile genuine. "I've known them since they were babies. Two more beautiful little boys, I'm sure I've never seen before—or since."

"We are not beautiful," announces Ferguson with a curl of his lip. It's enough to showcase his gap tooth, thus confirming their identities. He nudges his brother.

"Beautiful is for girls," agrees Jaime, though with reluctance. His mouth opens to reveal a similar gap, though his is marred by a dot of blacking on his lower lip and a slightly inexpert application of my favorite eyeliner to the tooth.

I struggle to suppress a smile. For all their resourcefulness, the boys haven't yet surmounted the obstacle of the intact incisor.

"Who needs beautiful when you can be dastardly?" I agree. I keep my tone light and inconsequential so they know I mean no harm. Even if I *did* believe they set up that entire episode on the boat to mess with me, I'm not going to tell on them to their grandmother. I'm a lot of unpleasant things, but a snitch isn't one of them.

Ferguson eyes me with misgiving. "What does dastardly mean?" he asks.

"Wicked and vile," I say, smiling to show how much I enjoy those particular attributes. "Pirates are dastardly. So are witches. And mediums, come to think of it."

Birdie coughs gently. "Mediums are the last true connection between the worlds, dear Ella, as I'm sure you know. Our work is of paramount importance."

"Of *course* it is," Sid agrees.

"Hear, hear," murmurs Nicholas.

"Meow," puts in Freddie.

I turn my head to smile at the kitten for her excellent timing, but my world suddenly grows black. I don't *think* I've reinjured my head, but the darkness that falls is so absolute that not even a hint of light is allowed in.

I realize what's happening the moment an image flashes across my darkened vision. It's the slideshow picture again, the brief glance at something not of this world. As before, nothing I did seems to have brought it on—and nothing I do is able to stop it now that it's arrived.

The vision is of a little boy, about eight years of age, his body held in a state of suspended animation. His skin is ghostly pale, his eyes shut, his limbs floating oddly in the air. It takes me a moment to recognize that strange buoyancy. It's not air that holds him thus. It's water. He's surrounded by it, *drowning* in it. I mentally will the boy to wake up—or at least to smile so I know whether he's Ferguson or Jaime—but the vision flashes off as suddenly as it turned on.

I open my eyes to find the entire room staring at me. It's the ideal moment to be honest about what I've seen, to prove to this room that I'm not—like Birdie White—some sham of a medium trying to leverage their pain and suffering for my own personal gain.

But I can't. The only sensation I have is one of deep, abiding fear.

It's always the children who suffer the most.

"You have to get the boys off this island," I say to Elspeth, doing my best to keep the hysteria out of my voice. Given the wide-eyed shock that results, I don't think I do a very good job. "As soon as possible and through any means necessary. Nicholas will take them. They can stay in a hotel, or he can take them back to his home until it's safe. They can't stay here. They need to leave."

Nicholas gently clears his throat. He's standing much nearer than he was a second ago, almost as though time and space have stopped making sense. "Perhaps you should sit down," he suggests. "Your head . . ."

As if it's capable of acting on suggestion, my head does start to throb. The ache is low and dull, but I barely heed it. "This has nothing to do with my injury. This is something else."

"You do look awfully pale," Sid says. She rises smoothly from her seat and makes a gesture for me to take her spot. "Nicholas, darling, bring her over here. I'll make her comfortable, and Ashley will pour her something to drink. It's been a trying day for us all."

"I don't want something to drink." I only have eyes for Elspeth. "Elspeth, I'm serious. Do they have somewhere else to go? Can you call your husband to pick them up, or maybe Otis can—"

One glance at Otis tells me that he's not going to be a likely source of assistance. The conciliatory mood that's had him mellowed all evening is gone, replaced by the snarling ogre of a man who first made my acquaintance.

"You're disgusting," he says, his voice thick with loathing. The sound is raw and emotional, and I shiver just to hear it. "Using children like this. Threatening their safety to get a reaction. Is there no end to how low you people will go, nothing that's sacred enough to be left alone?"

Although Birdie is presumably included in this tirade, Otis doesn't look at her. All of his anger is reserved for me and me alone. Not even having Nicholas at my elbow, his stance rigid and tense, is enough to shield me from it.

"You can say whatever you want about me," Otis continues bitterly. "You can accuse me of hoarding the gold on my boat and throw my dead wife and unborn baby at my head a thousand times over."

I'm about to point out that it was Birdie and not me who did that, but he's not finished. He looms closer, one finger outstretched.

"But you will not, cannot, *dare* not touch one hair on these boys' heads, or I will see to it that the only way you're carried off this island is in a body bag."

Even if I could think of a reply to a threat like this one, I'm too paralyzed to utter it. Otis's words are harsh and cruel, and the way he's saying them leaves little room for doubt as to his feelings about me, but I don't begrudge him a single syllable. It's about time someone else realized what kind of danger we're all in—not because of a stupid old curse, but because someone under this roof has already committed at least one murder.

If we're not careful, we'll *all* be carried off this island in body bags.

"I think you've said quite enough," Nicholas says, his tone more clipped and British than I've ever heard it. He doesn't just have a stiff upper lip; every part of him is rigid. However, that doesn't stop him from putting a protective arm around me. "Your message has been received and will be taken under consideration."

Somewhere in the back of my mind, I'm amused at how precise and formal Nicholas's speech becomes as he rises up in his role of white knight, but I'm unable to appreciate it right now. The way Elspeth is angling her body in front of her grandsons; the light horror that has dropped Sid's lower lip . . . Even Ashley, who doesn't seem to be affected by much, is starting to look uneasy.

Only Birdie remains unmoved by the scene unfolding in front of her, but that doesn't count for much, since she's mostly watching Freddie as she pads across the room to be groomed by her mother.

"Madame Eleanor won't hurt us," Jaime says, but more as a question than a statement of fact.

"You're not going to make us leave, Nanna, are you?" Ferguson asks. Although I wouldn't go so far as to say he looks scared of me, there is a taut wariness around his mouth that wasn't there before. "If we promise to be good and not get in any trouble?"

"You're not going anywhere," Otis growls. The boys shrink at the venom in his voice but stand their ground. "If anyone is leaving this island, it's those two."

The *those two* he refers to are, naturally, me and Birdie. I can't help thinking that this might all be a ploy—that Otis knows how close I am to finding an answer and that his sole objective is to get me out of the way—but it's a short-lived sentiment. If this is the case, he's a phenomenal actor. No one has looked at me with *that* much disgust before.

"I don't think anyone is going ashore in this weather," Birdie points out. She nods toward the nearest window. Sure enough, the lashings of wind and rain make it doubtful that anyone will be heading out to sea in the next few hours. "Perhaps we should make the best of things and let dear Ella try to reach her spirit guide."

This suggestion is, not unnaturally, met with violent opposition. Even Nicholas, who generally enjoys watching me work, is unable to support the idea of ghostly communion at this time.

"I think we ought to call it a night," Sid suggests before pandemonium erupts. She holds her hand out in a vague gesture of supplication and keeps it there until Nicholas takes it. "Please,

Nicholas, will you take me up to my room? I'm too scared to walk alone in the dark."

"Of course," Nicholas replies, but not before shooting me a look of apology.

I wave the pair of them off. Of all the things to fear inside this house, the dark seems like the least objectionable, but I'm not about to say so. Reminding everyone that they need to avoid being struck over the head or murdered in the bathtub isn't likely to win me any favors.

Sid's dismissal acts as a parting bell for the rest of the company. Otis stalks away without a backward glance, Elspeth bundles her grandsons off to bed, and Ashley lingers for only a few seconds before deciding that now might not be the best time to pester me about his book of poems.

In the end, only Birdie and I remain in the room. I'm afraid she's going to ask me questions about my vision, but all she does is nod toward my cats. "You weren't lying about your familiars, were you?" she asks. "I've never seen anything like it. You were gone for almost two minutes that time."

Two minutes? From my perspective, that vision had lasted no more than two seconds. I must have fallen deeper into a trance than I realized.

"Was it you who texted Nicholas?" I ask.

Her response to that is a bland smile and a slight inclination of her head.

"Why?" I demand. "What are you hoping to get out of all this?"

She answers my question with a few of her own. "What else are they capable of? Your cats, I mean. Will they be able to help you communicate with Glenn? Do you know something about the gold?"

"Aren't you even a little bit curious about what I saw? Those boys, Birdie. I saw one of them dead."

"Did you now?"

I stamp my foot, inadvertently startling Beast and Freddie in the process. They dash out the door, but I have no doubt they'll make their way to my bedroom later. Either that, or Nicholas's. Beast is much more likely to seek solace at his hands than mine.

"Don't you remember what happened the last time I saw someone die?" I demand.

"Yes." Her answer is simple, her indifference simpler.

"And that doesn't worry you? I probably shouldn't admit this, but that vision on the train was the first time anything like that has ever happened to me. I don't intend to make it a regular thing. If there's something I can do to prevent Jaime and Ferguson from dying, anything I can do to save them, I'm going to do it."

"Good on you."

It's more than I can take—these lies and manipulations, her calm façade in the face of all this horror. "I'm done trying to be your friend, Birdie," I say. They're some of the truest words I've ever spoken, and I feel liberated just to have them off my chest. "I don't know what you're doing here, but I don't think it's anything good. If you won't tell me how you knew that gold coin was in the wine cellar—"

"—Glenn showed me the way."

"If you won't tell me how you knew that gold coin was in the wine cellar," I repeat with awful deliberation, "and you won't tell me how you knew that Harvey Renault was going to die, then I can only assume that you were the one to steal the gold *and* to murder Harvey when he made an effort to come here and stop you."

"Oh, dear," she murmurs. "I've gone about this all wrong, haven't I?"

"Did you kill Glenn Stewart, too?"

"Glenn Stewart drowned in the bathtub."

I draw closer until our toes are touching. Even in this, she showcases her superiority to me. My leather T-straps have been damaged by all this salty sea air; her serviceable black trainers look incredibly comfortable and show no signs of disrepair from repeated wearings.

Something about those shoes gives me pause. They're the same ones she's had on since we met on the train, but this is the first time I'm really noticing them. The rest of her is so carefully crafted to look the role of a medium—the clothes and the hair and the mole that has once again moved to a higher point on her cheekbone than it was yesterday—that it doesn't make sense for her footwear not to match. Shoes like that denote stealing through corridors without making a sound, slipping down to boat docks and hitting unsuspecting women over the head when everyone else's back is turned.

"We know the location and cause of Glenn's death, yes," I agree, my voice cold. "But what we don't know is if someone pushed his head under the water and *made* him drown. What we don't know is if there were substances in his blood that might have made him susceptible to slipping under the surface. How can we? We're trapped out here on a remote island castle with no access to Barra or the people who might be able to answer these questions."

Birdie narrows her eyes. It's not a look of suspicion or of guilt—it's more like genuine thoughtfulness.

"This whole setup is designed for failure," I add. "An isolated house party might make a good setting for conjuring the dead, but it's not ideal when you want answers to real, important, life-or-death questions. As much as you might like to pretend we're here for the former, I think we can both agree that the *real* results will come from the latter."

I've said just about all I can on the subject without writing out a detailed confession of every fake ghost I've conjured in the name of quasi-science. I've also done all I can considering the current state of my head.

Still. There's one more thing I need to get off my chest before I go to bed.

"Also, if you would stop trying to get my boyfriend to leave me for Sid Stewart, I'd really appreciate it," I say. "He's not as easily won by female fragility as you think."

She tsks, undismayed, and shakes her head. "Poor Madame Eleanor. You might be able to see into the great beyond better than most, but you're blind if you think that."

Chapter 12

It takes Birdie less than twelve hours to cause another uproar.

I had the foresight to set my alarm early last night, as I was determined to wake up before the rest of the house to do some hands-on investigating. A visit to Otis's boat was to be my first order of business. A more thorough sweep of the boys' cavern was the second.

Which is why I'm so surprised when the distant cries that jolt me out of bed a good hour before my alarm goes off aren't, as to be expected, that of Birdie in a trance. Nor are they the sounds of Gloriana, Glenn, Harvey, Montague, Otis's wife, or any other of the half-dozen departed spirits she's conjured up communicating through her.

They belong to Sid. It's that circumstance and no other that has me jumping to my feet and wrapping myself in a sheet.

It doesn't take me long to determine which direction to take to find her. The castle is still clouded in darkness, but I'm starting to adjust to all this gloom and doom. Like a bat born and raised in darkness, I don't need to see. I have plenty of other senses to rely on.

Common sense, for example. Before I'm even fully aware of what I'm doing, I find myself turning in the direction of Glenn's room.

"Hello?" I call as I approach the bedroom door, which has been flung open wide. "Is everything okay in here?"

As I expect, Sid is waiting for help to arrive. She's sleep-rumpled but elegant; a pink satin robe flutters about her legs as I drag my sheet-wrapped body through the door. "Oh, Madame Eleanor. Thank goodness. You'll know exactly what to do."

Like my room, Glenn's former quarters are designed in a grand, historical style. There's not quite as much in the way of brocade and ornate carvings, but the four-poster bed, bookshelf-lined walls, and blue pinstripe wallpaper proclaim this a place of wealth and quiet dignity.

Or, rather, it *would* be a place of wealth and quiet dignity if not for the woman thrashing and moaning on the bed. From the look of her, all twitching limbs and fevered movements, you'd think she was in labor. A birth is one of the few life events I haven't presided over in the course of my career, but there's something about Birdie's legs twisted up in the tasteful blue sheets, kicking and struggling to get free, that brings the image to mind.

"What's happened?" I ask as I approach. It had been my intention to be polite but distant, refusing to give Birdie any more stage time than she's already claimed, but she really does look ill. I lay my hand on her forehead to find that she's clammy and cold despite the sweat that's broken out on her upper lip. "Birdie, what's wrong?"

Her eyes snap open. It takes a moment before she's able to focus enough to see me hovering over her—and when she does, she darts a hand out and clasps me around the wrist with a strength that seems almost superhuman.

"The curse," she manages before a spasm rocks her body and causes her to almost double over. "I warned you what would happen, told you how it would be if you didn't start to make some headway. We're running out of time."

"This isn't the work of a curse," I say as I whip the sheets away from her body. "It's probably food poisoning."

I'm tempted to add that it could also be the work of a woman who clearly intends to maximize the amount of attention that's put on her at all times, but I refrain.

"Where does it hurt?" I ask instead. "What's the precise location of your pain?"

She doesn't appear inclined to answer me, so I turn to Sid. "Can you tell me exactly what happened to put her in this state?"

Sid shakes her head, her hands worrying in front of her. From the amount of wringing and wrenching she does with those things, it's a wonder she has any skin left. "She was like this when I came in. All that moaning woke me up, and I thought perhaps it was . . . well, *Father*."

As if to confirm this, she glances over her shoulder to the connecting bathroom, where Glenn's death occurred. Birdie has yet to stage a scene from there, but that's not surprising. I'd be lying if I said we mediums didn't try to avoid bathrooms as much as possible—bathrooms and kitchens both. There's something about the ordinary functionality of those rooms that makes it difficult to set the right mood.

"She's going to be all right, isn't she?" Sid asks.

I don't answer, taken up as I am in trying to get a sensible answer out of Birdie. So far, her only contribution is to mutter "Gloriana," "the curse," or some combination thereof.

"It's working so much faster than before," Sid says in a failing voice. Lifting a shaking hand to her brow, she adds, "That attack on you yesterday, and now this . . . it knows what we're doing and is coming for us all."

I have no one to blame for that bit of nonsense but myself. I should have known better than to blame the blow to my head on the curse.

"Tell me what you need." A low, calm, capable voice sounds at my elbow, followed almost immediately by Nicholas's tell-tale scent—a light bergamot mixed with mint, and one of my favorite smells in all the world. "Medicine, a blow horn, some-one to sit on her chest for a few minutes . . ."

I fight to keep from laughing. Nothing about this situation is funny, but Nicholas has an uncanny way of knowing exactly what I need to hear.

"See to Sid, please. I can handle Birdie."

I cast a quick glance around the room, searching for some-thing that will help me make good on my claim. There's not much. Unless I want to strangle Birdie with the bellpull or smother her with a pillow—both of which sound more appeal-ing by the minute—I'm going to have to improvise.

"But first, hand me that water, would you?" I ask.

He hands me a ceramic pitcher from the bedside table. "There aren't any clean glasses."

"I don't intend to make her drink it," I say, and immediately dash the entire contents over Birdie's head.

Birdie is understandably displeased by my efforts at calming her. Her moaning turns to spluttering, and she even manages to open her eyes long enough to glare at me. However, the thrash-ing has stopped, and she's started breathing in deep and regu-lar—if damp—intervals.

"What did you do that for?" she demands. She makes an ef-fort to sit up. "How dare you attack me like that? How could you be so cruel as to—?"

She cuts herself off and falls back to the bed, unable to finish her tirade. That pained silence is when I realize for certain that she isn't faking. Any remaining color in her face has drained off, leaving a pale, shaking woman who suddenly looks twenty years older.

"That's better," I murmur. I use the sheets to wipe the water from her face. The mole on her cheekbone has all but disappeared by this time, a dark smudge on the sheets the only real indication it had been there at all. "Now, if you'll just tell me where it hurts."

"My stomach," she gasps as she curls into a ball and clutches the offending body part. "I think I'm going to be sick . . ."

She is, in fact, sick. Violently so, and with that same shaking lethargy that leaves me more unsettled than all her hysterics. The emptied water pitcher proves itself invaluable in this instance—as does Nicholas, who loses no time in whisking Sid to one corner of the room to dip her head between her legs and breathe deep.

I still think this looks more like food poisoning than anything else, but despite my ability to brew medicinal recipes using nothing but the herbs I grow in my garden, I'm no doctor. Any client with a *real* ailment I'm quick to send to Dr. MacDougal, our local family practitioner and a close friend of mine.

"I think one of you should find Otis and tell him to prep his boat for a passenger," I say to Sid and Nicholas over my shoulder. "I don't think she's in any immediate danger, but she needs to see a doctor."

"No!" Birdie's eyes pop open. She pushes me away and struggles to sit up once again. Regardless of what is ailing her stomach, her hearing seems to be working just fine. "You can't force me to leave this place. Not now. Not like this."

Like what? I want to ask. In pain and obviously unwell? Or when this is just the groundwork for yet another curveball she's planning on throwing at me?

"I have no idea what the tide is doing or what it means for setting sail, but the sooner she's evacuated, the better. Is Otis still sleeping, or will he be up and about already?"

Birdie doesn't heed me.

"*No.*" Her voice is stern, if feeble. "I won't be torn from our work before it's complete. And unless you can call upon the powers of levitation or teleportation, there's no way you're getting me out of this bed."

I imagine that the combined powers of Nicholas, Otis, and Ashley would be enough to carry out her forcible removal, but there's something about the set of her jaw that gives me pause. Birdie has already proven herself a woman of considerable determination; I have no doubt that if she loses this physical fight, she'll find a way to turn it into a supernatural one.

"Fine," I say, unwilling to argue further. I know a lost cause when I'm staring down its barrel. "Barring her evacuation, is there a doctor who might be willing to come out all this way to take a look at her? I still think we're dealing with a case of bad wine and too much fish at the breakfast table, but she needs to be seen."

"I only know of one doctor who makes house calls," Sid says doubtfully. "If you're certain we need him . . . ?"

"I am. Nicholas, please find Otis and accompany him to fetch the doctor. Recite a full list of Birdie's symptoms—her *medical* symptoms—and for the love of everything, leave Gloriana out of it."

He nods once. "Consider it done."

"What about me?" Sid asks faintly. She looks in no state to make a seaward journey, but I hardly need her to linger in the sickroom, adding more trouble than she allays.

"Get Elspeth," I say, thinking fast. What a situation like this calls for is someone with a level head and no drama about her. "And after that, um, set some water to boil?"

Nicholas hides his chuckle under a cough. I can only hope that Sid doesn't recognize this effort to get rid of her as easily as he does. Turning my back on the pair, I move to Birdie's bedside instead. Now that I've promised to bring the doctor to her, she's looking better, her writhing movements stilled and the cold, clammy sweat of her brow more of a ladylike glow.

"Perhaps we should take fewer wine recommendations from dead men from here on out, eh, Birdie?" I ask.

She doesn't answer me, either too weak or too smart to make the attempt. By the time Elspeth arrives to assist me, I suspect it's weakness rather than intelligence that's zapped most of Birdie's strength. She barely murmurs a protest as the pair of us set out to provide her with dry sheets, a clean and borrowed nightgown, a glass of water, and a cool washcloth for her forehead. They're hardly the stuff of a medium's trade, but they're much more likely to improve Birdie's state of health than any number of potions I might be able to concoct.

In fact, by the time we're finished making her clean and comfortable, Birdie is asleep. Her light snores are accompanied by an occasional shudder, and she's still much too pale for my peace of mind, but I'm grateful that she's able to get some rest.

"Sid won't be up here with the water for at least another ten minutes," Elspeth says as we both stand watching the rise and fall of Birdie's chest. "The stove wasn't lit yet, so it'll take some time to heat up. If you don't mind my asking, what did you want with—?"

"I don't." I interrupt her with a smile. "But I thought our task would be easier if Sid was busy and out of the way."

Elspeth doesn't answer my smile with one of her own. She's wearing the same weathered blue dress she's had on this entire visit. It matches her complexion, which is showing a decided gray in the feeble dawn light. She looks, in a word, exhausted.

"We make an awful lot of extra work for you, don't we?" I ask, a sympathetic cluck on my tongue. "I can't imagine what you must do to keep everything running for so many houseguests."

"It's not that," she's quick to respond. With a glance down at Birdie, she steps away from the bed and lowers her voice before speaking again. I'm not sure what to make of that precaution when she says, "I did as you suggested, Madame Eleanor."

"As I suggested?" I echo.

She makes a vague gesture with her hand, as though her palm is skipping over the waves. "The boys. Jaime and Ferguson. Last night in the gilded salon—you said I ought to send them away, and the sooner the better."

"They're gone?" For some reason, this news disturbs rather than pleases me. I want them somewhere safe, obviously, but not before I have a chance to talk to them one last time.

"Not yet, but they will be in two days' time. My sister—she lives on Barra—will take them, but she won't be ready to receive visitors until Friday. That's all right, isn't it? They can stay here until then?"

I have no way of answering that question with any semblance of truth. I have no idea how far into the future my visions can go, but two days seems like an awfully long time, especially considering the woman lying ill on the bed next to us.

The look of anxiety on Elspeth's face is so great that I have no choice but to nod. To heap an additional burden on the poor woman when she's already beset with so much would only be cruel. I can't imagine what kind of money she's paid to work at a place and a pace like this, but it can hardly be worth it. If I were in her position and happened to come across a box of gold during a routine spring cleaning, I'd scoop up a handful or two in recompense and feel no pang of guilt afterward.

"I'll miss having them around, but it'll be best for everyone this way," I say. And since now seems as good a time as any, I add, "Do you think they could be convinced to return my luggage before they go?"

The crestfallen expression that drops Elspeth's round cheeks is more than enough to make me wish I'd kept my mouth shut. "Oh, dear," she murmurs. "You suspect them, too?"

I smile to show that I'm not upset. "I've had my suspicions. They've been gallivanting about in two of my scarves for days."

"I'll make them return them at once, Madame Eleanor, on my honor. I would have from the start, only they promised they hadn't come near your bags."

"And you believed them?" I ask, laughing. "Don't look so upset. They've enjoyed every minute of those scarves, I'm sure, and they're more than welcome to keep them. But I'd be lying if I said there weren't a few items in my bags I'd like to get my hands on."

"They're good lads," Elspeth says, though it's more to convince herself than me. "They have awfully high spirits, though, and that school their parents send them to gives them no room to let them out."

"I like them immensely," I promise her. "Which is why I'm being so careful about their well-being, and why I'm not angry about the bags."

I toy with the idea of telling her about the gold coin they gave me but decide against it. Common sense demands that I accept the neat story about yesterday's episode—that the boys played a trick on me, that one of them was responsible for the blow to my head, even that they took the coins from my person once I was unconscious. After all, it's the most rational explanation. Even my earlier thoughts about Elspeth, that she could have easily scooped up a handful of gold coins at any point in her years of service on this island, might be laid at their twin door. They, too, have had more than enough opportunity in their short lives to come across that box of treasure and pillage it at will.

But they were scared—I know they were. Of Otis and of being caught, of taking even one more gold coin from that Styrofoam chest than they thought they could get away with.

They're sneaky little thieves, yes, but they're not stupid.

"May I see them before you send them off? Not"—I'm quick to add—"to berate them for my luggage, but to show that I'm not angry? So we can part as friends?"

There's no need for me to be so circumspect. Elspeth is more than happy for another opportunity to show her grandsons off.

"Of course, Madame Eleanor. I won't let them leave here without saying their good-byes. And I promise to ask them about your bags once more. Leastaways, I will as soon as . . ." She trails off and glances at Birdie. "There's no need to worry. The doctor will know what to do."

I can't tell if that's a question or a statement, but I decide on the latter.

"I have no doubt that this will all come to nothing," I say with a determination I'm far from feeling. Even if Birdie's illness turns out to be nothing more than that—an illness—there's no denying that the timing is portentous. "We'll have her back on her feet soon enough. And then . . ."

This time, it's my turn to trail off. Getting Birdie well is obviously the most important thing, but I have no idea what comes after that.

Yes, you do, Winnie says.

For once, I'm not happy to hear my sister chime in. What she's saying—what she's implying—is that the next turn of events is the death and sea burial of an innocent little boy.

"Not if I have anything to say about it," I mutter.

Elspeth doesn't appear to hear me. Winnie, however, does.

Sorry, Sis. But I told you to turn around while you had the chance.

The doctor arrives in good time, carrying with him the bracing scent of the sea.

To be fair, all the men who gather in the hallway are redolent of salty brine and chilly air, but only the doctor dares to enter so hallowed a sickroom while seaweed clings to the bottom of his shoes.

"Knock knock!" he calls in a broguish singsong. There's no need for the announcement. If the heavy footfall hadn't warned us of his arrival, then the fact that Ashley has been stationed at the window watching for Otis's boat to pull into view for the past hour would have done the trick.

Still, it's nice to hear someone being cheerful. I've *tried* to keep up our collective spirits, even going so far as to listen to Ashley recite his poetry, but there's only so much I can do with Birdie lying in bed and moaning anytime I try to leave the room.

"I hear you're feeling a little under the weather," the doctor adds.

Birdie's only response to this is a loud sniff and a glance that dares me to abandon her. There's no need for it. As I have a vested interest in the outcome of this examination, I don't plan on going anywhere.

When standing side by side next to Ashley, himself a small man, the doctor is revealed to be of a level height. However, whereas Ashley is best described as *dapper*, no such appellation could be applied to the medical man. His prematurely balding head seems disproportionately large for his body. His eyes are small and close-set, his build that of a child's, and the diamond-patterned jumper he's wearing looks as though it belongs on a court jester.

Something about him seems familiar.

Nicholas coughs from the hallway. "We'll, ah, just give you some privacy, shall we?" he asks. "Ashley? Otis? I'm sure Eleanor can handle things from here."

I easily recognize his tone as one of veiled command. It might sound like a polite request, but he has every intention of standing there, one arm gesturing at the company, until every last person follows him downstairs.

In the normal way of things, he'd have been successful at it, too. When Nicholas Hartford III gets uppity, he also gets his way. But that's not accounting for Otis. The trip to Barra hasn't improved his mood any. In fact, from the scowling way he's standing in the doorway, his arms crossed and his huge great-coat dripping all over the floor, it's obvious he has no intention of relinquishing his current position.

"They may stay," Birdie says, her voice rising feebly from the blankets. She lifts a hand before dropping it back to the bed again, as though the weight of it is too much for her to bear. "Whatever the doctor discovers is likely to affect us all."

The doctor tsks. "Only if it's contagious—and even then, there are ways we can reduce the spread."

My eyes meet Nicholas's, and we both relax. It's absurd to hold a medical examination in a room crowded with people, one of whom is likely a murderer, but at least the doctor seems to know what he's about. As he bustles to Birdie's side, the feeling of familiarity grows until it clicks like a key turning in a lock. That comforting brogue, the ease with which he comes to the rescue, the recently pared fingernails . . .

My heart leaps to my throat. This is no ordinary doctor. It's the doctor from the train, the one in the kilt. The one who tended to Harvey the moment his heart attack struck.

I glance down at Birdie, wondering if this is yet another of the tricks she manufactures with ease, but her eyes are closed, and she doesn't seem the least bit interested in the events taking place around her.

"I don't think it's anything contagious," I say in a failing voice. In small towns and island communities such as these, it's not uncommon to run into familiar faces and stumble over coincidences. In fact, it's part of the reason that so much superstition abounds in them. It's easy to draw connections when there are a limited number of people and places to draw connections *to*. Eventually, everyone's path is going to cross.

But this is too much, even for me. This doctor could very easily be the last person to have seen Harvey Renault alive.

"She's been experiencing vomiting, nausea, a rapid pulse, pallor, and clamminess," I say, reciting her symptoms in an attempt to quell my own rapid pulse, pallor, and clamminess. "There's been no spike in her temperature, but she claims to feel cold, so we heaped her with blankets. Have I about covered it, Birdie?"

She manages a wan smile. "So good of you, dear Ella, but what's the use? What ails me can't be cured by modern medicine."

On the contrary, modern medicine is all we have. Medicine and science and cold, hard facts—which I'm going to extract from this case if it kills me.

Don't say it, I mentally warn Winnie. My cats are currently lording over a bowl of cream in the kitchen, so there's a good chance my sister is with them instead of me, but I don't want to risk it. Avowals of death on any front are no longer welcome.

"We've been pushing fluids, but she hasn't been able to stomach much else," I add. "My main concern right now is whether you think it's safe for her to stay here, or if we need to take her to a hospital. She doesn't want to leave the island, but—"

"She doesn't understand," Birdie says to the doctor with a sad, knowing smile. "She doesn't see, as the rest of us do, that Fate has much bigger plans."

"Birdie, I think we can all agree that Fate would like to see you restored to your usual health," I say tightly. "Or, at the very least, the Stewarts would like to see it."

"Oh, yes," Sid agrees from the other side of the room. Her voice is almost as faint as Birdie's. "The last thing we want is for Gloriana to claim another victim."

"Gloriana?" The doctor is jolted into a response. Gone is the kind, soft-spoken medical professional in whom I had some hope of finding rational discourse. The moment the curse is mentioned, he's all nervous sweat and shifty eyeballs. "She's here? *Now*?"

Sensing how close I am to losing my temper, Nicholas pulls me away from Birdie's bedside, leaving the doctor to conduct

his examination without me. As loath as I am to let a believer—
even a medically trained one—loose on that woman, I need the
space.

In a move of much less wisdom, Nicholas keeps pulling me
until I'm standing in the hallway where Otis lies in wait. He ac-
knowledges me with a tight, unpleasant grimace. "Is she going
to live, do you think, or should I fetch the undertaker before a
storm rolls in?"

"She'll be fine." I follow the line of his vision to where the
doctor presses a stethoscope against Birdie's stomach. His
movements are calm even if his demeanor isn't. "There's nothing the least bit mysterious about what ails her. Anyone who's
taken a first-aid course would tell you the same thing."

"Oh, so you're a trained medic now on top of everything
else?" Otis asks. The question is a rhetorical—and sarcastic—
one, because he follows it up with, "Why am I not surprised?
There seems to be no end to your long list of accomplish-
ments."

"I'm sorry it took so long for us to get back here," Nicholas
says without so much as a blink for Otis's outward hostility.
"We stopped by the hardware store on Barra to see if we could
get our hands on a backup generator."

"Really? That didn't even occur to me. What a good idea."

Otis chokes out a bitter laugh. "You think? Unfortunately,
they were out of stock. It's too bad we didn't try to buy one last
week. Apparently, they had three, but someone had the foresight to buy them all up the day you arrived."

"What?" I turn to stare at Otis. "Someone bought three generators? At once?"

"Odd, isn't it?" he muses, rubbing his hand along the scrubby
growth of his jaw. "When old Booker who runs the place hasn't
sold that many in the past year? One might almost suspect that
this enveloping darkness was brought upon us on purpose."

As much as I'd like to hold Birdie accountable for this one, there's no denying that she's been almost entirely in my company since the train ride up here. Unless she shopped early, hopped on a plane, and then got on the train with me somewhere south of the Scottish border, she couldn't have bought those generators without my knowing about it.

"It *has* been awfully stormy," I suggest. "Perhaps the lightning is taking out the electricity in lots of people's houses."

Otis's response to this is a disbelieving snort. "And I wear this eyepatch because I like the way it makes children run screaming in the opposite direction."

I ignore the obvious implications of this. "So there won't be any electricity for the foreseeable future?" I ask. "The old generator is absolutely unfixable? Because of . . . lightning?"

He doesn't miss my meaning. "Yes, it is absolutely unfixable. As to whether or not lightning caused it, I'll leave that up to someone as all-seeing as you. *Something* caused the short and fried the control board. I'm no expert, but it would have had to have been a particularly vengeful god who shot a bolt that strong down from the heavens."

I nod my understanding, careful not to let any of my feelings show. What he means is that it would have to be a particularly vengeful god or a curse working overtime. Or, as is much more likely, someone who wanted to make sure the atmosphere here is as gloomy and sinister as possible.

By this time, the doctor has completed his examination of Birdie. He wraps his stethoscope around his neck and calls us back into the room with an air of suppressed agitation. "It's exactly as I suspected," he announces. "This woman has been poisoned."

Not surprisingly, this bit of information acts on the room like a five-alarm fire. There are shrieks, squeals, poetry on the inevitability of death . . . and, in Otis's case, a low, muttered outburst before he stalks angrily from the room. I'm tempted to follow him. The last thing I want to do right now is calm a bunch of hysterical fools who are rapidly eroding my last nerve.

Of everyone, Birdie takes the news the best. She rests against her pillows as one resigned, even going so far as to cross her hands over her chest in an approximation of her final interment.

Nicholas clears his throat and, in his usual careful and methodical way, asks the question foremost in both our minds. "When you say she's been poisoned, would you like us to understand that she was purposefully given something to cause her harm?"

The doctor doesn't, as I hope, adopt the matter-of-fact approach I'd hoped to get out of him. Instead, he smooths the straggling strands of his hair and adopts a lofty tone. "This woman is suffering from intestinal and digestive upset related to the ingestion of toxins. As to the intent behind it, I'm sure you know that better than I."

I won't do it. I won't say her name.

The doctor does it for me. "It isn't Gloriana's usual method, as I understand it, but I'm not an expert in her ways. I prefer to leave such speculation to you."

"Is she going to recover, at least?"

"Oh, yes. A little rest, plenty of fluids, and she'll be as good as new."

A wash of relief moves over me, disproportionately large for a woman I care for as little as Birdie. As much as I might deplore her tactics and playacting, I don't want her to suffer for *real*. "And are there precautions we should take to ensure our own safety?" I ask. Not unhopefully, I add, "As in, evacuate the island? All of us—even the children?"

The doctor has the audacity to chuckle. "My poor dear. You have nothing to fear. Just stay away from the kippers, and I'm sure you'll be fine."

"Kippers?" I echo. "You mean it's *food* poisoning? I was right all along? She was poisoned by her breakfast?"

His eyes shift uneasily. "I can't say for sure, mind you, but that does seem to be the most likely cause of her gastric distress. Between you and me, I've never cared for Elspeth's way with a fish."

I can only stare, openmouthed, as I contemplate the doctor. There's no doubt in my mind that he did this on purpose—setting us all in upheaval, making it seem as though there's a malicious poisoner skulking in our midst.

In other words, he's just as bad as everyone else. Eight years of medical training overturned by the mention of one stupid curse.

"Bad fish?" Birdie says, disappointment rendering her normally low voice a little high.

"At breakfast?" Sid adds.

"'Life, within doors, has few pleasanter prospects than a neatly-arranged and well-provisioned breakfast-table,'" quotes Ashley.

Taking control of the room after this is no easy task. I accomplish it not through kindness and sympathy, but by informing the Stewarts that the only way for Birdie to heal is with rest, relaxation, and complete silence for the remainder of the day—and that I will enforce this plan if it means I have to curse them in a way that rivals that of all the vengeful queens of Britain's past. Birdie opens her mouth to argue, but she catches sight of my fulminating gaze and snaps her lips closed again. So, too, does the doctor. As soon as he sees how close I am to losing it, he murmurs something about going to find Elspeth and having a room readied for the night.

"An excellent idea," Nicholas murmurs as he gathers up the rest of the assembled crowd. "You don't know Madame Eleanor well enough yet, Sid, but her curses are exceptionally frightening. I've known grown men to cross the street whenever she happens to pass."

This playful sally does much to restore my equilibrium—and to clear the room, which is even better.

"I like that doctor," Birdie says as soon as we're left alone in the room together. Without all the people bustling about, it feels much darker than before. The corners are shrouded in shadows, the flickering candles doing little to dispel the gloom. "He seems to know what he's about, wouldn't you say?"

I give the pillow underneath Birdie's head a liberal thump. "No. I think he's at least six eggs short of a dozen."

"So obliging of him to have come out on a moment's notice, too. I can't imagine it's comfortable, getting hauled out here without any warning, but I understand that the family has come to depend on him for such things."

I hesitate, mistrusting her tone.

"Why, he came out just last month when Glenn had his accident. Dr. Fulstead, I believe he said his name was."

At mention of the doctor's name, I can only stare at her, mouth agog, my heart thumping so much it's like there's someone inside it, frantic to get out. Somewhere in the back of my mind, I know she's only doing this to get a reaction out of me—playing her games, dipping into her bag of tricks. Unfortunately, as much as I wish I could pretend not to be affected, I *can't*.

If what she's saying is true, then the doctor wasn't just the last man to see Harvey Renault alive; he was the last to see Glenn Stewart, too.

And he's been hand-delivered to this island. To me.

"The weather being what it is, there's no saying when he'll be able to return to Barra. Why, we could have him with us for the duration of our stay."

"Birdie!" I drop my hands and blink down at her. Although there's no denying that she looks like a woman currently suffering from food poisoning, there's none of her moaning or thrashing, no signs that she's about to succumb to the beckoning of her old friend Death. "You did this on purpose, didn't you?"

She closes her eyes and settles more comfortably into her pillow. "I'm sure I have no idea what you're talking about, Madame Eleanor."

That *Madame Eleanor* isn't lost on me. She's careful never to use the name when we're in the company of other people. When the Stewarts are around, it's always *dear Ella* this and *dear Ella* that, a transparent—if effective—way of putting me in my place. When we're alone together, she has no qualms about using my real name.

"You knew I wanted to talk to the doctor," I insist. "You knew there was something suspicious about the way Glenn died, and that the only way we'd get any answers is if we talked to the person who was called in when it happened."

Birdie neither confirms nor denies this, which is as good as a signed confession. I'm emboldened to continue.

"He's the same doctor from the train, the one who rushed to Harvey's aid. Did you know that, too? Did you know he had ties to both men?"

She doesn't answer me. She merely holds out her hand, keeping it level until I place my palm against hers. I'm not sure what it's for until a small envelope falls out of her sleeve and into my hand. Birdie's movements are so subtle, so practiced, that I honestly have no idea how she manages it.

Not that it matters when she says, "Dispose of that for me, would you? There's no telling what might happen if it falls into the wrong hands."

I turn the envelope over, but it's unmarked and unremarkable save for a slight bulge that indicates some kind of powdery substance inside.

Poison.

"It's a pity about the fish," she murmurs without opening

her eyes. "Herring, I think. It was quite delicious, but I doubt Elspeth will have the nerve to serve it again after this."

I know, without realizing why, that nothing I say or do will extract the truth out of Birdie now. She plans to maintain the pretense of her role as medium at all costs—even if it means giving herself a violent stomachache in the process. Not even to me, and not even when we're alone in a room together, will she admit that she finds everything about this case just as suspicious and dangerous as I do.

What I don't understand, however, is what it's all for. Everything Birdie has said and done on this island is grounded in science, in fact, in reality. She puts on a good show, yes, and knows more about this family and its inner workings than mere research could account for, but she's just a woman. Like me. She's just trying to find the gold. Like me.

But if she knows that Glenn and/or Harvey was murdered, why isn't she saying so? Why is she here, putting herself in harm's way, when she should be calling in the entire Scotland Yard? Why is she feeding me inside information only to retreat behind her mystical veil when I start to get close to an actual answer?

It's almost as if she's hiding something. *Protecting someone.* But who?

"I'll get rid of it," I promise, closing my fist over the poison. "In the meantime, is there anything I can do to make you more comfortable? I'd like to have a chat with Dr. Fulstead, but I don't want to leave you if you need anything."

She waves her free hand at me. "I'll be fine. Elspeth promised to bring me a bit of hot wine before bed to settle my stomach and boost my energy for the trials ahead. You run along and do what you need. Our doctor friend should be nice and uneasy now that he knows Gloriana walks amongst us. I'm sure he'll be very receptive to whatever you have planned."

In this, as in all things, she's absolutely right. Loath as I am to admit it, Dr. Fulstead *will* be easier for me to handle if he's on edge. There are so many things I want to say to her, not the least of which is a heartfelt *thank you*.

"Oh, and Eleanor?" she adds before I have the chance. "Proceed with caution. If there's one thing I've learned over the years, it's that truth has an uncomfortable way of making the spirits restless."

Chapter 13

"I'm not sure I follow." Nicholas steps back and surveys his handiwork, his eyes narrowed in shrewd appraisal. "*Why* are we dressing you up as a Halloween ghost?"

I glance down at myself. True, the white bedsheet I've wrapped around my body is a little more obvious than I'd have liked, but I'm not in a position to cavil. I'm running out of time—and supplies.

"I don't know what you're talking about." I shake out my hair until it flows in long waves to my waist. Combined with the sheet and the dark rings that are starting to take natural shape under my eyes, the overall effect is close to what I'd been hoping for. "I'm not a Halloween ghost. Halloween ghosts are silly. I'm mystical and effervescent."

"Hmm."

"And don't make judgmental sounds like you're atop some high and mighty steed over there. You and Otis seemed to get mighty friendly over the course of a single day. Did you forget the part where I was attacked on board his boat?"

He has the decency to look abashed. A slight tinge of color

touches his cheekbones, his lips quirked in a rueful smile. "Yes, well. You did tell me to get close to the suspects."

I lift one hand—rendered eerily pale by the liberal application of decades-old talcum powder I scrounged out from underneath a bathroom sink—and point at him. "I told you to get close to Birdie."

"I thought you'd be pleased at my show of initiative."

"You don't think he's guilty."

Nicholas pauses and considers his next words. He'd like to flatly deny my accusation, but he knows better than to lie. Sniffing out deceit is my second-greatest skill.

Sniffing out murderers is my first.

"How can you tell?" he asks.

I tilt my head and study him, unsure how to explain it in a way that he can understand. The reality is that Nicholas is a difficult man to read. He's careful to keep his emotions on a tight rein. He's always polite, always charming, always correct—and until you've reached the inner circle of his heart, you can never really know him.

But I do. It's my gift and my curse—to see people, to understand them, to *know* them.

"It's why you sent me here in the first place," I say. "Not, as you'd like me to believe, because you thought I'd enjoy this vacation more than Malta, but because you're genuinely worried about your friend. Sid loves her cousin—more than anyone else in her family, at any rate—and you're afraid that if he's the guilty one, it would break her heart."

"It *would* break her heart."

I know it would. I also know that this sentiment—while it does Nicholas justice—gives him a blind spot. It's the same blind spot that brought me into his life in the first place. When his own house was plagued by ghosts, he hired me not because he wanted to, but because he had to. It was the only way he could gain perspective—a harsh, abrasive, realistic perspective.

My harsh, abrasive, realistic perspective.

"He has the most motive, Nicholas. He also has the means, the temperament, and the intelligence to pull it off."

A frown tugs at his lips. "I know."

"And despite what Elspeth says, I don't believe Jaime and Ferguson were playing a trick on me yesterday. They got that gold coin from Otis's boat, and they genuinely thought I would find the rest of the treasure on board."

His frown deepens. "I know that, too."

I place my palm on his cheek and hold it there. As a romantic gesture, it's not much, but it's all I have. I'm not soft and clinging, and I never will be.

And there's the truth in a nutshell. I'm not one of the Sid Stewarts of the world. I'm a Birdie White. I'm a scary talking puppet, a plague on this household, a cheating and manipulative liar who will stop at nothing to get her way. Although there are times when I'm sure Nicholas knows this—admires it, even—I can't help thinking that he won't always view it as something positive.

"What is it?" I ask. "What's on your mind?"

He sighs and brings my hand down until it's gripped tightly in his. "I'm wishing I'd whisked you away to Malta while I had the chance, that's all. I don't like this."

I know exactly how he feels. In fact, it's why I'm wearing this ridiculous getup in the first place. It's the only way—the only *safe* way—to proceed with my investigation. If Birdie's actions have proven anything, it's that there *is* someone weaving a malicious spell over this family—not a long-dead monarch or a malicious spiritual entity, but a living, breathing person who's capable of irreparable harm. She wouldn't have summoned the doctor otherwise, wouldn't have risked her own health to try and get real answers.

"I know you think I look silly, but this is the best way." I hold out the envelope Birdie gave me, gently opening the folds to reveal the white powder inside. "Don't touch it. It's what was used to poison Birdie."

It says a lot about Nicholas that he doesn't evince more than the mildest show of surprise. "Should I ask?"

"I didn't give it to her, if that's what you're thinking. On the contrary, *she* gave it to me. She thought I might want a private chat with the doctor and felt that a sudden and violent indisposition was the best way to go about it."

He blinks—slowly at first and then gaining speed, almost like a butterfly taking flight. "I see."

"You don't, but that's okay." I fold up the envelope and stow it in my bedside table. "I'm not a hundred percent sure what Birdie's game is yet, but I'm not going to waste this opportunity. I need to talk to Dr. Fulstead and discover what he knows about the nature of those deaths. For all we know, we might be dealing with nothing more than a series of interconnected coincidences, and the gold will turn up in some box at the bottom of a wardrobe somewhere."

"I thought you didn't believe in interconnected coincidences," he says.

"And I thought you didn't believe in mediums," I counter before giving my sheet an ominous waggle. "But you have to admit I make a convincing show."

I don't bother knocking on the doctor's door. Stealth and surprise are my best allies, and I intend to make the most of them. Stepping silently into the guest room, I find the doctor seated at a desk in the corner, his fingers busy with a paper and pen. He leaps to his feet at the sound of my entrance.

"Good God!" His fright is genuine; the scrambling way he conceals the scrawled pages behind him is not.

"Hello, Dr. Fulstead," I say as I glide into the room. I keep my voice pitched low, almost deep enough to match Birdie's.

It's too bad I didn't think to grab her white feather and thread it in my hair. The added touch would have helped. "I'm glad to find that you haven't yet retired."

He realizes I'm not an eerie vision, but a woman of mysterious powers and persuasions, and blinks his recognition. "I'm afraid I don't sleep as well as I used to," he explains. "One of the vagaries of old age."

"A small price to pay for the wisdom that accompanies it. May I sit?"

I wait only until the doctor's head begins to bob before pulling a chair in front of the door and sitting in it.

"I thought you were Gloriana," he says as I settle the folds of the bedsheet more becomingly around me. "You looked so pale as you walked in."

"Gloriana isn't a ghost," I say, but with much less exasperation than every other time she's been mentioned. Ghostly pallor is the exact impression I was hoping to give. "She's an *influence*. She won't manifest herself physically or start throwing objects around like a poltergeist. He powers are much more subtle . . . and dangerous."

He appears concerned but not surprised by this reading of the Stewart specter.

"Please." I gesture for him to resume his seated position. "Rest. Relax. I'm here for a friendly chat, that's all. Something is troubling you."

He sits, but not in a way that signals rest or relaxation. "How can you tell?"

Well, for starters, because literally *everyone* on this planet is troubled by something. It might be as big as murder or it might be as small as uncertainty about what to make for dinner, but no one is completely worry free.

"Because you're a doctor," I announce, stating one of the only pieces of truth I have at my fingertips. "A healer. A bringer of comfort."

"I am?" He glances up at me and, seeing that I mean no harm, straightens in his seat. "I mean, I *am*."

"You dropped everything to come to this family's aid when they needed you."

He nods, his head bobbing up and down like a buoy at sea.

"You've always done that—watched over them, protected them. Even when they don't realize they need you, you're here."

He nods again, his shoulders returning to their squared, confident position. "That's true," he says, as if realizing it for the first time. "I protect people."

Things are progressing exactly as I hoped they would, and I feel a sudden pang that no one else is around to witness me at work. Birdie, for example, might appreciate the subtlety of my methods. Otis, too, could learn a thing or two from my tact. My best work always seems to be my least appreciated.

"You *do* protect people," I agree, sweeping up my arm and allowing the folds of the bedsheet to fall. In the semi-darkness, I have no doubt it looks very grand. "From illness and disease, from pain and despair. But the one thing you can't protect them from is themselves. You couldn't protect Glenn from himself, could you?" At the sudden flash in the doctor's eyes, I'm emboldened to add, "That's why you're here. You want to atone."

"Who told you that?"

You just did, I think but don't say. "Had he already passed when you arrived?" I ask instead.

He ducks his head in a gesture of affirmation. "There was nothing I could do. Not by the time I was called. The mischief had already been done."

Mischief could mean a lot of things, including that Glenn had fallen asleep or suffered from a minor condition that hastened his death. Then again, it might also mean that someone held him under the water by force.

"He doesn't hold you accountable for it," I say, extending

my hand in comfort. When Dr. Fulstead doesn't reach back for me, I decide to take a leap. "Neither does Harvey Renault. There was nothing you could do by the time you reached him."

The doctor bolts upright, his spine straightening as though a rod has been shoved straight through it. "Harvey Renault?" he demands. "What do you know about him?"

I toy with the idea of admitting that Birdie and I were on the train that day, drinking gin and tonics while Dr. Fulstead pared his nails, but I don't. Birdie certainly wouldn't resort to such a mundane thing as truth.

"You went to him the moment help was needed." I speak as though I'm seeing the event through a cloud rather than memory. "Without hesitation, and when no one else would go to the rescue."

"How do you—?"

"The train car was red. He was wearing Oxford wing tips."

"You saw him?"

I neither confirm nor deny this question since the truth is more complex than that. Besides, I'm less interested in my own experience of the events than I am in his. "Did he really suffer from a heart attack, or was it something more . . . *mischievous*?"

He doesn't miss my meaning. With a nervous shake of his head, he says, "I wasn't his official doctor, Madame Eleanor. It's not my place to say."

"Perhaps not, but you've been in practice long enough to recognize the symptoms when you see them. Did you know that he was Glenn Stewart's solicitor? That he, too, was tied to this family?"

"What?" He visibly blanches, and he swivels his head as though looking for a quick means of escape. Since he's in a room that overlooks the cliff, he's not likely to find one. "*No. It's not possible.*"

"Not only is it possible, but it's a fact."

He bolts up out of his chair, his pallor so pronounced that he matches my sheet. "I did everything I could for him."

"I'm sure you did."

"His attack was a severe one—and from what I understand, it wasn't his first."

"So I heard."

"If you want to talk to anyone, it should be the woman I was called here to attend. She was on the train that day—did you know that? I *saw* her."

I hesitate, fearful that this recollection will lead to another of a similar nature—namely, that I, too, was present on that fateful trip—but he doesn't appear to have noticed. "I didn't think anything of it at the time, but she entered through the front of the car. She could have easily passed Harvey on the train—in fact, I *know* she did. She came down the center aisle where he was seated."

Dr. Fulstead isn't telling me anything I don't already know. There's always been a suspicion that Birdie is more involved in this than mere chance allows—his confirmation only strengthens it. What I *want* him to tell me is whether or not Harvey's death was a natural one or if it was brought on by, say, poison.

Before I have a chance to continue my interrogation, Dr. Fulstead turns it on me. "Why have I been brought to this island?" he demands. "What do you want?"

This ferocious turnabout takes me aback, but I answer with my usual calm. "You were called to attend a sick woman," I say.

"Yes, and I did that. My job is finished. You should have no further need of me." His eyes narrow, and he takes in the sight of me—the *full* sight of me, bedsheets and scraggly hair and all—with sharp suspicion. "Wait a minute."

I wince, fairly certain I know what comes next.

I'm not wrong. The doctor points his finger in accusation. "You were there, too. With the sick woman on the train." He backs away, stumbling over his chair and sending it careering into the desk. The pages he'd been at such pains to hide flutter about like leaves caught in the wind. It looks to be a letter, though I have no idea who he'd be writing to—or why. It's not as if the postman makes regular visits to Airgead Island. "You two are in this together."

Tempting as it is to deny this claim, I refrain. Like it or not, Birdie and I *are* in this together. She's secretive and sneaky and is hiding something. She uses people and pretends to believe in ghosts for her own ends. She's also smart as all get-out.

"I didn't kill Harvey Renault, if that's what you're thinking," I say.

"N-no," he stammers, his eyes growing wide. "I know that."

"And I'd never even heard of Glenn Stewart until I was summoned to this island. I have witnesses who can corroborate that."

"Of course, of course." He bobs his head in a subservient, pandering way that showcases his disbelief—and his fear. It's that second one that hits me the hardest, especially when he pauses, and his voice drops almost to a whisper. "Wha—What are you going to do to me?"

To him? Nothing. I have a few follow-up questions, obviously, and it would be nice if he didn't think I was a murderess and a liar, but I'm not going to force the issue.

"Your fate is not in my hands, I'm afraid. Birdie's, however . . ." I shake my head in a move that isn't wholly faked. I don't know what Birdie's fate is, but I doubt it's going to be the one either of us has in mind. "I'm sorry to have disturbed you, Dr. Fulstead. It's late, and you were obviously in the middle of something when I came in."

This quick apology does little to soothe him. He gulps and runs a hand across the bald crown of his head. "Yes. Yes, I was."

"I'm not what you think, you know," I say with a grimace at

my attire. Perhaps the sheet was a *touch* overdone. "I'm only trying to help this family, to bring them peace."

"Are you?" he returns.

It's not meant as a critique, I know, but I can't help taking it that way. I might have come here with the expectation of being entertained, but somewhere in the past few days, the Stewart family problems have become my own.

"I am," I say, though by this time, it's more for my benefit than Dr. Fulstead's. "You have my word that everyone is going to make it off this island alive."

Chapter 14

When I wake up in the morning, it's to find a pair of floral-patterned trousers, a ruffled silk blouse, and a pair of pantyhose sitting at the foot of my bed. They're accompanied by a note stating that they're all that could be found to fit me.

They do fit, but they also make me look like a piece of 1970s outdoor furniture. Since I'm a *clean* piece of 1970s outdoor furniture, I decide to run with it. I wasn't looking forward to another day in that velvet dress.

While my appearance has taken a turn for the better, my brain is just as befuddled as it was when I went to bed last night. Rest has brought no clarity or comfort; my dreams, if I had any, have been lost to the night.

I poke my head out of my room and make a quick survey of the dark hallway, trying to decide where to begin today's adventure. My stomach tells me to start with breakfast, but my cat directs me otherwise. Although Freddie is nowhere to be seen, Beast is sitting outside Birdie's bedroom, standing guard like a sphinx half-buried in sand. The cat shows no sign of pleasure as I draw closer, but her eyes shift and she allows herself to indulge in a regal yawn.

"Some familiar you've been so far," I mutter as I draw closer. "I thought Birdie brought you here to help."

Beast's only reply is a twitch of her whiskers.

I knock lightly on the door so as to avoid rousing the entire household. "Birdie?" I call. "Birdie, are you awake yet?"

There's no answer.

"Hello?" I call again, a little louder this time. When I still receive no reply, I try the doorknob.

I feel a quick pang of guilt as I step inside. There's a hush about the space, the heavy quiet of deep slumber. Considering that Birdie poisoned herself yesterday, sleep seems like a valid way to spend the morning. The decent thing to do would be to wait until she's had some time to recover before I pounce, but I'm hoping that the early hours will catch her off guard.

I tiptoe closer to the bed. The first thing I notice is another pile of clothing at her feet, though hers doesn't have an accompanying note.

"Come on, Sleeping Beauty." I poke at the lump huddled under the blankets. "I know the doctor prescribed rest, but it'll have to wait. You can sleep when you're dead."

When she doesn't respond, I move to the window and pull the curtains open. It would be too much to say that beams of sunlight fill the room, but the watery gray sky is less ominous than it has been in days past.

"I had a chat with the doctor last night," I say, placing myself in the light of the window much the way my cats do. "Not a very forthcoming chat, unfortunately, but an interesting one. He knows we were on that train with Harvey, and it scares him. That's something, right? He wouldn't be scared if it was just a heart attack that had carried him off."

Birdie doesn't reply to that, either.

"Weren't you yammering at me just the other day for having a lie-in?" I ask, poking her a little harder this time. "Who's the lazy houseguest now?"

When I'm greeted once again by nothing but silence, alarm grips me by the throat. That alarm turns to a panic that crushes my windpipe when I realize that Birdie hasn't moved—not even to breathe—since I entered the room.

"No." My hand is shaking as I yank the bedspread down, but I force it to keep moving. Some of the talcum powder from last night lingers, giving my skin an eerie translucence. "It can't be. She isn't."

But it can be, and she *is*.

Death isn't a new concept to a woman like me. I've managed to build an entire career around it. I've stood over my sister's grave and heard her to speak to me from somewhere beyond it. I've faced it head-on and emerged triumphant.

In that moment, looking at the body of Bridget Wimpole-White lying cold in her bed, I fear it for the first time.

Gloriana did this, I think. And then, *no*.

Before I can fully give way to my sense of terror, I check Birdie for signs of life—breath, pulse, a twitch of an eyelid—but to no avail. All are extinguished and, if my quick assessment is any indication, have been for quite some time.

As it just so happens that we have a doctor currently residing under our roof, summoning him seems like the best first step. I'm strangely loath to leave Birdie alone in this room, so I stand on the threshold and call his name. He appears sleepily in his doorway a few seconds later.

"Please come quickly. It's Birdie. She's not breathing. She's not moving. She's—"

I don't need to say more. With an alacrity I can't help but admire, the doctor dashes across the hall to come to my aid. He doesn't seem to mind that he's wearing nothing but a nightshirt, his legs like white sticks protruding from the hem.

"What's this?" he asks as he pushes me aside. "Has she taken ill again?"

"No, not ill. *Dead*."

He doesn't believe me. That much is obvious from the way he makes a tutting sound and goes to Birdie's bedside, prepared to find a woman prostrate but not debilitated by her condition. It doesn't take him long to come to the same conclusion as me. He goes so far as to attempt chest compressions, but it only takes a few before he realizes it's an effort in futility.

"I'm afraid she's gone," he says as he steps back from the bedside. There's a sense of finality about that step, especially when he accompanies it with a theatrical gesture that Birdie would have been the first to applaud. Lifting the sheet covering the lower half of her body, he brings it to rest over her face. "We're too late. There's nothing we can do to save her now."

I open my mouth and close it again, at a loss for words for what might be the first time in my life.

"We should notify the household," he says when I'm unable to supply him with anything but the ineffective movements of my jaw. "Sid, or—"

I shake my head with a vehemence that sets the strands of my hair fluttering. "No," I say, my voice croaking but operational. "Don't do that."

The doctor's eyes narrow, and he looks at me with the sharp appraisal of a man who recently heard me claim that no one else in this house was going to die. There's nothing I can say and even less I can do to convince him that I have any authority here, so I don't make the attempt.

"Sid will only be upset by this latest . . . development," I explain somewhat feebly. "Who we want in this situation is—"

"Elspeth!"

Actually, I was going to suggest that Nicholas would be the most helpful person at this point in time, but the doctor's idea isn't without merit. "Yes, perhaps," I agree, but that's as far as I get. Dr. Fulstead wasn't making a suggestion so much as an exclamation. I turn to find Elspeth standing in the doorway to

Birdie's room. She's bearing a tray that holds a pitcher of water and a decanter that smells strongly of coffee. Without waiting to fully assess her condition, I rush forward and take the tray from her.

And a good thing, too, because the moment Elspeth takes in the sight of Birdie lying motionless under a sheet, her knees begin to buckle.

"Dr. Fulstead—" I say, but he's already on the case. He rushes to the older woman's side and helps her as she staggers to a nearby chair. Her face is as white as Birdie's sheet, and her hands, now empty of the tray, shake.

I pour some of the coffee into the mug provided on the tray and hold it out.

"Drink this," I suggest. "It'll put some heart in you."

She accepts the mug but doesn't drink, her attention too fixed on the bed. "Not again," she moans in what is rapidly becoming the mantra for this particular case. "Not like this. Is she—?"

"I'm afraid so," I say, interpreting her sudden sob as an inability to say the word aloud. Dead. Gone. Yet another victim of the curse.

Or, you know, of the *murderer*.

"The doctor and I came in and found her like this." I touch the bottom of the mug and tilt it up. "Take a sip and you'll feel much better. If you brought it for Birdie, I'm sure it's strong enough to do the trick."

Elspeth manages a smile and even swallows a mouthful of the potent black brew, but it doesn't do much to restore her color.

"This isn't your fault, Elspeth. Birdie was ill—we knew that. Maybe her ailment was worse than we thought. Maybe she had a preexisting condition. It's important that we don't jump to conclusions."

I pause, recalling that Birdie's particular *ailment* had been self-inflicted. I have no idea what kind of poison was in that envelope, but I do know that it's currently sitting in the top drawer of my bedside table.

"Um, would you two excuse me a moment?" I ask. The doctor doesn't look too eager to let me out of his sight, but he's also too wary to put up a protest. "Don't go anywhere. I'll be right back."

I dash across the hall to my own room. I'd like to think that my intentions are honorable—that I'm bringing the doctor the poison so he can ascertain what it is and determine if it contributed to Birdie's sudden death—but there's an element of self-preservation in there, too.

Nicholas wasn't wrong that day at the pool when he called me unsinkable. I will *not* be going down for poisoning Birdie.

The first bedside table I check is empty save for an ancient leaflet on the perils of chewing tobacco. Thinking I must have gotten the two confused, since they're similar in design, I scramble over my bed to check the other. It's even emptier than the first one. Pulling the drawers out and checking underneath them reveals nothing, nor does peeking behind them.

It's not a very thorough search, and the lack of light means I might have easily overlooked something, but I know—in my heart of hearts—that no amount of searching will reveal that envelope.

Like the elusive hidden gold, it's nowhere to be found.

I return to Birdie's deathbed with slow, deliberate steps. A few minutes ago, I *might*, had I really put my mind to it, been able to convince myself that Birdie's death was accidental. A wrong dose of the poison she self-administered, an overindulgence in breakfast fish, even that preexisting condition I hinted at to allay Elspeth's fears—any of them could have been pinpointed as the culprit.

That missing envelope of poison tells a different story. A

darker, more sinister one. One through which we must all tread carefully.

My own tread is so careful that my feet make almost no sound as I approach the bedroom door. Sneaking up and eavesdropping hadn't been my intention, but the sound of voices causes me to pause before I head in.

"She's not wrong," the doctor says. "It *is* possible that this is nothing more than nature meandering on her usual course. Without knowing Ms. White's full medical history, I can't say for certain what carried her off."

Elspeth's voice is so soft that I'm unable to distinguish her reply.

"I know," the doctor says gravely. "The similarities worry me, too."

They don't say more, but I don't need them to. In a place where another man so recently died, *similarities* can only mean one thing.

"Sorry about that," I say as I enter the room once again. It's just as hushed and full of death as before, but Elspeth seems to have a better handle on herself. "What have we decided?"

The doctor clears his throat, his eyes shifting left and right. "I, ah, believe now might be a good time to notify Ms. Stewart."

I bite back a groan. Rousing Sid and informing her that the curse has struck again is the last thing I want to do. Her hysterics will be immeasurable—as will the amount of work I'm going to have to do to allay them.

"She's not going to take this well," I warn.

"One can hardly blame her. Most people find sudden death alarming."

I can only assume that Dr. Fulstead is referring to my own lack of alarm. I could very easily pander to him and adopt the air of a woman stricken with fear, but what's the use? It's not going to bring Birdie back, and it's certainly not going to help us find who did this. What *is* going to help us is to discover what the doctor and Elspeth were talking about before I came in.

"You might want to find Nicholas first," I suggest. "Sid will appreciate having him there when you break the news."

Dr. Fulstead shows every sign of wishing to remain exactly where he is. I'm afraid he's going to insist upon it, but his shoulders eventually drop in capitulation. "Don't tamper with the body, if you please," he says as he makes one last survey of the room, memorizing its contents and the exact placement thereof. "I'll be back as soon as I'm able."

He doesn't, as I hope, shut the door behind him. For me to close it now would only be to draw attention to the fact that I want privacy with Elspeth, so I have to make do with dropping to my knees in front of her.

"Elspeth, I know you're upset right now, and that you probably want a moment or two to collect your thoughts, but I need you to tell me what you and the doctor were talking about."

She blinks down at me, moisture gathering in the corners of her eyes. No tear escapes, but I can tell she's close. "What we were talking about?" she echoes.

I scoot closer, my toes bumping hers. "The similarities the doctor mentioned. He was talking about Glenn, wasn't he? Glenn and Birdie? The ways they died?"

She stiffens and sits up straighter, causing coffee to slosh over the edge of her mug. It spreads across the faded blue fabric of her dress like a bloodstain. Seeing it, she blanches and swallows. "Glenn never told me anything about feeling under the weather," she says, a plea underscoring her voice. "Not a word—not a single complaint."

I wish I could let her off the hook, or even take more time to build a sense of comfort before plunging in, but I doubt I'll get another opportunity like this one. Birdie's death has knocked Elspeth out, emotionally speaking, like a bomb going off and flattening everything in its path. There's never a more ideal time to get the truth out of someone than when all the pieces are scattered.

"He didn't have to tell you, did he?" I urge. "You knew. You always knew. No one understood Glenn Stewart like you did."

A small sob racks her body but is stifled almost as quickly as it escapes. "He wasn't a man who liked having his wounds touched," she explains.

I nod my understanding, finding this easy to believe. Otis is cut of the same cloth. I imagine it's why he's so willing to embrace the pirate look and pirate profession, making a game of the scars he wears on the outside. It's the only way to keep people from poking at the very real and very painful scars that haven't yet had a chance to heal on the inside.

"What were his symptoms?" I ask.

Her eyes meet mine in a stricken bid for sympathy. "Nausea, night sweats, fatigue. I could tell from his sheets. But he was on the mend, Madame Eleanor, I know he was. He ate a good breakfast that morning, had his usual walk down to the dock, and then . . ."

"And then decided to take a nice, warm bath?" I suggest.

She ducks her head. It's not an absolute confirmation of what I'm suggesting, but it's close enough. And the story fits. Oh, how it fits. A slight illness preceding death is a great way to allay suspicion, especially since Glenn was an old man who lived in an isolated place. Even something as trifling as the flu could have carried him off.

Birdie White, however, was a woman in her prime. And what ailed her was no viral infection.

Unfortunately, there's no way I can tell Elspeth about the poison Birdie ingested without putting myself at risk. Even if I did still have it in my possession, what on earth could I say to explain it? That a dead woman gave it to me? That Birdie willingly ingested a toxic substance that would lead to her death less than twenty-four hours later?

Honestly, if I didn't know better, I'd almost think she gave it to me on purpose, knowing full well that I'd end up being blamed for her murder.

That would have been something, wouldn't it?

The sound of Birdie's voice causes me to whirl around. Crouched as I am near Elspeth's feet, I have very little balance to begin with. There's nothing but the dangling edge of Birdie's death sheet to catch myself on, and I don't dare make a grab for it. The result is that I topple over, narrowly avoiding a collision between my skull and the side of the bed.

Elspeth's housekeeping is up to such high standards that there's nary a speck of dust underneath the mahogany bedstead. Nor, since the castle closets number in the dozens, is there the usual household clutter of clothing, photographs, or other stored keepsakes.

There is, however, a suitcase. No—I'm sorry—*four* suitcases, three of which are battered and well-known to me, and one of which looks suspiciously like a floral-patterned carpetbag. I have to fight a strong urge to yank those bags out from under the bed and dive into the glory of clean underclothes and my favorite white shawl—and to tell Birdie's inanimate form exactly what I think of it.

"This should have been the first place I looked," I mutter. I *knew* it was suspicious that Birdie's eyebrows remained immaculate this entire time. She had to have been touching them up to keep them looking so sharp.

"What's that, dear?" Elspeth is up and out of the chair, a look of maternal concern on her face as she helps me back to my feet. "Is everything all right?"

No, everything is not all right. My nemesis and the only real lead I have in this case is dead. She's had access to our luggage this entire time, and through means that are just as mysterious as everything else that's been happening since I boarded that train.

And to top it all off, I'm almost *certain* I just heard her speaking to me.

"I'm sure there's a rational explanation for everything," I say, more to comfort myself than Elspeth.

It doesn't appear to work on either of us. Mostly because *rational explanation*, in this case, means someone running around this castle and killing people at will. Strange as it seems, I almost wish we were dealing with a curse instead.

"I don't believe it." Sid's voice carries down the hallway in a shrill vibrato that pierces through the walls. "I *won't* believe it. Not until I see her with my own eyes."

As one, Elspeth and I dash for the door, doing our best to prevent our hostess from viewing the spectacle of Birdie's prostrate form. No good can come of it; even if Sid weren't emotionally overwrought, there's something grisly about the entire household shuffling in and peering at Birdie as though she's an exhibit at a zoo.

"Madame Eleanor, is it true?" Sid demands as soon as she catches sight of me in the doorway. Both Nicholas and the doctor have escorted Sid down the hall, one on each side of her like supporting columns. "Is she in there? Is she . . . gone?"

I nod at Elspeth, who quietly shuts the door behind her. Since that room is now an active crime scene, it should probably be locked, but there doesn't seem to be a key.

"There now, Ms. Stewart." Elspeth draws forward with a soothing cluck. "Why don't you let Madame Eleanor and Mr. Hartford take you somewhere you can be comfortable? There's naught you can do for our guest now."

Sid visibly blanches. "So it *is* true?"

My eyes catch Nicholas's, which are as troubled and surprised as I expect to find them. I imagine he's thinking of the poison.

Either that, or he's noticed my floral trousers.

"I'm afraid it is true," I say, and prepare to catch Sid as she inevitably swoons.

Strangely enough, my words only cause her to draw a deep breath and straighten her stance. She's as pale as the white satin pajamas she's wearing, and I can see that this news has come as a severe blow, but she remains standing.

"That's it," she announces. Withdrawing her arm from Nicholas's, she turns to the doctor and issues instructions with the ease and rapidity of a woman accustomed to dealing with unexpected corpses. "Rouse the rest of the house—with the exception of the boys, of course—and ask everyone to convene in the gilded salon."

"The gilded salon?" Dr. Fulstead echoes.

"It's as good a place as any to break the news," Sid says. "Father always sat there when he had the chance. Birdie liked it, too. She said it reminded her of Versailles. Elspeth, would it be asking too much for you to bring some refreshments? Nothing heavy, but coffee, perhaps, and some Danish?"

It seems the height of cruelty to ask the poor woman to go rustle up breakfast after what she's just been through, but Sid's words act like a balm. With a nod of approval at being given something concrete to do, Elspeth agrees.

"I know just the thing," she says. To the doctor, she adds, "Ashley will still be abed, but Otis is likely to be down by the docks. He should be easy enough to find."

At her most efficient, Elspeth is almost impossible to ignore. This moment is no exception. With a duck of his head, Dr. Fulstead goes off to do her bidding.

"Now, Madame Eleanor, show me Birdie, if you please," Sid says, still with that air of calm authority. I can't decide if I'm more impressed or alarmed by it until she adds, "I promise not to go off in a swoon, so you and Nicholas needn't look at me like that. I never got a chance to see Father. It's one of my biggest regrets."

I don't know what good it's going to do her to look at the corporeal remains of a woman she knew less than a week, but I don't know what harm it can do, either. Stepping aside, I snick open the bedroom door and allow Sid to enter.

"Ellie . . ." Nicholas says the moment we're left alone in the hallway. His use of my nickname says everything he doesn't—namely, that we're crammed together inside a tight spot with no means of escape.

"I know," I say, grimacing. "And this isn't even the worst part. There's more."

There's no opportunity for me to tell him *how* much worse things are about to get. The information that the poison is missing and that Glenn and Birdie died under similarly questionable circumstances is going to have to wait. Sid emerges from the bedroom, ashen but intact.

"I think I'd like the support of your arm," she says as she presses a handkerchief to her forehead. I assume she's talking to Nicholas, but I'm the one she reaches for. "Thank you for giving me a moment alone with her. She seemed rather peaceful, don't you think? The doctor said my father looked peaceful."

"Death *is* peaceful," I assure her as we begin our slow and laborious descent down the stairs. Sid wasn't joking about wanting my arm to support her—she's pressing down with what feels like her full body weight. "I know you have a somewhat tempestuous relationship with death as of late, but it's not always a bad thing, I promise."

Nicholas clears his throat, forcing me realize what I've just said—and how I've said it.

"Losing Birdie is terrible, of course," I hasten to add. "A tragedy for us all. I only meant in the general way of things."

Since the conversational burden seems to be mine and mine alone, I take a moment to add, "Thank you for the clothes, by the way. That velvet dress of mine was starting to become downright rancid."

"Clothes?" Sid pauses to blink at me, taking in the sight of my new apparel as if seeing it for the first time. "Oh. I didn't notice. Did Elspeth finally find your bags?"

Now it's my turn to blink in bewilderment. I stick a finger in the ruffles and give the shirt a tug. The neckband is suddenly feeling awfully tight. "These aren't yours?"

Sid's trill of laughter is genuine, if a little forced. "I ought to have offered you something of mine days ago, but with one thing and another, I kept forgetting." She pauses and looks at me anew. "Now that I think about it, those might have been my mother's. Are they Laura Ashley? That's how my brother got his name, you know. My mother adored her clothes."

"You didn't leave these on the foot of my bed?" I think of the similar stack of clothes at Birdie's feet and suppress a shudder. It's possible that Elspeth was the one who brought us both something to wear, but it's equally likely—if not more—that the murderer was looking for a good excuse to slip in and out of our rooms.

"No, but I'd be happy to see if there's anything else of my mother's that might fit you. She was almost exactly your size."

I thank her for the offer and leave it at that. Nicholas is watching me with the keen scrutiny of a man who knows I'm onto something, but he leaves it at that, too. As much as I'd like to rip these clothes off and dive into the bags under Birdie's bed, I don't dare.

Not until I have some answers.

And not until I get some of that coffee from Elspeth, either.

Everyone is gathered in the gilded salon when we arrive. Candles have been lit in their holders and the lamps set out, illuminating the room enough for us to hold a rational conversation. There's something about the warm, yellowing light of it that brings solace at a time when we need it most.

The entire party is present, with the sole exception of

Elspeth, who is most likely putting together the breakfast requested by Sid.

"Ms. White will have to be taken to the mainland," the doctor says by way of initiating the conversation. He stands in front of the fireplace with his hands behind his back, looking as authoritative and capable as he had that day on the train. There's something about an emergency situation that brings out the best in him. "We can't leave her here, and I imagine the coroner will want to perform an autopsy."

"But didn't you say she had food poisoning?" Sid asks from her perch on the arm of an overstuffed leather davenport. Her brother is on the seat next to her, the pair of them holding hands in a way that makes my heart wrench. Whatever else might be said about those two, loss has been a very real and painful thing in their lives. "Food poisoning could kill a person if it was bad enough, couldn't it?"

Dr. Fulstead coughs lightly. "That's what the autopsy will tell us. The sooner we get her to the mainland, the sooner we'll all have the answers we seek." His gaze moves across the room as he speaks, landing on each face as he does. There's something ominous about the way he does it, as though each of us is being marked. It's almost as if he knows that one of us is a murderer—that one of us could very easily murder again.

"I'll prep my boat as soon as we're done here," Otis says. "I assume you'll be coming, Dr. Fulstead?"

"Of course. I can be of no use to the poor woman now."

Otis signals his agreement with a short nod. "Sid, I think you and Ashley should pack your things and join us." At Sid's wince, he draws close and pats her shoulder, allowing his hand to linger. "I know it's not ideal. But you won't be able to tell that she's on the boat with you, and you can hardly wish to stay here any longer. It's not . . ."

Several words spring to mind to complete that sentence: ideal, safe, *sane*. Even if Birdie's death is nothing more than yet another coincidence in an impossible lineup of them, a few more days of this will have all of us foaming at the mouth.

"I'm not going anywhere." Sid shrugs off Otis's touch and removes her hand from her brother's clasp. Once again, she's proving to be more resolute than her appearance suggests.

There's something about it that snags my notice. I'm all for people finding their strength in adversity, but she's been undergoing an assault of bad news for over a month—for her whole life, really. The death of a houseguest under mysterious circumstances should be the thing that breaks her, not the thing that puts her back together again.

"I'm sorry, Otis," she says. "I know you'd prefer to whisk me away to safety, but you can hardly expect me to leave now. We have to get to the root of this problem, or people are going to keep dying. It's our duty. Gloriana demands it."

At mention of the curse, Otis releases a soft oath. "Ashley, would you please talk some sense into your sister? This is getting ridiculous. Neither one of you can accomplish anything by staying in this dark castle and worrying yourselves to death. The longer you remain, the deeper you fall into this stupid, superstitious farce."

"'For he is superstitious grown of late,'" quotes the poet.

At a look from me, Nicholas takes a step in front of Ashley. I'm not saying Otis would *murder* his cousin, but he'd be justified in planting him a strong right hook.

"This is our responsibility, Otis," Sid says, her voice soft but determined. "You know that as well as anyone—better, probably. Mother, Father, Nadia, Harvey, and now Birdie . . . How many more people have to suffer before you finally start to believe?"

I can only assume that Nadia is the name of the long-dead wife, because the look that crosses Otis's face is so fierce that I'm no longer certain he won't resort to murder to vent his wrath. I wouldn't put it past him to burn this entire castle down—with us in it.

Oh, please. Don't you think that's a touch dramatic?

At the sound of Birdie's voice once again intruding on my thoughts, I give a startled twitch. It's followed almost immediately by a feeling of foreboding so deep that it touches my bones.

Once, and I was willing to chalk it up to a figment of my imagination. Twice, and I can only wish my imagination ran that deep.

"Nope," I say aloud. "I'm not doing this. Not for all the gold in the world. I refuse."

"What do you refuse?" Sid asks, just as the voice sounds again.

I told you someone here was going to die. I bet you're sorry now that you didn't believe me.

Even though I know how it makes me look, I slap my hands over my ears.

"Eleanor, why don't you go down to the kitchen and give Elspeth a hand?" Nicholas suggests. His voice is careful—*too* careful, that of a man talking to someone on the edge. "I'm sure we can handle things from here."

On the contrary, I'm beginning to doubt that *any* of us—with the apparent exception of Sid—can handle what's happening on this island. There are too many unknowns, too many questions we don't even know how to ask, let alone answer. In an effort to buy myself some time, I place my hand to my temple and hold it there.

You look like a buffoon when you do that, Birdie says.

She's right, you know, Winnie agrees. *I've always thought you should come up with something more . . . sophisticated.*

I can't help it—I laugh. It's the laugh of a woman who's reaching the edge of her sanity, who's starting to question the color of the sky and which way is up, but I can't help it. I can't imagine what I've done to be cursed like this.

"That didn't stop you from copying it," I tell Birdie. "By the way, if you're going to linger for a while, the least you could do is help me out. Tell me the cause of your death, or at least where to find that blasted gold."

This eminently sensible suggestion is met with silence.

Nicholas clears his throat and draws my attention. I glance around to discover the entire party staring incredulously at me.

"Is it . . . Birdie?" Sid asks, her eyes wide and her mouth slightly parted. "Were you just talking to her?"

I see no reason to respond with a lie. There are more than enough of those floating around already. "Yes."

"From beyond the grave?"

I grimace. "I think it's safe to assume as much."

My words are like a starting bell for reactionary outbursts.

"What did she say?"

"What does she want?"

"Has she seen Gloriana?"

"Does she know where the gold is?"

I can only close my eyes and wait for the barrage of questions to abate. I know enough of communing with the dead by now to know that it will never be as simple as making a query and getting an answer. If I can't get my own sister to tell me what I want to know, I have no idea how I'm supposed to control Birdie.

"She says 'I told you so.' " I say with a shrug of helplessness. "That's the gist of it. She wants us all to remember that it was she who predicted someone would die under this roof."

Not surprisingly, this revelation doesn't do much to still the undercurrent of fear in the room. In fact, the only person who seems mildly appreciative of Birdie's sense of humor is Otis, who laughs outright.

A light knock on the door to the salon is followed up by the rattle of an incoming tray cart. The doctor rushes to help Elspeth as she enters. Impossible though it seems in the half hour that's passed since we last saw her, she's managed to put together a feast. A tower of cakes and other dainty pastries, a steaming pot of tea, and what look to be awfully strong spirits for ten o'clock in the morning beckon.

"Are we sure that's safe?" Ashley asks as he eyes a particularly decadent Victoria sponge cake. "It looks delicious, as always, but until we know what happened to Birdie . . ."

Elspeth's face falls. I feel an almost ludicrous pity for her—caring for her grandsons, keeping the castle in order, being blamed for Birdie's self-poisoning, and receiving nothing but the mildest thanks for it all.

"I, for one, am ravenous," I announce. "Thank you, Elspeth. I hope you don't mind if I end up eating that whole cake. Your cooking is always delicious."

She blushes her pleasure so rosily that I'm tempted to allay fears by adding that Birdie herself vouches for the safety of the refreshments. I don't do it, however. The link between me and a recent poisoning is already stronger than I like. I'm not deliberately putting myself on the hook for another.

"Yes, thank you," Sid echoes, though I notice she doesn't rush to cut herself a slice. "And don't worry—I'll take everything back to the kitchen when we're done."

"No, you'll be packing your things and getting on a boat with me," Otis reminds her. "In fact, I think all of us should go. Immediately."

For once, I find myself in agreement with him. If this were a game of Clue, we'd want to lock everyone in the castle together, pitting wits and uncovering evidence that would eventually lead us to the murderer. But life isn't a game, and I'm worried. As long as that poison remains somewhere inside these walls—and with someone who isn't afraid to use it—we're all in danger.

I had no idea you were so squeamish, Birdie says.

I ignore her. It's not squeamish to want to live. It's not squeamish to recall that there are two little boys whose lives are endangered with every second they remain here.

"He's right," I say. "No good can come of us lingering. We should all get ourselves to safety while we still can."

"You're giving up?" Sid asks. Her brows are pulled tight, her lips twisted in a moue of displeasure. "After everything that's happened? After all we've been through? You'll just let Gloriana free to vent her wrath?"

In that moment, not even Ashley at his most poetic could touch Sid for soulful entreaty. Her hands are cast up in supplication, the fate of the entire world hanging from them.

"Please, Madame Eleanor," she adds. "I'm begging you not to abandon us. Not now. Not when we're so close. Without you, there's no chance we'll ever discover what happened to the gold—or to Father. You're the only hope we have."

"Well . . ." I falter, unable to ignore how desperately she wants to stay and find the gold. Even that bit about her father was added only as an afterthought, as though the treasure is her real ambition—has been her ambition all along. I can't help remembering the feeling I had yesterday that Birdie was hiding something, protecting someone. That feeling is still there, but I'm starting to wonder if *protect* was the right word.

"Personally, I'd like to stay and see this thing through," Nicholas says, clinching the matter. He adds, almost apologetically, "But if Eleanor thinks we ought to go, then I'm willing to accede to her wishes. I know better than to doubt her intuition—or her sister's."

This proves too much for Otis. "You don't *believe* her," he says, angry spittle forming in the corners of his mouth. "You can't possibly think that she talks to dead people."

Nicholas lifts his brow. "Of course I do."

"But—" Otis glances back and forth between us. "No. It's not possible. She makes it up. It's all a sham. You said so—I distinctly remember you saying so."

. "On the contrary, what I told you was that she puts on a

good show. Which she does, as you've seen for yourself. The talent behind it, however, is authentic."

"Then how many fingers am I holding up?" Otis swiftly pulls his hands behind his back. It's a common trick among those who have no confidence and even less imagination. "Ask your dead friend about that."

"First of all, it doesn't work like that," I say, fighting a strong urge to roll my eyes. "And second of all, you're not holding up any fingers. You have your hands in a pair of fists in an effort to trick me."

"How the devil?" He pulls his hands out from behind his back and stares at them, as if the answer to my sapience lies in the flesh. "Is there a mirror behind me or something?"

Nicholas chuckles. "No, but even I could have guessed that one."

"So what does this mean?" Sid asks, looking from one face to another. "Are we staying or going?"

There's a note of anxiety in her voice that clinches the matter. It's not anxiety over her own safety or the safety of her guests; it's anxiety over whether or not we plan on seeing this gold-hunting expedition through to the end. That much resolution, and this late in the game, is impossible to ignore.

"Birdie thinks we should stay," I say with a decisive nod. "She doesn't want to have died in vain."

"She said that?" Otis asks, suspicious. "Out of the blue? She can just pop in whenever?"

I heave a sigh that's only partially faked. "Apparently. Believe me when I say that I'd gladly hand her over to you if I could. The last thing I want is to spend the rest of my life with Bridget Wimpole-White gazing over my shoulder and keeping up a running commentary."

As if just now realizing the implications of this newest twist in the Eleanor Wilde mystical saga, Nicholas physically balks.

"Dear God," he says. "The rest of your life?"

I laugh. There's nothing funny about any of this, but the look of horror on Nicholas's face leaves room for nothing else. My sister has never yet intruded on moments of real intimacy, and I doubt she ever will, but there's no saying what a woman like Birdie will do.

"Don't worry," I say, and give his arm a squeeze. "I haven't yet attempted an exorcism, but after everything else I've managed to pull off, how hard can it be?"

Chapter 15

When I return upstairs, it's to find the note that accompanied my clothes is gone. So, too, is the entire stack of clothing on the foot of Birdie's bed. It's been replaced by the sleeping, purring mass of my two cats, who seem to be taking an awfully macabre interest in her mortal remains.

"It's going to take a couple of us to carry her down," Nicholas observes from somewhere a few feet behind me. "You have approximately five minutes to snoop around before you'll miss your chance."

"I don't snoop; I investigate," I retort, but leave it at that. Five minutes doesn't leave me with much in the way of time. "Quick—see if there are still four bags under the bed and take them to my room. If nothing else, at least I can change out of these clothes."

"I think you look nice in those ruffles," he says, but doesn't hesitate to carry out my orders. And a good thing, too—if he wasn't being so helpful and supportive, I'd have a thing or two to say about a man who thinks Laura Ashley clothes suit my aesthetic.

"Is it safe to assume these are yours?" he asks as he easily balances all four of the suitcases.

"Yes. I thought the twins were behind it, but Birdie must have had them this whole time, the lying sneak."

With a furtive glance down the hallway, we dash across to my room, where Nicholas safely bestows the suitcases in one corner. Dropping to my knees in front of the smallest of them, I zip it open and inspect the contents. That my belongings have been rifled through is without question. I'm not the neatest packer in the world, but everything had been more or less folded when I left my cottage. It's now a tangled mess of clothes, jewelry, and—thank goodness—the white scarf that had been the last thing Winnie ever gave me.

The other bags are similarly vandalized. Nothing is missing, but the herbal remedies I brought with me have all been opened, and my ghost-hunting tech looks to have been tampered with at least a few times.

In fact, after making a survey of the contents, I realize that the only things missing are two scarves in bright shades of red and blue.

I rock back on my heels. "*That* must have been what Ferguson and Jaime meant," I say with a shake of my head. Since Nicholas has yet to ask the question I'm sure is on his lips, I glance up and add, "At one point, they mentioned bribery in conjunction with Birdie's name. She must have tried getting information out of them by promising to outfit them in my pashminas."

"Not very polite of her," Nicholas murmurs. He scrubs a hand over his jaw. "Although she must have known that you'd notice them wearing the scarves and piece the truth together. Especially if she was only hiding these bags under the bed. You could have gone into her room and found them at any point."

I stare at him. He's not wrong. Not only would it have been easy for Elspeth to unearth the bags during one of her cleaning rounds, but that room has been unlocked for the entire duration of my stay. Birdie almost assuredly examined my own room from top to bottom—how could she possibly know that I wouldn't do the same?

"You think someone planted them?" I ask, and immediately shake my head. "No. She had to have taken them. It fits with everything else she's done."

There's a questioning tilt to Nicholas's head, but I can hear footsteps in the distance. The cortège must be on its way. I only have time to explain, "I know it sounds far-fetched, but I could almost swear that she was more interested in helping *me* find the gold rather than searching for it herself."

"That's one of the nicest compliments you could give her," Nicholas replies as he helps me to my feet. "It obviously didn't take her long to realize that you're worth two dozen of her."

It's an incredibly sweet thing to say, but it's a bunch of malarkey, and he knows it. I can only assume that all this murder is addling his brain; the next thing I know, he'll be flowering me with saccharine sentiments and encouraging me to invest in more ruffled blouses.

Otis and Ashley arrive upstairs to carry their burden down to the waiting pirate boat. Since the removal of Birdie's remains isn't going to help me solve this case—and because it turns out I'm more squeamish about this sort of thing than I realized—I duck out and leave them to their work.

I want nothing more than a few minutes of quiet time to reflect, think, and—the Good Goddess willing—come up with a plan that will scare the murderer into revealing himself. Imagine my dismay, then, when I reach the bottom of the stairs to find a trap lying in wait for me.

"There she is!"

"Show her what you did!"

"Madame Eleanor, you won't believe it!"

I put a smile on my face and greet the twin boys. They've

been recently brushed and scrubbed—prepped, no doubt, for their upcoming journey—but all the soap in the world couldn't subdue their natural spirits.

"It worked!" Jaime flashes me a not-so-toothy grin and holds out his hand, where a small white pebble rests. "I kept saying the spell over and over again, and bam! It popped right out."

"I didn't think it would work that fast," Ferguson confides. A burgeoning sense of respect peeps out from his lowered lashes. "What other spells do you know? Can you turn people into frogs?"

"Or . . . pirates?" Jaime suggests.

The mention of pirates recalls me to a sense of my surroundings—and my duty. Crouching to their level, I put on my sternest and most serious expression. "I'm happy that you were able to remove your tooth, but I need you to tell me something very important."

The boys' twin gazes shift toward one another.

"You're not in trouble," I hasten to add, but that's obviously an expression they've heard many a time in their small lives, because it only increases their wariness. "I need to know one thing. Did Birdie White—the woman who passed away—give you two the scarves I saw you wearing the other day?"

Their eyes begin moving again, but I speak up before they have a chance to make contact.

"That's a silly question, because I already know the answer. She *did* give you those scarves."

"How d'you know that?" Ferguson asks.

With more hope than suspicion, Jaime adds, "Did you see it in a crystal ball?"

"I don't use a crystal ball. I see things in my mind's eye."

This doesn't appear to impress them. Ferguson crosses his arms and watches me speculatively. "If you can see things in your mind, then why d'you need us to tell you anything?"

It's a fair question, and one I'd have been sure to ask when I was that age. Unfortunately, the certainty of youth has long since left me. All I have left is wisdom and the ability to strike fear into people both young and old.

"It's okay." I shrug and resume a standing position. "You don't have to tell me anything. I have no power over you. But don't be surprised if you get a visit from the police while you're with your great-aunt. They'll have quite a few questions about the bribes you took from a dead woman."

From the wide-eyed shivers that move through the boys, I'm afraid I took things too far. It's one thing to threaten adults with the hand of the law, quite another to frighten children that way. But it turns out the shivers are more delighted than fearful, and the next time they share a look, it's one of gleeful capitulation.

Ferguson drops his voice to a near-whisper, forcing me to lean in to hear his confession. I wonder if priests and vicars get this same thrill when they hear the sins of others. There's something delightfully suspenseful about it.

"She wanted to know where Nanna keeps the silver," Ferguson confides.

I'm oddly disappointed by this. "The silver?"

Ferguson casts a darting look around and, seeing no one, adds, "And where to find the key to get it."

"Did you tell her?" I ask.

Jaime nods. "It was easy. The silver isn't locked up. It's in the kitchen."

This revelation proves to be equally disappointing, if only because of Birdie's lack of ingenuity. When I resort to bribery, I like to make sure it's worth my while—which the Stewart family cutlery is decidedly not. Two pashminas seems like a steep price for such paltry information.

"That's it?" I ask, probing further. "She didn't want to know about secret hiding places or the wine cellar or chests of pirate gold?"

Ferguson shakes his head. "The only one who keeps asking about the gold is you."

Yes, and a good thing, too. I've been left holding the gilded torch, as it were. If I don't do something to yield tangible results, no one will.

Then again, someone did kill Birdie less than twenty-four hours ago. She may have been closer to the truth than I realize.

"Well, she did *try* all the spoons," Jaime adds with a self-conscious prod at the hole in his smile. "Even the big ones. They barely fit in her mouth."

Several thumps from the top of the stairs warn me that a body will soon be heading this way. As blasé as the boys seem to be about this whole death thing, I'm not eager to put them face-to-face with a corpse.

"She tried them?" I echo. "You helped her do this?"

"Well, we didn't 'xactly *help*," Jaime admits. "She didn't know we were there. I think she wanted it to be a secret."

The thumps from upstairs are accompanied by a groan from Ashley and a quotation on the ephemeral nature of death, so I give the boys a nod and allow them to hasten off. I only wait until their small figures round the corner before taking myself off in the opposite direction.

And *not*, as a bystander might assume, because I'm disinclined to come face-to-face with a corpse myself. In this instance, I have a much more important task to undertake.

Bridget Wimpole-White. In the kitchen. With the silver.

It might not be the slam dunk I've been looking for in terms of this case, but if my suspicions are correct, it's a step in the right direction.

To prove to Birdie—and myself—that subtlety is much more likely to yield results than the bribing of children with stolen scarves, I join Elspeth in the kitchen.

As usual, she's hard at work, stoking the wood fire and

standing over bubbling pots. She's still wearing the faded blue dress with the coffee stain, but her serene cheerfulness appears to be restored.

"They're taking Birdie down to the boat now," I inform her. "I came to see if you needed anything."

"Isn't that sweet of you," she replies. "You've been a most helpful guest."

A twinge of guilt rises up from my stomach. On the contrary, I'm neither sweet nor particularly helpful. Nicholas might look at me and see someone worth admiring, but he's blinded by the throes of affection. It's the Otises and Birdies of this world who see me for what I really am.

"Sid asked if we could use the silver service this evening," I say, lying through my teeth and proving my point to perfection. Nothing could heap more work on this woman's head than to dine in stately grandeur. "I thought I'd help by making sure it's all polished. I imagine it tarnishes easily in this climate."

Elspeth turns to look at me, a look of surprise on her face, but she doesn't raise a protest. "To be sure, if Ms. Stewart wishes it. You'll find it in that cupboard by the woodpile. Will we be using the good plate, as well?"

I'm not willing to push my luck—or her workload—that far.

"No, just the silver. I made the mistake of telling her that it's a lunar metal." When Elspeth responds to this with a bewildered blink, I add, "It's very cleansing. It should help to restore balance in the house."

My duplicity works. Elspeth shows no more interest in my doings than a mild remark that I'll find the silver polish in the top drawer of the cupboard.

I begin to regret my actions as soon as I realize how much silver the Stewart family has in its possession. Forget the missing gold—there's more than enough of this second-best metal to keep them in riches for generations to come. Fortunately, it's all in good repair. Whether because Elspeth stays on top of things, or because Birdie herself took a rag and aluminum silicate to the spoons, everything gleams like it's come straight from Buckingham Palace.

Angling my back to Elspeth, I lift one of the spoons and put it to my mouth. I don't, as the twins suggested, pretend to eat from it. Instead, I bite.

And nearly chip a tooth in the process.

"Ouch," I mutter as I almost drop the spoon. I catch it just in time, quickly replacing with another and testing the metal again. It's still strong, still hard.

In other words, it's not melted-down pirate gold masquerading under a silver veneer.

I could have told you that, comes a voice I'm starting to recognize all too well. *That was one of the first things I checked.*

I don't point out the obvious—that the things Birdie *could* tell me number in the thousands. The entire knowledge of the universe might be at her fingertips now that she's dead, but unless she starts sharing it with me, it's basically useless.

The acrid tang of fire fills my nostrils, so I pause in my pretense of polishing the silver. "Oh, dear. I think something on the stove is burning. Do you need a hand before I start setting the table?"

"I haven't burned a roast in this oven since the day it was brought in," she says with a dignified air. "In aught truth, I haven't burned a roast in this oven since the day *I* was brought in."

I'm about to ask her when exactly that was—how many years of her life have been spent in service of the Stewarts—but the burning scent is growing stronger. It's not filling just my nostrils now; the whole room seems to be swirling with it, though there's nothing but a few motes of dust in the air.

"Are you sure it's not something on the back burner?" I give up on the spoons and join Elspeth at the enormous, fiery stove. She's noticed the smell by now and, like me, seems concerned as to its source.

"Maybe something spilled over." Elspeth opens the oven door. The waft of air that hits us is rich and hot and meaty. I might question such a heartily carnivorous choice when we've all recently touched a corpse, but it smells too good to bother. "That's odd. I don't see anything amiss."

The back kitchen door bursts open in a whirl of brimstone-scented air. Elspeth and I turn as one, the older woman's elbow knocking into a saucepan and sending the contents flying. I'm too busy trying to avoid scalds from the tomato-laden broth to notice who's standing on the threshold, but that question is answered for me as soon as he speaks.

"'The triumphal arch through which I march, with hurricane, fire, and snow—'" Ashley begins.

"Bless you, Mr. Stewart, coming in here all in a tiz," Elspeth interrupts him before he can weave one of his tangled linguistic webs. "You know I don't understand poetry any more than that doormat you're standing on. You'll have to tell me in plain speaking. I was always a sad case when it came to your Romantics."

I can't help but admire the deft way she handles him. I wish I'd feigned a similar lack of education, but it's too late now. Besides, with the door hanging open like that, we're being bombarded with more than the just the scent of smoke. A damp, smoldering seepage starts to fill the room.

"Fire," Ashley says on a gasp. Now that I'm paying closer attention, he's looking decidedly disheveled. His mustache is no longer combed flat, and there's a smudge of what looks like soot along one side of his jaw. "Down on the dock."

"Fire?" Elspeth cries with an alarmed look at me.

"The dock?" is my contribution.

Ashley decides to answer my question first. He grimaces and rubs his hand along his jaw, causing the sooty patch to spread. "It's Otis's boat. Someone lit it on fire. In a few more minutes, it'll be gone."

* * *

"Oh, dear." Elspeth is the first to react to the sight of the sinking hull of Otis's tour boat. Neither of us took the time to grab a wrap, but she had the foresight to bring a dishtowel with her. She's holding it to her mouth now, her words muffled but strong. "That doesn't look good."

Her comment is an understatement to end all understatements. I'm no seafaring expert, and the whip of the wind is blowing salty, smoky water in my eyes, but that's a sinking pirate ship if ever I've seen one. A blast of what looks to be a cannonball has formed a huge hole on one side of the boat, making it dip sideways under the slapping waves. The flames are concentrated on the main cabin, which is blazing up as though it's made of, well, wood.

"Nooo!" Otis cries. He's so close to the flames that they reflect orange and gold on his skin. "Not my boat. It's gone too far this time."

Considering that Birdie's body is lying shrouded and unattended at the top of the dock, and she's the third in the spate of recent deaths that can be laid at the curse's door, Otis's comment seems a little drastic. His expression is wild as he struggles to free himself from the grip Nicholas has on his shoulders.

"I have to get to the cabin," he says, fighting and bucking against my beau's restraining arms. "I have to secure the hold."

If he were paying heed to anything but the loss of his livelihood, I could have enlightened Otis on the futility of his efforts. Nicholas Hartford III is a deceptively strong man. He might look long and lean, but he's carried me over fields and along tunnels and through much more difficult scenarios than this.

"Otis, don't," Nicholas says, his voice as strong as the rest of him. "You can't possibly board her in this condition."

"But my navigation equipment! My logbook! My—" He casts an anxious look at me and swallows. "The rest of my belongings."

I have no idea what else he was going to admit to storing on board the boat, but it doesn't matter. We stand there, a silent and forlorn group, watching as the remaining flames start to fizzle. It's all they *can* do as the boat continues to keel sideways. I have no idea when that hole was put in the side, but the boat must have been taking on water long before the fire was set. What we're witnessing are the final death throes.

As if in solidarity, the sky itself starts to churn up billowing black clouds that swell on the horizon. From here, they look like plumes of smoldering smoke, the last gasps of a ship that will never again sail the seven seas.

"I can't afford another like her," Otis says as the boat creaks and groans with eerily human-like sounds. "I'm ruined."

I'm not so removed from financial hardship myself that I fail to appreciate the enormity of Otis's despair, but we're facing a bigger problem than mere loss. His boat was sabotaged with intent and with malicious ends in mind.

"Someone did this on purpose," I say. I'm sure this has occurred to everyone standing on the dock, but someone has to move the conversation along. Like it or not, we're going to have to face the fact that we're stranded on this island.

Together. With a murderer.

As if understanding our predicament, a rumble of thunder breaks out above our heads. Nicholas glances up, only to be hit in the eye with a huge splash of rainwater. He whips out a handkerchief to wipe the moisture away before realizing the futility of his actions. After one more ominous boom, the rain starts to fall—not a trickle or a drizzle, but an oceanic sheet that drenches us within seconds.

"What do we do now?" Elspeth asks. She hasn't made a move to protect herself from the elements. I find it odd until I realize that she'd have to walk past the body in order to make it to cover.

"We'll have to take Birdie back up to the castle," Otis says, his gaze also alighting on that unmoving shroud. "We can try to get out a request for help, but it's not likely that the call will make it through in these conditions. My ship's radio could have done it, but . . ."

We all look to the smoking, half-submerged wreckage, our thoughts shared and unspoken. That radio isn't going to do us a particle of good now.

"Elspeth and I will notify the others," I say. "You three will have to find a way to get Birdie somewhere safe and dry. The wine cellar, perhaps. She'd like that."

No one finds anything odd in this pronouncement. The men nod their assent and bend their attention to the task of carrying Birdie—no light burden—back to the house.

Taking Elspeth quietly by the hand, I lead her back up the stairs. Since she's still a little too quiet for my taste, I take it upon myself to speak in the hearty tones of one who's accustomed to women dying on remote islands and escape boats sinking in fiery crashes. "I'm not sure where Dr. Fulstead is hiding himself, but I think Sid is lying down on her bed," I say.

A few days ago, I might have taken Sid's fragility as yet another sign of her inability to cope with real-world problems, but now I'm starting to think otherwise. Her absence is too conspicuous, too well-timed. *Too much like an alibi.*

"If you'll let the doctor know what's going on, I'll attend to Sid," I add.

Elspeth, in her kindhearted way, assumes I plan to take Sid some supporting broth and comforting tea. I don't bother correcting her. What I have to offer Sid isn't sustenance—it's an interrogation.

I don't share these thoughts with Elspeth, who squeezes my hand as we make our way up to the castle. "The boys, at least, will be delighted," she says with an attempt at a smile. "They were none too excited to be carried off before the adventure was over."

The boys. For Elspeth's sake, I bite back a groan, but it takes some doing. The one good thing about all this was that Jaime and Ferguson were finally going to be toted off to safety. Now even that reassurance is going to be denied me.

It's with a heavy step and an even heavier heart that I find my way to Sid's bedroom. I peeked inside during my first few days at the castle and found little there to interest me. Like most of the rest of the house, it's decorated as a tribute to the spirit of acquisition. Heavy furnishings, beautiful treasures, and impeccable wallpaper might make for a pretty room, but it doesn't make for a very inviting one. Even the few personal items Sid brought for her stay—toiletries and clothing and a small alarm clock in the shape of a bird—do little to dispel the stifling pomp of it all.

The door is ajar when I arrive at the threshold to her bedroom. Manners demand that I knock before I enter, but from where I stand, I can just make out the sprawl of her body across her bed—either deep in sleep or determined to give the appearance of it.

"Oh, Madame Eleanor, is that you?" Sid sits up and stretches, a yawn parting her lips. "I was having such a good dream. Isn't that odd, with everything that's been going on?"

It doesn't take her long to realize something is wrong. Most of it is the way my body is shaking, since I'm drenched to the marrow and feeling the full effects of the storm, but part of it is the way I have yet to speak. I can't help it—I'm trying to figure out how to frame my next words.

"What is it?" Sid asks. "What's happened to make you look like that?"

I'm careful to keep my expression neutral and my tone flat. "I'm afraid there's been an accident."

Sid blanches convincingly, but I don't buy it. A few days ago, she'd have out-and-out screamed or fainted at such a piece of news. "Not . . . Otis?" she asks. "Or Nicholas?"

I shake my head. "Not that kind of accident. It's your

cousin's boat. I'm afraid it's no longer a viable means of transport."

Her lips press together in a thin line.

"Someone sabotaged it—broke a hole in its side and then set a fire to make sure the job was done. It's currently making its way to the bottom of the ocean."

"I see," she says, a faint crease between her brows. "Then I suppose this isn't a good time to notify you about the phones. I tried to call ahead to warn the coroner that we'd be coming, but it's always difficult to get cell reception in stormy weather."

I wish I could say that I find this surprising, but I don't—not the news nor her delivery of it, which almost rivals my own in terms of matter-of-factness. "Are you sure it's the storm?" I ask, watching her. "It's not someone jamming the signal?"

At this, Sid makes a convincingly wide-eyed show of alarm. She *does* look genuinely concerned to be trapped on this island without any means of communication, but that could be because, well, we're trapped on this island without any means of communication.

I told you the way back wouldn't be nearly as calm.

I breathe deep and will Birdie to perdition. "If all you're going to do is sit there and smugly tell me 'I told you so' every time something goes wrong, then you might as well flitter away," I say to her. "I have neither the time nor the patience for your antics. Go haunt someone else."

Even in this, Sid is showing herself to be inured to shock. "Birdie again?"

"Yes. It seems she was right about a lot of things, drat the woman."

As I say the words aloud, I realize how true they are. This entire time, I've been lamenting how Birdie always seemed to be one step ahead of me, as though she had direct access to some clairvoyant hotline available only to her. She knew where and how Harvey Renault would die. She predicted and/or controlled the weather. She knew where to find the first gold coin. I wouldn't go so far as to say that she's *psychic*, but she has had an advantage over me.

Either that, or she had an accomplice.

As if on cue, I could almost swear that I hear the low-throated, echoing laugh of Birdie in the distance.

"Well, that's it, then," I announce, eyeing Sid with new—and unnerving—clarity. "There's only one thing left to do."

I can't tell if I'm more excited or daunted by the prospect, but all of my training and experience has brought me to this one moment.

"One thing?" Sid echoes. "What?"

"I'm afraid we're going to have to hold a séance."

Chapter 16

I've never done more—or less—to prepare for a séance in my life.

A Madame Eleanor séance isn't an affair that happens every day. They've always been my pièce de résistance, the grand show at the end of a haunting, a way to lay all fears—and all spirits—to rest. My tactics have been perfected over the years, and typically include everything from wind machines and voice throwing to electromagnetic artifice.

In other words, they're a bunch of malarkey. As such, it generally takes me a few days and a lot of careful planning to get everything set up where I need it to be.

That's what makes today's séance so strange. For once, I've done no advance planning. There's no artifice, no behind-the-scenes trickery. Nothing has been rigged up in the background, and I've elicited no outside help. It's just me, my cats, and a room full of people who would prefer to be literally anywhere else right now.

"I need everyone to hold hands," I say to the assembled group. We're seated at a large, round table that I had Nicholas drag into the gilded salon. It's not the darkest or the most mystical room in the castle, but we've spent so much time here since this whole thing began that it feels the most fitting.

"I've placed a few of Birdie's personal effects in the center of the table, so if you could focus on them, that would be a big help," I add. "Think of her. Remember her. Call to her."

I have no idea how effective any of this will be, especially since the personal effects in question are, well, questionable. I couldn't admit to having unearthed the bags hidden under her bed without casting further suspicion on my head, so I had to make do with her purple fringed shawl, a few lingering shards of one of the wine bottles she smashed, and a lock of her hair that I shamelessly cut from her deceased head.

If the expressions on the gathered faces are any indication, they're equally unimpressed by my offerings. However, it seems anticlimactic for me to sit here with Freddie on my lap as I try to get some sense out of Birdie, so they'll just have to play along.

"Here, Birdie, Birdie," Otis calls in a purely sarcastic manner. Of everyone, he was the most difficult to coax into agreeing. It took Sid pointing out to him that the only alternative was to sit playing backgammon for the next two days until McGee shows up with his regular delivery. Between that and the likelihood of Birdie's body reaching the festering point, he decided to acquiesce. "Come out, come out, wherever you are."

Sid slaps his hand. "Hush. You know that's not how this works. Madame Eleanor needs to concentrate."

"Are you sure I should be here for this?" Dr. Fulstead asks. Of all of us, he seems the most nervous. He's seated on my right, his hand damp with perspiration. "I'm not one of the guests, and I don't know anything about the spiritual world."

"Of course you're welcome," I say, tightening my grip. Sweaty palms aren't my favorite thing, but I'm afraid he might try to make a run for it if I let go. "There's nothing secretive or dark about this. It's just a gathering of people remembering a dear friend."

Nicholas coughs.

"Well, an overbearing acquaintance, at the very least," I correct myself.

"Can we play?" asks Ferguson from one corner. Children at a séance is never a good idea, but Elspeth and I are equally loath to let them wander the island at large. While fires are being set and women are being poisoned in their beds, it seems wisest to keep them within eyeshot. I gave Ferguson a ball of yarn and told him to keep Beast occupied, but it's obvious he's about as impressed with the cat as the cat is with him.

"I'm a powerful wizard now," Jaime insists. He's given up on Beast and is making a finger cradle from the yarn. "My other tooth is already coming loose."

He's too far away for me to make out the details, but the quiet determination of the next few seconds leads me to believe that he's doing his best to wiggle his second incisor free.

"Then keep up the good work. The power of the séance might help things progress." Before he has a chance to argue—or to ask me about other spells to while away the next hour—I turn to Ashley, who's seated on my left. His palm, unlike the doctor's, is bone dry and paper thin. It feels almost like holding hands with a mummy. "Ashley, why don't you begin? Tell us something that struck you about Birdie upon your first meeting."

It takes him a moment to decide on the right thing to say. When he does, it's not, as I expect, a florid burst of poetry, but a much more prescient truth. "I never did understand what brought her," he says. "*You* were invited, obviously, but we'd never even heard of her before. What did she want, coming here as she did?"

"The gold," I say, not mincing matters. "You heard her admit that if it's cursed, haunted, or possessed, she knew about it. I'm guessing we could also add *if it's worth anything* to that list."

Everyone looks mildly uncomfortable at this piece of truth, so I waste no time in continuing. Mild discomfort is a great first step in any séance.

"She knew that your family was in possession of Gloriana's Burden," I say with a careful glance at each face. "She knew the exact history of the curse as well as the value of the gold. She knew where in the wine cellar to look for the box, but she didn't seem surprised to find that it was empty."

I think, but don't add, that although she drew everyone down to the wine cellar, she waited until I was in the room before she extracted the box. Based on the weight of it, she knew as well as I did that it couldn't possibly contain the missing gold, but that hadn't surprised her in the slightest.

Because she'd been setting us up. She'd been setting *me* up.

"Well, Birdie?" I ask, somewhat rhetorically. "What do you have to say about that?"

To my surprise, she answers on cue.

I'm not going to do everything for you, dear Ella.

And that's it. That's all Birdie says—all she does. As has been the case since the moment we met, her only plan is to throw me into the middle of a mess, bow out of the way, and watch what I do.

So I show her.

"She was a fraud," I announce.

Otis grunts. "Well, obviously."

"No, I mean it." I hold up a hand to prevent Otis from saying more. I half expect Birdie to chime in with a roaring defense of her own capabilities, but all that happens is that Freddie stands up from my lap, emits a tiny pink yawn, and settles back down again. "She was no more capable of predicting the future than you are."

"I?" Sid asks with a blink.

"Yes, you—all of you. Everyone here." I lift a finger and move it in a circle around the table. "Bridget Wimpole-White was a fake and a fraud, but the one thing she knew from the beginning, the one thing she banked on, is that I'm *not*. Since we first sat together on that train, her sole objective has been to serve as my right hand. The first thing she did upon hearing about the curse was to ask how I planned to counteract it. She unearthed a gold coin in a wine cellar and immediately handed it over to me for safekeeping. She sent for my cats when I needed them. She brought me Dr. Fulstead."

I wait in case lightning should decide to strike me dead and counteract my claim, but all I hear is the shocked silence of the room I hold captive. It's my moment of glory.

"Someone hired her to find that gold," I say, taking pleasure in stating the words out loud. "The only way a fraud like Bridget Wimpole-White could have known as much as she did was if someone had been feeding her information the entire time. But the one thing she didn't know—the one thing she *couldn't* know—was the gold's actual location. And do you know why?"

No one answers, even though I'm fairly sure by now that they've all figured out what I have.

"Because the person who hired her didn't know, either."

I glance around the table once more, my gaze skimming over the faces of the gathered party, each more troubled than the last. Many of my own thoughts are echoed there. There are stolen glances and uncomfortable squirms as everyone starts to understand the implications of what we're dealing with.

For a moment, I toy with the idea of lying—of saying that I know who the guilty party is and waiting for the outburst to follow—but a glimmer of gold on the edge of the painting of the hunting dog catches my eye. It's an ugly picture even without the heavy gilt frame, but there's something about the overt ostentation that pushes it to the next level.

I blink as another painting in a similarly heavy frame comes into focus. Then another. And another.

I almost gasp as I realize the truth of what I'm looking at. There's one more thing Birdie knew that I didn't, one more thing she hid from me from the start. Her first task upon arriving on this island was to find and test the family silver to see if it was gold.

Because if there's one way to ensure that no one finds a giant box of gold coins, it's to hide it in plain sight. It's to change its shape and put it on display.

"What is it, Madame Eleanor?" Sid asks, her voice yanking me back to a sense of reality. "Are you all right? You look as though . . . Well, as though you've seen a ghost. Do you know who hired her? Did she tell you?"

I don't answer. My mouth is too dry, my pulse too fluttering. On the one hand, I've accomplished exactly what I promised to do in coming to Airgead Island—I've located the gold. It's here in this room, shining down on us as we commune with the dead. It's been here all along, adhering to the rules of that silly curse and everything it threatens.

On the other hand, there's no way I can say as much out loud. The one thing I haven't revealed to this gathering—the one thing it's too dangerous to say out loud—is that because Birdie discovered too much, or because the person who hired her didn't like the way she was going about the process, they killed her. They killed her the exact same way they killed Glenn. If someone in this room was willing to hire—and murder—Birdie in pursuit of the gold, there's no saying what they'll do once they realize I've found it.

Kill *me*, most likely. Possibly everyone in this castle. There's no way they're getting their hands on it otherwise. Not now that I've revealed the truth to everyone in this room.

"We have to get off this island," I say. It's a mere echo of what I've been trying to drive home this entire time, but my voice is firm with resolve this time. As long as we're stuck here, we're all at risk. We can't call for help. We can't put Birdie in the hands of capable forensic scientists. Accidents and illnesses can strike without risk, and the curse blamed for the whole. "I don't care what we have to do. It's not safe for any of us here."

"You didn't answer her question," Otis says. His expression

has taken on a keen intensity, the brutish lines of his face deepened by exhaustion and grief and maybe something more. "Did she tell you who hired her?"

"No," I say, unable—and unwilling—to lie while so many lives are at risk. "But I'm not kidding about the rest. We have to find a way to safety, even if it means one of us has to swim to Barra."

I glance around the room once more. This time, I don't see anything worth note—and I mean that literally. In the corner where Beast sits and calmly cleans her fur, there's only an abandoned ball of yarn. Jaime and Ferguson must have used the distraction of my discovery as an opportunity to slip away.

"The boys—" I say as I jolt to my feet. All the blood from my body drains and pools in my gut. "Elspeth, did you see where they went?"

"Oh, dear," she says, but not in a way that signals alarm. "I warned them to stay close, but you know how boys will be . . ."

I do know it, unfortunately. I also know that I'm the only person who realizes just how much danger the boys are in. The one thing—the only thing—that Birdie White was successful at from the start was believing in me. If I'm going to pick up the reins and finish this for her, then I'm going to have to do the same.

Starting—and ending—with my vision of a little boy drowning at sea.

Chapter 17

"There's nothing to be so upset about, Madame Eleanor. It's a shame they ran off the way they did, but they won't come to any harm." Elspeth shakes her head. "I might not be able to see the future, but I can see that much."

As much as I'd love to believe her, I have too much experience with visions of death to accept her words at face value. "I'm sure they are, but I need to see them with my own eyes."

"And so you will, once you've had a nice cup of tea."

If there's a polite way to refuse such kindly maternalism, it's not something I've learned in my lifetime. "Elspeth, *please*. I know it sounds silly, but this is a matter of life and death."

For what is probably the first time since I've met the woman, Elspeth allows an expression of annoyance to cross her face. I know what she's thinking—that we were all in the gilded salon together, that no one could have harmed those boys without a witness—but that's only part of the story.

"Whoever hired Birdie might think the boys know more than they let on," I say—*plead*, really, my voice cracking near the end. "I didn't want to say anything during the séance, but we need to consider the likelihood that Glenn, Harvey, and Birdie were all killed in pursuit of the gold. We can't let Jaime and Ferguson be next."

Something about either my words or my tone finally breaks through. Elspeth sucks in a sharp breath.

"There's a whistle hanging by the back door," she says. "If you stand outside and blow, they'll head back from wherever they've run off to."

"You want me to whistle for them? Like dogs?"

She nods. "It's not orthodox, but it works."

I lose no time in pulling a thin, silver whistle from a hook near the kitchen door. How they're supposed to hear it over the gale of the storm is more than I can say. The wind whips around me in a howling twist, my skirt flapping against my legs and my hair in tangles.

As soon as I bring the whistle to my lips and blow, I understand the reasoning. This sucker is *loud*. The sharp whine carries over the rocks and past the waves, adding to the tempestuous backdrop with its mournful cry. No animal could make this sound; no human, either.

A ghost could, though. Or a woman frantic to find a pair of rambunctious little boys.

"How long does this usually take?" I poke my head into the door to ask.

"Not long. They're never out of earshot."

I have no idea how long Elspeth considers earshot to be, but I count to two hundred without catching a glimpse of anyone. Bringing the whistle to my lips again, I blow harder. If it sounded like a ghost before, it's a whole cacophony of spirits this time. Anyone sailing nearby is likely to think that Airgead has succumbed to the curse, the entire island falling dead and dormant through Gloriana's rage.

After the next two hundred seconds pass by, Elspeth joins me at the door, wiping her hands on a dishrag.

"This isn't like them," she says, and puts her hand out for the whistle. She gives it only a cursory wipe before placing it to her mouth and repeating my efforts.

The sound of footsteps a short distance away cause both of us to relax—until we catch sight of the tall figure trotting up to us. "I checked down at the cavern," Nicholas says without preamble. I haven't yet had an opportunity to tell him about everything I've discovered or suspect, but the nice thing about him is that he doesn't need to know. I want those boys found, which means he'll move heaven and earth to find them.

He nods at the whistle in Elspeth's hand. "Is that what they normally answer to?"

The sight of Nicholas also putting forth his best efforts to track down her grandsons has Elspeth growing even more concerned. She blinks up at him. "Ever since they were wee ones. It's never failed to bring them running. They're good boys. No one here would hurt them."

A grandparent's doting fondness isn't a thing to be implicitly trusted, but I find myself agreeing with Elspeth. It's difficult to imagine anyone on this island taking things that far. Not Sid, not Ashley, and not . . .

I stop, remembering the boys' inherent fear of Otis.

"Perhaps they're hiding inside the castle," Nicholas suggests before I can go too far down that road. "They wouldn't hear the whistle if that were the case."

"They're not ones to stay indoors if they can help it," Elspeth says, worry rendering her voice wobbly. "Usually because I find a way to put them to work. Madame Eleanor, you don't think—?"

I don't bother answering. We all know what I'm thinking because it's a sentiment we share. I *knew* we should have gotten them off this island days ago. I *knew* it was too risky to keep them on hand.

"Oughtn't we to ask the rest of the party to join in the

search?" Elspeth reaches out and grips my arm with an intensity that makes me wince. "The more people we have out looking, the faster we'll find them."

"No." Nicholas says it for me. The familiar lines of his face are pulled taut with worry, his expression growing more troubled the longer we spend here. "Until we know who we can trust, it's best to keep the search small."

This affects Elspeth more strongly than all the rest. As Nicholas takes himself off to continue his search, I take her by the hand. "It's not a big island," I soothe. "If they're still here, we'll find them."

I can't imagine what made me choose my words so clumsily unless it's the fact that I'm just as worried about those children as she is.

"If they're still here?" she echoes, blanching. "Where else would they be?"

I've already plunged my foot in, so I see no use in backing out now. "I warned you about my vision, remember? I told you it wasn't safe."

"But the curse has nothing to do with them," Elspeth protests, though much feebler than before. Her nerves seem to be getting the better of her, her whole body shaking as the minutes tick by. "It's only the Stewarts who are affected by it. I don't understand. Why would it bother with the boys?"

"It's not the curse I fear. And it's not the curse you should be worried about, either. The gold is safe enough where it is. What we need to watch out for is someone who would be willing to go to great lengths to get it."

When she glances up, her gaze is sharp. "What do you mean, the gold is safe?"

I see no reason to lie. The more I can impress upon Elspeth the idea that our villain is of human rather than supernatural origin, the greater the chances that she'll tie those boys to her apron strings and refuse to let them out of her sight.

"I mean, I know where it is. I found it."

"The two gold coins?" she asks sharply. "The ones you lost?"

There's something about the shrill quality in her voice that gives me pause. It's not the sound of a woman distressed for her lost grandsons; it's the sound of a woman who's being confronted with an unpleasant truth.

I've been confronted with enough of those in my lifetime to *know*.

"No," I say, choosing my words carefully. "I mean the entire treasure. I found it."

"No." That's all she says—that one word, that one *no*.

"Yes," I counter as the next piece of the puzzle slips into place. "But there's no need for me to tell you, is there? You already know where it is."

"Where are my grandsons?" Elspeth demands.

"I have no idea," I admit. "How long have you known about the gold?"

"What have you done with them?"

I shake my head. "How long, Elspeth?"

She doesn't answer me, but that's okay. I don't need her to. Her silence confirms everything I suspect. After all, she said it herself during one of our first encounters—she's the caretaker here, the keeper of Airgead Island. As long as she lives, she has a home to call her own . . . a home in which an entire room is gilded with pirate gold worth enough to buy half a dozen such islands.

I take a wide step back. Since I'm on the side of the kitchen without the stove, pots, pans, and knives, there's nothing I can grab to defend myself. The closest thing I can find is a broom, but it's so old that the wood looks as though it would snap at the first sign of struggle.

Still, I reach out and grip the splintery handle. If I can't take one sweet, old, murderous lady down with a broom, then I'm not worthy of the name Eleanor Wilde.

"You took those coins from me that day on the boat, didn't you? Smashed me over the head and stole them?"

"I don't know what you're talking about," Elspeth says. "I'd never hurt a living soul."

I take another step backward, my shoulder blades brushing against the stone wall. There's nothing left for me to do but raise the broom. Somewhere in the dim recesses of my mind, I know that this doesn't make sense—that if Elspeth knew about the gold all along, then she couldn't have been the one to hire Birdie to find it—but my fight-or-flight responses have kicked in by now. I care less about her motives and more about the fact that we've all been duped.

"You won't get away with this," I warn. "Sid and Ashley will discover the truth eventually. So will Otis. He won't be willing to give up all that gold without a fight."

"What makes you think he doesn't already know?" Elspeth counters.

This remark takes me so much aback that I don't register the sound of footsteps coming down the hall. They're lighter than those of Nicholas, with a random, frantic pace. They're also accompanied by the squelch of sodden shoes. I'm about to call out and warn whoever it is, but Elspeth releases a sigh of relief.

Not Otis, I pray, and am rewarded for my piety by the sight of a small, damp head poking in the door.

"Ferguson!" Elspeth cries as she runs to her grandson with her arms outstretched. "There you are. You'll be the death of me. Where did you and your brother go? I told you not to wander off."

In the normal way of things, this return to the scolding, loving grandmother would have had me heaving a sigh of relief, if not yet relinquishing the makeshift weapon in my hand. But there's something about Ferguson's upturned face, so despairing, so *alarmed*, that I throw the broom and drop to my knees in front of him.

"Where is he?" I demand. "Please tell me he didn't go in the water."

His face screws up, and huge, droplet-sized tears start trickling down his cheeks. "I told him not to, Madame Eleanor. Honest, I did. But we've been working on a raft for months and it was finally ready to go and he said you needed to find help—"

"No," moans Elspeth. She staggers where she stands, and with such force that I have no choice but to hold her up. Embracing a woman who lately threatened me might not be the wisest course of action, but I have no other choice. She looks as though she, like Harvey Renault, might die of a heart attack right here and now.

She turns on me with a look of intense loathing, but I don't dare let her go.

"What have you done?" she demands. "What will happen to my grandson?"

If there's anything I can do to help it? Nothing.

I shuffle Elspeth over to the nearest chair and drop her unceremoniously into it. Without waiting to hear her input on my plans, I turn to Ferguson. Shrugging out of my shawl and kicking off my shoes, I make one simple and terrifying request.

"Show me which way he went. There's no time to find the others."

Several thoughts clamor for precedence as I follow Ferguson out into the dark, swirling, *freezing* air of the Outer Hebrides in November. Elspeth's knowledge of the gold's whereabouts is up there, as is the fact that she named Otis as a coconspirator. That I still don't know who hired Birdie is also high on the list.

But nothing compares to the idea that Jaime is on that raft because of me. Cold, alone, most likely scared out of his mind—if not worse. The rational part of my brain tells me to wait for Nicholas, warns me that to plunge into the ocean with all of two dozen swimming lessons under my belt is madness.

The rational part of my brain, however, has nothing on my heart. There's already been too much pain—too much death—in this place. I won't lose someone else.

"Ferguson, I need you to find Nicholas and tell him what you just told me," I say as I reach the end of the dock. It looks ominous with the wreckage of Otis's boat still moored to it, but I focus less on that pile and more on trying to gauge the distance between me and the raft in the distance. It's difficult to make out anything except for the relentless rain and the small, bobbing speck that's carrying Jaime, but I figure it can't be more than a football field or two. "Let him know I'm going after your brother."

Ferguson's lower lip wobbles, and a splash of something that might be rain but is more likely a tear hits his upper lip. "He's going to be okay, isn't he? You can swim out to get him?"

I've spent most of my life lying to people for my own ends. This time, the lie is one hundred percent for someone else.

"Yes," I promise. "I'm an excellent swimmer. I'll have him safe and sound in no time."

Ferguson accepts me at my word. With a squaring of his shoulders and complete confidence in my ability to swim through ocean currents like a mermaid, he turns and dashes back to the castle to find my backup.

I wish I could say that my own actions are as assured, but my hands are shaking, and it feels as though a rock has lodged itself in the pit of my stomach. There's just enough time for me to hope that it won't weigh me down any more than is necessary before I force myself into a diving position and plunge off the dock.

There are levels of cold in this world, and I like to think that I've experienced quite a few of them. For example, the chill of a fall morning in Sussex is less severe than the windswept shores of the Outer Hebrides, but both are charming in their own way. What I feel as I hit the water, however, isn't the least bit charming. This isn't cold. It's bone-chilling. If I were to place an icebox in the center of Antarctica and turn an air conditioner on high, I doubt it would touch the sensation that envelops me. For the first twenty seconds, I'm afraid that the numbing cold will literally kill me—not because of the temperature, but because my limbs are in such a state of shock that they don't seem to be working. The water freezes my muscles into immobility and sucks any of the remaining oxygen out of my lungs. It's more painful than I expect, too, like a deep punch to my solar plexus.

But then I hear her—not Winnie, my champion and beloved sister, but Birdie.

You think this is cold? she asks with a laugh. *You should try being dead.*

It's enough to get my heart pumping and my body moving again. I won't die this easily. Not if it means I'm going to end up where she is, with nothing better to do than taunt every defenseless medium who happens by.

Drawing on the buoyancy that's genetically coded into my bones, I allow myself to rise to the surface. I don't go nearly as fast as I'd hoped, but all that swim practice has strengthened my lungs. As soon as my head hits the air, I suck in a deep and grateful breath that's only 50 percent saltwater. Angling my body in what I hope is the correct direction, I begin a slow, painful breaststroke toward the raft.

The exercise does wonders in warming my body. I know, deep down, that this feeling won't last, and that the moment I stop moving is the moment I'm likely to stop swimming forever, but I don't allow myself to dwell on it. I can't. It's all I can do to fight the current that's threatening to pull me under.

Fortunately, I seem to have caught the water at slack tide. Although there's much more to the pull of the waves than I was expecting, it takes me only a few minutes to make it past the break. Once I pass that boundary, the water becomes less violent, more like a cauldron set to simmer rather than boil. I'm even able to pause long enough to make a quick survey of my surroundings. I could wish for more sunlight to guide me, but I haven't spent the past week in a dark castle for nothing. That bobbing mass to my right is the raft, I'm sure of it.

Either that, or a shark. I'm heading that direction regardless.

Distance and time stop meaning much after a few minutes. So too does the cold and the wet and everything except for the repetitive motions of my arms and legs. Unfortunately, I don't seem to have gained on the raft by much more than a few yards. The same forces that are propelling me out to the vast nothingness of the ocean are doing their best to send Jaime on his way, too.

As much as I try to subdue the image of his little body sinking through the waves, it's my constant companion throughout the ordeal. It keeps my limbs moving even when exhaustion threatens to pull me under, forces me to breathe deeply and regularly even as waves crash up over my head.

Fatigue and fear have started to set in when I see the boat coming to our rescue. It moves quickly and effortlessly through the waves, covering more area in a matter of seconds than I have in the entire past ten minutes. With a shout that's immediately drowned in a mouthful of saltwater, I lift my arm and wave. I have no idea how or where Nicholas was able to track down a rescue vessel this quickly, but I'm not about to question it. Especially when a tight, painful spasm in my calf threatens to overtake me.

"I'm here!" I cry, though I doubt Nicholas hears me. I'm forced to shift to the side in favor of my cramping calf, but now that I know help is on the way, my panic starts to ebb. "Get to Jaime first. I'll be fine for a few more minutes."

I may as well not have spoken. Not only is it futile to try and shout over the sound of the boat's engine, but it's already making a beeline straight for the raft. All I can do is struggle to stay afloat and watch as Jaime's rescue is enacted before me.

Except . . . The cramp in my leg intensifies, forcing me to cry out and dip under the swell of an oncoming wave. The murky gray-blue of the ocean is all I can *literally* see, but the image of that boat is bright and clear in my mind's eye.

That doesn't look like anyone I recognize piloting the vessel. McGee, maybe? Or, if I'm very lucky, a member of Her Majesty's Coastguard?

I manage to break up through a wave. My lungs hurt almost as much as my leg does by the time I return to the sweet, oxygenated surface, but I don't dwell on it. I'm too busy trying to make out the details of the rescue. As if aware that I'm watching, the captain of the small fishing boat turns to face me. His form seems tall from this distance and, considering how my head is starting to swirl from the lack of air, particularly ominous. It's impossible for me to make out his features, but I could almost swear that a dark, mocking smirk crosses his face.

A devil in his sneer? I think.

There's no opportunity for me to discover whether or not I'm right. Just as I watch the figure help Jaime from the raft, my other leg starts to seize up. I'm half afraid that Birdie is going to talk me through the act of following the light, but that's one mythology I'm happy to put to rest.

There is no light. There is no tunnel.

There's just dark and cold and the burning sensation of all the air leaving my lungs.

Chapter 18

Like Sleeping Beauty, I awaken to a kiss.

It's not a particularly good kiss. After a year of tender embraces in the arms of a man like Nicholas Hartford III, I've grown accustomed to a certain amount of finesse. I like a little pressure, a little persuasion, and a lot of passion.

None of those are taking place this time. The man with his lips pressed against my mouth is rough and brutal, and he seems insistent on pushing all the air from his own lungs into mine. When a tight band of pressure releases from around my chest and a splurge of seawater fills my mouth, I suddenly realize why.

With a splutter and a cough, I empty what feels like the entire contents of the ocean from my lungs. My whole body is shaking with cold and adrenaline, but one thing I know for sure—I'm alive.

"Jaime," I croak, my throat raw.

"I'm here, Madame Eleanor," a small voice says. It sounds just as miserable as I feel, but I'm too grateful to find the boy alive to care. Even though my limbs feel weighted down with water and fatigue, I reach out and pull him into my arms.

He's wrapped in a blanket, but that doesn't seem to prevent his small body from being wracked by shivers. His teeth chatter, and his lips are blue, and I rub my hands up and down his body to try and get his blood pumping. That's when I realize that the shivering isn't coming from him so much as it is from me.

"Here." A heavy wool blanket falls over my shoulders. "You'll catch your death if we don't get you warmed up soon."

I don't recognize either the voice or the man it issues from. That he's my savior, I know without question. He's decked out in a waterproof slicker, a hood over his head to protect him from the spray. He's an older gentleman, tall like a smokestack, and straight-backed despite his age.

"Thank you so much for coming to our rescue," I say. "A few more minutes, and I fear we both would have been lost."

The man's only reply is a grunt. Since he's steering the small powerboat back toward Airgead Island, I'm willing to forgive his taciturnity.

I turn my attention to the boy in my arms instead. "What were you thinking?" I demand, wrapping Jaime in an even tighter hug. "You could have been lost or frozen or—*worse*."

The boy wriggles in an attempt to get out of my hug, but he gives up after a few seconds. I think he must realize that the embrace is more for me than him.

"You said you needed help," he says, a slight whistle in his speech from his newly gapped teeth. "I went to find some. Nanna says you should always help others, even if it's scary."

An interesting sentiment from a woman currently hoarding a room full of gold, but I let that pass.

"And so you did," I reassure him. "You rescued us all."

Our savior at the helm grunts.

"You, too, of course," I say. "But you're not going the right way. The dock is on the other side of the island."

"We're not going to the island."

The cold and recent oxygen deprivation have slowed down my responses, so it takes a moment before this remark registers. When it does, I find I'm not wholly against it.

"Yes," I say through my chattering teeth. "Maybe that's for the best. I can call the police, bring reinforcements back with me. But I'm not sure I understand. Who are you? And how did you know to come pick us up?"

"That doesn't concern you," he says with another grunt. Although there seem to be a lot of guttural noises emanating from his throat, the accent is a cultured one. For some reason, I find this more alarming than the fact that we've now completely passed Airgead Island by. Seeing the castle in the daytime—even a daytime as overcast as this one—is a new experience for me. It looks just as forlorn and ominous as it did the night I arrived, but beautiful, too.

"Are you taking us to Barra?" I ask, a panicked waver in my voice. Considering how close Jaime and I are to hypothermia, we don't want to delay going ashore for too long.

"That depends."

I'm almost afraid to ask. "On what?"

He turns toward me. His face is shadowed by the hood of his rain slicker, but I can still tell that his expression isn't a kind one. "On whether or not you give me what I want."

There isn't enough room on the boat for me to back away, but every instinct I have tells me to do just that. There are few things I have to offer a man like this one. Since I look like the bedraggled remains of week-old seaweed, I doubt it's my virtue he's after. I obviously have no money on my person, and my worldly possessions are few.

The one thing I do have in abundance, however, is information.

With a gulp, I allow my gaze to move from his face down his body. As if aware of my scrutiny, he holds himself perfectly still. I skip over his chest and his hands, work my way down his legs . . . and stop only when I reach his feet.

Oxford wing tips.

My gaze snaps back up to his face, which has gone from not kind to downright sinister.

"Harvey?" I ask, barely able to credit the sound of my own voice. "Harvey Renault?"

Either his laughter is silent, or it's so soft that I can't hear it over the rush of blood to my head. It's deeply disturbing either way.

"You *are* good, aren't you?" he says. "Birdie was right about that, at least."

Since my arms are still wrapped around Jaime, he's able to tell that my whole body has gone rigid with tension. He whimpers softly, but I tighten my hold in a way that signals reassurance. Having come this far to save him, I'm not about to let any harm come to him now.

I hope.

"Birdie was right about a lot of things," I return, forcing my voice to remain calm. "Except, it would seem, your death."

He returns his attention back to steering the boat with another of those soundless laughs. "Clever of me, wasn't it? Or did you think that was her idea? I hate to disillusion you, but Bridget Wimpole-White wasn't nearly as smart as she wanted you to think."

Ha. As if I hadn't known that from the start.

"She was smart enough not to trust you," I counter.

He releases another of those grunts and turns the boat sharply to the right. I'm grateful for the distraction that the driving forces on him, as it gives me a chance to start sifting through the barrage of facts pelting me like raindrops.

Harvey didn't die on that train. Harvey didn't die on that train, and Birdie knew it.

"Was I supposed to be in awe of her ability to predict death? Was I supposed to think her the real deal and cower in the face of such prowess?" A thought occurs to me. "You broke the generator and stole our luggage, didn't you? And fed her information. You wanted us to think her omniscient."

He doesn't answer, which I take to be as good as an assent. Besides, it makes sense. The more powerful we believed Birdie to be, the more likely we were to buy into her nonsense. It was the perfect cover for finding the gold. Not only did holding us in her thrall give her an opportunity to search the house at her leisure, but it ensured that if someone—say, Elspeth—did know where the gold was hidden, they would be more likely to give up the location in their fright to be free of the curse.

Except . . . it hadn't worked. Elspeth has never been afraid of the curse. Otis isn't scared of it, either, even though Harvey took pains to ensure that he'd be on the island with the rest of us. Which was why Birdie, in her desperation to get results, was forced to turn to me instead.

For all the good that did me.

"I learned my lesson the first time," Harvey says. He cuts the engine to the boat so suddenly that Jaime and I are thrown off balance. We stumble but are so weighted down by our wet blankets that we don't fall overboard. "So don't think I'm going to offer you what I offered her. I'm done letting a pack of fake mediums call the shots, just like I was done letting Glenn and those stupid kids of his sit on a treasure they have no intention of spending. You'll tell me where the gold is, or I'm throwing that boy over the side of the boat and watching him drown."

Jaime whimpers and clings tightly to my waist, his head pressed against my side. My heart wrings to feel it. Like the child he is, he's averting his face from the monster in hopes that it will make him go away.

"What makes you think I know where it is?" I ask in an effort to buy myself some time. A way out of here is beginning to take shape in my mind, but it's not a pleasant one. "If you couldn't force the location out of Glenn while he was alive, why would I be able to do it now that you've murdered him?"

Harvey takes a step toward us. The entire boat rocks in response, as if it, too, is quaking in fear of what comes next. "Call it a hunch. You're a smart woman and an observant one. You haven't spent a week on that island without learning a thing or two about its inhabitants."

No, I haven't. Nor have I spent a lifetime dabbling in the paranormal without learning a thing or two about myself. To the outside world, I might not be as renowned or celebrated as Birdie White, but that's okay. I don't need to be. My confidence will probably never match hers, and I can only dream of being as capably devious someday. For now, I only know what I can do. I only know what I have seen.

I also know that what I can do and what I can see are just one part of a much bigger picture—a much bigger plan.

"Jaime, can you swim?" I whisper, my mouth grazing the boy's ear.

He whimpers but nods. It's not a very reassuring response, but it's all I have. With a silent call out to every protective power in the universe, I yank the blanket from his body. Waiting only for Harvey to halt in sudden surprise, I place my hands on Jaime's back and push.

"Then *go*," I say as he plunges into the ocean. His body falls in the exact position from my vision, his limbs immobile, his head disappearing under the waves. My every instinct tells me to jump in after him, but I stand my ground.

Turning to face my would-be rescuer, I swallow and force a smile.

"Now," I say in what I hope is the same evil nonchalance he used to threaten the boy's life in the first place. "What were you saying about finding that gold?"

Chapter 19

"You're crazy." Harvey stares at me with a look of surprise, his mouth agape and a glint of what I could almost swear is fear in his eyes. "Are you crazy? What did you do that for?"

I wish I could peek over my shoulder to see if Jaime has surfaced, but I don't dare. To do so would ruin what little upper hand I've managed to gain.

I shrug. "I don't like to be threatened."

Harvey brushes past me and peers out over the water. He doesn't appear to be alarmed by the sight of the boy surviving his fall, which has the effect of alarming *me*. Surely Jaime must have surfaced by now?

Harvey gives a short laugh. "I should have approached you at the outset. I was sure the other one would be more easily bought."

I don't bother telling him how correct he was in that original assumption. There's not a dollar amount in the world that could justify the killing that's been done in pursuit of that gold—not in my eyes and not, I think, in Birdie's. Once she realized the true state of affairs on Airgead Island, she was quick to take steps to rectify her error, to push me toward the truth in her stead.

"How much did you offer her?" I ask, and not just because I need to draw his attention away from the water.

"Fifteen percent. For you, I'll double it."

"What's the doctor's cut?"

Harvey gives another of those silent laughs. "Fulstead? That old bleater wouldn't know a medical emergency if it bit him on the nose. Come to think of it, he didn't. He took one look at me clutching my chest on the floor of that train and gave me up for dead."

"But—"

"That man hasn't had a working medical license in twenty years, Madame Eleanor. Everyone calls him 'doctor' out of respect, but no one who wants their loved ones to live calls him in. Well, except for other relics like Elspeth and Glenn."

That makes sense, too, now that I think about it. I've always felt that Airgead Island is a sort of time capsule—an ancient place run by ancient people who adhere to ancient superstitions and beliefs. Elspeth in her faded and timeless blue dress, McGee in a fisherman's sweater that could have been woven and knitted three hundred years ago, the pair of them standing watch over a castle that refuses to evolve past the sixteenth century.

And for what? To serve as a stone fortress standing watch over a cursed fortune for all eternity?

In a way, I'd be doing the Stewarts a favor by telling Harvey where the gold is and letting him loose to steal it at will. It's the easiest solution, the neatest way to free them from the curse's power. Once the gold is gone, they can move on with their lives, happy in the knowledge that justice will be done to their father's murderer in the form of Gloriana burdening someone else for a change.

"Forty percent," Harvey says, as if sensing the trend of my thoughts. "That's as high as I'm willing to go."

As tempting as it might be to dream about all the ways I could spend that kind of money, it's only a fleeting thought. This man has done terrible things in pursuit of that gold. He killed his friend. He killed *my* friend.

Do you really mean it? I had no idea you felt that way.

I grin. It's a slow and careful grin, more for Birdie's benefit than Harvey's, but I have the felicity of seeing him quaver at the sight of it.

"Or what?" I counter. "You'll poison me the way you did Glenn and Birdie? You'll throw me over the side of this boat and watch me drown alongside that little boy?"

He's understandably confused by this sudden turnabout. "You murdered that boy, not me. And I'll tell everyone—see if I don't. You pushed him as callously as if you'd been planning it all along."

"I did," I agree. "And I'd do it again in a heartbeat."

A small head pokes up on the other side of the boat, directly behind Harvey. Jaime looks cold and wet, but he flashes me his gap-toothed smile despite everything. It had been my intention for him to swim to safety rather than around in circles, but this works, too.

"Yet you have the audacity to stand there looking at me as though *I'm* the bad guy?"

"Yes, I do," I say. Jaime is reaching for one of the emergency oars on the side of the boat, but his movements are slowed by the cold and his desire to stay hidden. I do my best to keep Harvey occupied—a thing accomplished with one of the easiest and most difficult things in the world. The truth. "See, the one thing you don't realize is that I saw a vision of you on the train that day. The red car, the spilled tea, the shoes—it was all real, and it was all coming from me. The only thing I didn't see was your death. I just assumed that was the outcome, since I was going off what Birdie told me. That phone call Ashley received the first night from the station—it was you, wasn't it? Informing him of your own death? You wanted to make sure everyone was good and scared before we started the search for the gold."

"So what?" Harvey's face is starting to turn red, his burgeoning anger at odds with his desire to placate me. Without me, he knows he has no chance of finding the treasure. "What does that have to do with anything?"

"It worked," I say. "I *was* scared, but not for the reasons you think. I was mostly terrified of myself, of my newfound ability to predict death."

His look of disbelief tells me what he thinks of that newfound ability.

I allow a smile to spread across my face. "But I was wrong. You're alive. I didn't see a vision of death. I saw a moment in time, a piece of the plot. That's all."

By this time, Jaime has managed to pull the oar all the way out and is holding it like—dare I say it?—a pirate's sword. I have no idea what part of Harvey he plans to hit with it, but at this point, I'm not picky.

"I assumed when I had a similar vision of Jaime that I was seeing his death, too. But I'm not that good. I doubt I ever will be." I draw a deep breath and brace myself, my feet planted firmly as Jaime prepares to thrust. "To be honest, I'm kind of glad. I don't want to see people die. If the universe wants to give me an occasional glimpse of a lottery ticket, I'm not going to turn my nose up at it, but my ambitions stop there."

Harvey has no idea what I'm talking about, but it doesn't matter. With a lunge that would have done the pirates of Stewarts past proud, Jaime drives the oar into Harvey's back. It's not enough to knock him overboard or even to bring him to his knees, but it startles him—oh, how it startles him.

An old man with a weak heart. An old man who's already suffered two coronaries. An old man who recently murdered his childhood friend for something as meaningless as money.

There's nothing I can do to save him. Even if I were medically trained enough to stop a heart attack after it's already begun, rescuing Jaime from the water takes every last bit of strength I have. I heave him the rest of the way on board before falling into a collapse, both of us clutched together, drawing what comfort and heat we can.

"You're okay now, Jaime," I murmur into his ear, holding him so tight that it feels as though my frozen bones will crack. "He can't hurt you now."

"You mean it?" he asks. "You're not just saying that to make me feel better?"

I shake my head and hold him tighter, watching as the clouds above us begin to open up. It's the first real sign of hope I've seen since I got here, and I welcome it with my whole heart. Birdie White might have had a good working relationship with her old friend Death, but I know now that my job is a different one.

I'm not here to prophesy for the dead. I'm here to care for the living.

Chapter 20

Fortunately for the outcome of this tale, Jaime knows how to pilot a boat.

In addition to being unable to stop a heart attack from killing a man, I also seem to have missed the course on starting an engine and plunging a fishing boat through oceanic waves. It takes a very small, very wet, very resolute eight-year-old to do it for me.

"See, Madame Eleanor?" Jaime says through teeth that chatter so much I'm afraid he's going to lose the whole mouthful. "I told you I could get us back."

"So you did," I agree, my own jaw clenched so tight that I have to force the words out. "You saved the day."

"*We* saved it," he corrects me.

Those words mean a lot more than he realizes, especially once he brings the boat up to the dock. From the looks on the faces of those gathered there, I'm not going to get much else in the way of gratitude.

"Eleanor, you perfect *idiot*," Nicholas says as soon as Jaime cuts the engine. He practically pounces on me, yanking me out of the boat and propelling me into his arms. "Do you have any idea how stupid it was to go after him like that?"

"My boy! My poor boy!" cries Elspeth, doing much the same to her grandson. "You're soaked to the bone. You'll get pneumonia. Or hypothermia. Or both."

"Tell them it wasn't my fault," Ferguson cries. He's looking both chastised and sullen, his face drooping so much he resembles a basset hound. "Tell them I had nothing to do with it."

These recriminations might have continued unabated, if not for a low cough from Otis. "I hate to interrupt when you're all so busy, but can I ask why Harvey Renault's corpse is on the bottom of this boat?"

The answer to this question doesn't come from either me or Jaime. At just that moment, Ashley bursts out from the hidden stairwell, his hair plastered against his forehead and his velvet smoking jacket ruined from the rain. "I saw it all!" he says as he tumbles our direction. "I was watching through the telescope the entire time. Madame Eleanor pushed Jaime out of the boat. She tried to kill him. And when that didn't work, she killed Harvey Renault instead."

I groan, but the sound is swallowed by a fresh wave of reproaches and questions. Whether because I succumb to a maidenly swoon for the first time in my life or because I, too, am about to come down with some combination of pneumonia and hypothermia, my knees give way underneath me.

"We need to get these wet clothes off them," announces Dr. Fulstead. "Get them dry. Cover them in blankets. Hot tea. In that order."

Even though I know about his lack of medical competence now, I've never heard such wise and wonderful words.

"Yes," I manage. "Blankets. Tea."

My one-word responses seem to awaken a sense of justice in my audience. As if only now noticing that I'm tiptoeing up to death's door, the censure changes to concern. As much as I'd like to fall into it, embracing the hero's welcome as my due, I turn to Otis first.

"He didn't die on the train."

Much to my relief, Otis understands me. "Yes, thank you. I gathered as much."

"He killed your uncle."

"I'm starting to realize that, as well."

"He killed Birdie, too."

"I'm not surprised. I was tempted once or twice myself."

"Let's take this inside, if you please," Nicholas says, his voice gruff. It rumbles through me, adding to my shivers. The thought of trotting all the way up those stairs, of lifting the dead weights of my legs over and over again, almost causes me to go off in that swoon again. Sensing this, Nicholas swoops me into his arms. "This is the second time I've had to carry you up these stairs, you know."

"I could make it, if I had to," I say, my voice only partially cracking. His body is so warm, so *comforting*. "I could always crawl."

"The devil you could."

I snuggle closer and allow myself the luxury of his embrace. Birdie had been right about a lot of things—too many for my comfort, if the truth be told—but this was one thing she got wrong. On the train, she told me that women of our profession are better off living and working alone, relying on no one but ourselves. And in a way, it's true. In order to become a *real* success, I'd have to be an island, a rock, a tower of strength capable of standing for centuries despite the battering of the seas.

But that's not what I want. I'm no Sid Stewart, it's true, but I'm no Birdie White, either.

I'm Eleanor Wilde, and that's good enough for me.

"But I don't understand." Sid hovers over me, her expression one of mingled anxiety and awe. "How could you be sure that Jaime wouldn't die when you pushed him into the ocean?"

"I didn't *push* him," I protest. Now that I'm wrapped up like a mummy and reclining on the couch in—where else?—the gilded salon, I'm feeling much warmer. And much better able to defend myself. "I gave him a small nudge, and I made sure to ask if he could swim first."

It's obvious from her look of anxiety that she doesn't find this comforting.

"Yes, but where did you want him to go? Back to the island? To Barra? What on earth were you thinking?"

As if in response, the small, purring bundle on my lap shifts. I manage to get a hand out from under my blankets and settle Freddie back to sleepy contentment. She hasn't left my side since Nicholas brought me in here and laid me down, her body heat doing wonders to warm me up, both inside and out.

My pet, my familiar, my connection to the other realm.

With an inward sigh, I realize what I have to do. Commanding Birdie and Winnie to silence—and willing Nicholas to stop laughing at me from across the room—I place my hand to my temple and do what I do best.

"I had a vision, a presentiment. In a flash, I saw what I had to do to bring Harvey Renault to justice. I knew Jaime would be safe as long as my protective cloak was over him."

"Ohhh," Sid says, falling to the nearest chair in relief. "I understand. It was a magic thing."

Sure. Why not? Stranger things have happened this day.

"So Birdie and Harvey were working together all along?" Sid asks. "They killed Father and faked Harvey's death and tried to make us give up the secret of the gold's location?"

She looks a lot like I feel: exhausted. Soon after the rest of us took shelter inside the castle, Otis was able to use the radio on Harvey's boat to get a mayday call out. McGee is on his way with a fleet of strong men, but it'll take them a few hours to get here. Jaime was bundled off to bed and put under the strict guard of Dr. Fulstead, but I don't have any such luck. I'm facing what amounts to a firing squad. Everyone is on edge and full of questions.

"I don't think Birdie was in on your father's death," I explain. "Once she realized how far Harvey had taken things, she started to have second thoughts. It was why she was working so hard to feed me information—to force the truth to light as well as find the gold."

"As if we have any idea where it is," Ashley says. He's sitting with one leg crossed elegantly over the other, the slight damp of his hair the only indication that he's exerted any effort today. "We wouldn't have gone through all this trouble in the first place if we had."

Elspeth and Otis share a look that doesn't escape my notice.

"About the gold," I say.

Their look transfers itself to me.

"It's gone."

As I expect, this news is greeted in an outburst of emotion. Ashley and Sid are outraged, Nicholas curious, and Otis downright perplexed. Only Elspeth regards me with anything approaching understanding.

Holding up my hand, I command the room to silence. "Birdie took it. She found it the first night she was here."

I beg your pardon?

"It was in the wine cellar all along," I say. "It was the first place she looked—she was pretending to get a bottle of port at the time. She left that one coin in the box so you'd think she was still looking for it. That gave her time to make arrangements for its transportation without anyone being the wiser. She double-crossed Harvey. She never had any intention of sharing it with him."

That is a bald-faced lie and you know it.

"By now, it's long gone." I sigh as though I, too, feel the pain of such a loss. "I can only imagine that's why she died the way she did. Harvey was the one who snuck into the castle and poisoned her, of course, but we all know who was really responsible."

"Gloriana." Sid and Ashley breathe the name as one.

Take it back, Madame Eleanor. Take it back right now.

"The moment she smuggled those coins off this island, she transferred the curse to herself. In a way, that makes her your savior. She freed you. You'll never have to worry about the gold or about Gloriana again."

The only sounds I get from Birdie this time are angry splutters. Which is interesting for a lot of reasons, not the least of which that I didn't realize ghosts *could* splutter.

" 'Peace, peace! He hath awakened from the dream of life,' " Ashley says in a spurt of poetic fervor. Sid isn't too far behind him, murmuring something about how she always knew she could count on me to save her.

"Technically, it was Birdie who did the saving," I point out, but to no avail. Sid has already rushed to my side and pulled me to her bosom in a grateful and crushing hug. Now that I know she's not conspiring to murder us all in the name of the gold, I recognize it as the newfound strength of hers that it has been all along.

The idea is reinforced when she professes a wish to check on Ferguson and Jaime, eschewing the company of both Nicholas and Otis up the stairs. She opts instead for her brother, the pair of them walking tall and straight out of the room, their auburn heads together as they discuss a future free of Gloriana and all her burdens.

"I don't suppose you're going to enlighten us as to *how* Birdie arranged to remove those coins without anyone on the island knowing about it," Otis says the moment the pair disappears from view.

"How would I know?" is my easy rejoinder. "Apparently Harvey came and went all the time without anyone being the wiser. I think he used the small inlet near the twins' cavern. A resourceful medium could do the same."

Otis shifts so that his good eye is facing me, and then he stares with it. *Hard.* "You know very well that Birdie never found the real gold."

"I don't know anything of the kind," I say, meeting his stare without a qualm. There's no doubt in my mind that Otis knows the gold is in this room. Elspeth admitted as much right before I went dashing into the ocean, and he admitted as much right now. This whole time, he was only trying to protect his cousins.

In fact, he's still doing it right now.

"I'm just a medium," I say, perfectly innocent. "A conduit. I can only relay what I hear."

"She must have had Harvey plant that coin in the wine cellar weeks ago for the sake of their ruse," Otis says. "It was a fake."

"You think? How interesting."

"You can't play the fool with me. I used to carry similar ones myself, but small boys and rude passengers kept stealing them, so I had to replace them with cheap plastic ones." He takes one looming step closer. "That's why you were hit over the head on my boat, you know. So Birdie could take it from you without casting suspicion on herself. She couldn't risk either me or you inspecting the coin too closely and realizing what she was up to."

"You seem to have a lot of confidence in my intelligence all of a sudden."

Otis wavers between exploding in a rage and laughing. I sit quietly and pet my kitten, waiting to see which way he ends up leaning.

It's the latter.

"I can't decide if I like you or loathe you," he says between deep, cracking laughs.

In the background, Nicholas coughs gently. "That's part of her charm, I'm afraid. I often feel the same."

It's Elspeth's turn to speak now, which she does kindly and with the maternal air she's been wearing ever since I returned to Airgead Island with her beloved grandson intact.

"It's much better for everyone this way," she says as she tucks the blankets more firmly around my body. She glances up at the paintings adorning the walls, and I have the satisfaction of watching as Nicholas realizes what the rest of us already know.

"It's here," he says, releasing a soundless whistle. "It's been here all along."

Elspeth nods. "Glenn had the frames made up after his wife died. The kids were such wee things when it happened; he didn't want them to suffer any more than they had to. This way, the gold will always stay on the island where it belongs."

"With you as its keeper?" I suggest, accepting her ministrations with gratitude. It's nice to be fussed over sometimes.

She lifts her head in an assent. "Until my time is through and another is called to my place."

This seems like an awfully boring fate for the next person hired to tend to the castle, but I don't remark on it. Hopefully, Elspeth occasionally takes one of the many treasures lying around here to line her own pockets. God knows she's earned it.

"What Sid and Ashley don't know won't hurt them," Otis adds in a soft voice that matches the one he uses with his cousin. "And since you've seen fit to eradicate the curse on their behalf, they'll never be troubled by it again."

As if to disprove this optimistic assertion, a crack of thunder sounds in the distance. It has the effect of causing Elspeth to jump, but the rest of us are perfectly at ease.

At least, we are until the lights flicker, sputter, and turn themselves back on.

The brilliance of a gilded room with candles burning *and* the overhead chandelier glittering with electricity is almost too much. I'm blinded by so much luminous, bedazzled décor, but Nicholas only laughs.

"This is the last time I let you talk me out of an island paradise," he says. "Next time, we're going to Malta and scuba diving like normal people."

The idea of purposefully going into the ocean—even a warm one—causes me to shudder so much it dislodges Freddie from my lap. "Don't even joke about that. The next time you send me anywhere, it had better be landlocked, or I'm staying home."

You know, there is a Tudor home in Shropshire that Birdie's been telling me about, Winnie says. *She really does know all the haunted hot spots around here. It might be worth a visit.*

"Winnie, no," I moan.

Her laugh is light and musical and accompanied by Birdie's low chuckle. Otis and Elspeth look at me as though I'm a few pancakes short of a stack, but Nicholas only heaves a resigned sigh.

"Don't worry," I say with a reassuring smile. "I'm sure Birdie will leave just as soon as we lay her body to rest."

Don't count on it, dear Ella, comes the easy reply. *As it turns out, our work has only just begun.*

Can't get enough of Ellie and her friends,
Both earthly and not?
Be sure to watch for more installments of
The Eleanor Wilde Mystery series
And don't miss
SÉANCES ARE FOR SUCKERS
And
POTIONS ARE FOR PUSHOVERS
Available now from
Kensington Books
Wherever books are sold